THE ANGEL'S CHASE

Also by Cap Daniels

Book One: *The Opening Chase*
Book Two: *The Broken Chase*
Book Three: *The Stronger Chase*
Book Four: *The Unending Chase*
Book Five: *The Distant Chase*
Book Six: *The Entangled Chase*
Book Seven: *The Devil's Chase*
Book Eight: *The Angel's Chase*
Book Nine: *The Forgotten Chase* (Spring 2020)

I Am Gypsy

We Were Brave

THE ANGEL'S CHASE

CHASE FULTON NOVEL #8

CAP DANIELS

ANCHOR WATCH
PUBLISHING
** USA **

The Angel's Chase
Chase Fulton Novel #8
Cap Daniels

This is a work of fiction. Names, characters, places, historical events, and inci-
dents are the product of the author's imagination or have been used fictitiously. Although many locations such as marinas, airports, hotels, restaurants,
etc. used in this work actually exist, they are used fictitiously and may have
been relocated, exaggerated, or otherwise modified by creative license for the
purpose of this work. Although many characters are based on personalities,
physical attributes, skills, or intellect of actual individuals, all of the characters
in this work are products of the author's imagination.

Published by:

ANCHOR WATCH
PUBLISHING
** USA **

13 Digit ISBN: 978-1-951021-00-9
Library of Congress Control Number:

Cover Design: German Creative

Printed in the United States of America

Dedication

This book is dedicated to...

My friend, Pastor John Grossmann, upon whom a character in these novels is based.

Many of the moral battles my protagonist, Chase Fulton, wages in these novels are based on my own questions, beliefs, doubts, fears, and shortcomings that have been a part of my life for decades. I receive dozens of emails every week from readers, and I always do my best to personally respond to each of them; however, some of those emails stand out from the others. One such email came from a gentleman named John Grossmann, a pastor in Ohio. I'll never know exactly why, but something about his email made me start a conversation with him about my faith. Maybe it was just chance, luck, fate, or some other mysterious force, but that conversation has become a friendship and a student/teacher relationship. John takes the time to patiently listen to my doubts and questions about my faith and provides answers I've sought for decades. He has no agenda other than sharing his wisdom and understanding of God and faith. John is changing my life, one email at a time, from a long way away.

I introduced a character named Singer in book five, The Distant Chase, who is an unlikely and sometimes humorous character. Singer is a deadly sniper who has the ability to change the dynamics of a battlefield from a great distance away from the actual fighting. Interestingly, Singer also has a habit of singing gospel hymns while sniping. Those are two worlds we rarely expect to collide. It is becoming clear that Singer exists in this series to help Chase resolve the issues that haunt him so deeply, and I believe that is exactly what my friend, Pastor John Grossmann, is doing in my life.

Special Thanks To:

My Remarkable Editor:
Sarah Flores—Write Down the Line, LLC
www.WriteDowntheLine.com

As I do in every book, I must give credit where credit is due, and my editor, Sarah Flores, deserves far more credit than she gets in the creation of this series. Her heart-of-a-teacher approach to making me a better writer with every new book is the single greatest element in my pursuit to becoming the best writer I possibly can. Aside from turning my manuscripts into readable novels, Sarah has become my friend and trusted advisor in almost every aspect of publishing this series. I truly hope I never have to create a story without her.

The Angel's Chase

CAP DANIELS

Chapter 1

Why Twenty-One?

The echoing report of the rifle fire sent chills down my spine as the seven men, all dressed identically, held their position with practiced precision and moved as one. The second volley of fire sounded, and everyone around me shuddered, knowing a third volley was only seconds away, and nothing could be done to stop its coming.

When it came, the knowledge that the rifles had fired their last round was no consolation. The echoes of the twenty-one rounds wafted through the valley below the national cemetery as the bugler, somewhere behind the gathered crowd, blew the soul-wrenching notes of Taps. Two of the pallbearers, now tasked as the flag team, lifted the American flag from the coffin, pulling it taut with a crisp *pop*. Not a sound could be heard except the order of the rifle squad commander. "Order...arms!"

Every member of the squad executed the order robotically, as if linked by some invisible binding that caused their arms to move in perfect synchronization. The rattle of the rifles as the butts struck the ground beside each man's right foot was a mechanical reminder of the finality of the rifle salute and the life of one of America's finest warriors.

With precision matching that of the rifle squad, the two men folded the flag into a perfect triangle, with the brilliance of the white stars against the blue field reminding every heart in the gathered crowd of the purity represented by those stars.

After the formal, ceremonial inspection of the folded flag, the Army captain in command of the honor guard burial team accepted the Stars and Stripes and knelt on one knee at the feet of Margaret Butterworth Joyner, Major James "Smoke" Butterworth's sister and only living member of his immediate family.

"Ma'am, on behalf of the President of the United States, the United States Army, and a grateful nation, please accept this flag as a token of your loved one's true and faithful service."

With quivering hands, Margaret embraced the flag and managed a trembling, "Thank you."

The captain stood, and with spotless white gloves, saluted Smoke's sister and the flag in a motion of slow, measured cadence. Following the salute, the captain turned on his heel to face the commander of the rifle squad and receive the second token he would place in Margaret Joyner's waiting hands.

In an identical kneeling position as before, the captain placed three rifle cartridges on top of the flag on Margaret's lap. "Ma'am, please accept these in remembrance of the three volleys fired in salute to Major Butterworth by the United States Army Honor Guard under my command."

Margaret placed her left hand over the cartridges and her right against the left side of the captain's face in an intimate expression of her appreciation. She whispered, "Thank you. Jimmy wouldn't have wanted all this fuss over him, but he would've been proud of you boys."

* * *

After Smoke's funeral, the drive back to Saint Marys, Georgia, began as an exercise in individual reflection...at least for me. Reliving the last conversation he and I had the night before he took his own life left me burdened and blessed with the responsibility for the men who'd served under him, in defense and preservation of freedom, through countless deadly missions. He and his men had fought, bled, and in some cases, died side by side all over the globe. The remaining men of Smoke's team now looked to me, a man with no formal military service, for direction and leadership. Each of those men were battle-hardened warriors and patriots of the highest order, but at their core, they were soldiers awaiting orders for where to go and what to do next. In Smoke's eternal absence, the eyes of his men fell upon me, and mine fell upon my partner and most trusted brother-in-arms, Clark Johnson.

"What happens now?" I whispered.

Clark grimaced in pain. "If you're asking me, I say we go home, hang up these stuffy dress uniforms, and get back to work. If you're asking yourself, that's a conversation you should have when you're alone and far out of earshot of your men."

Wisdom such as Clark's is rare and can't be bought on a college campus or gleaned from any textbook. It's hard-earned wisdom, often trimmed in blood, and always soaked in sweat.

I met his gaze. "How are you feeling?"

"I've got a broken back, seventy-four broken ribs, and a two-hour drive with a van full of knuckle-dragging trigger pullers. How do you think I feel?"

"You've only got three broken ribs," I reminded him.

"Let me break three of yours, and then you can decide if it feels like seventy-four."

"Point taken."

Clark, along with five other men—Stump, Mongo, Snake, Singer, and Smoke—had encountered an ambush high on the Khyber Pass, in the mountains of Afghanistan and Pakistan, where they suffered catastrophic injuries, and ultimately the loss of three of their six-man team. Stump, the helicopter pilot, didn't survive the crash of his Hughes 500 Little Bird. Rodney "Snake" Blanchard fell victim to a murderer while in a hospital on an Air Force base in Germany. And finally, James "Smoke" Butterworth took his own life as a result of the guilt and unfathomable psychological torture of leading a team into such a deadly ambush.

Brinkwater Security, the defense contractor who'd tasked the team to defend the munitions supply train across the Pass, made the political decision to abandon Clark and the others on the mountain after the ambush.

With the help of a Defense Intelligence agent named Bimini and a Tajiki chopper pilot with an affection for American green-backs, I rescued the team from the top of the Khyber Pass. Every surviving member was injured, but Clark's condition was by far the worst. Despite orders by numerous doctors to remain in bed and allow his back and ribs to heal, he refused to be bedridden. He was one of the toughest men who'd ever lived, but the agony on his face told the story of the immense pain he was suffering.

"Why twenty-one?" asked Penny Fulton, my wife of less than a month, and the most astonishing woman I've ever known.

Despite my education as a psychologist, I rarely had any clue what women were talking about, and my new bride was no exception. "Why twenty-one what?"

"At the funeral," she said, "they fired a twenty-one gun salute. What's the significance of that number?"

Sometimes questions arise for which the answer is assumed to be common knowledge, but in reality, it is known by few. Why is hot on the left and cold on the right at the kitchen sink? I found Penny's question to fall into this category.

It was Jimmy "Singer" Grossmann, one of the finest snipers in the world, and legendary crooner of Southern Baptist hymns, who finally answered my wife's question. "Even though they fired twenty-one shots, that wasn't a twenty-one gun salute. It was a three-volley salute. There's a big difference."

Singer had the full attention of everyone in the van, and I was relieved to know I wasn't the only one in the group who didn't know the difference.

"In the days when wars were fought on battlefields across open expanses of land, on which men would face each other and fall to their deaths in droves, it became necessary at times to stop the fighting long enough to clear the bodies from the battlefield and carry the wounded to the rear where they could be cared for. When this gruesome work was done under cease-fire conditions, both sides would signal their dead had been carried away and properly cared for by firing three volleys of fire into the air, signaling the battle could then continue. That's exactly what was done today when we buried Smoke. The rifle squad signaled our dead had been carried away and properly cared for, and our battle could continue. Our work isn't done. It was merely paused while we buried our dead."

Silence sucked the oxygen from the air as the awesome reality of Singer's words fell over us.

Chapter 2
Staff Meeting

Maebelle met us in the circular drive when we pulled up to the Bonaventure Plantation, the magnificent home and property that was a pecan plantation during the nineteenth and twentieth centuries. The property had been handed down through generations of the Huntsinger family until most recently, when Judge Bernard Henry Huntsinger passed it on to me. Judge Huntsinger, known to everyone who knew him as "the Judge," was apparently my mother's great uncle. The Judge's great-granddaughter Maebelle and I were the only remaining heirs in the Huntsinger family.

"Is Clark all right?" were the first words out of Maebelle's mouth. She, like most women Clark met, had instantly become infatuated with him and took on the role of nursemaid and personal chef.

I helped my friend from the van, and it broke my heart to see him in so much pain. "No, Maebelle. He's not all right. He's in a lot of pain, and he's too muleheaded to go to bed."

She brushed past me and took Clark's arm. "Come on, you stubborn old man. I have a plate made for you and a fresh pitcher of sweet tea, just the way you like it."

He looked around Maebelle at me and shrugged. "It's a curse. What can I say?"

"You're a curse," I said as he let Maebelle gingerly lead him up the stairs.

Penny hip-bumped me. "Jealous much?"

I laughed. "No, not jealous. Just amazed. How does he have that effect on women everywhere he goes?"

Penny put on her mischievous smile. "He's a pretty man, and chicks dig the uniform."

"I need to get myself a uniform."

She raised her eyebrows. "Oh, no you don't, Chase Fulton. I'm the only chick who needs to be digging on you, and I like you just fine without a uniform. In fact, I like you without any clothes at all."

I slid my hand into hers. "What more could any man ask for?"

"If you ask Maebelle, sweet tea just the way *he* likes it."

"Apparently," I said, "but I remember promising a certain somebody a honeymoon. Would you happen to know if that certain somebody is packed?"

"That certain somebody lives on a boat with you." She poked her finger into my chest. "And everything she owns is aboard that boat, so no packing required."

"Let's get these guys settled and check the weather. I don't see any reason we can't set sail on the next outgoing tide."

* * *

Clark's wasn't the only plate Maebelle had prepared. She was a world-class chef, trained at the Culinary Institute of America— or "the CIA," as the Judge liked to call it.

Gathered around the table were Marvin "Mongo" Malloy, the six-foot-eight-inch, muscle-bound teddy bear who could rip an oak tree out of the ground with his bare hands; Singer, the Southern Baptist sniper; NCIS Special Agent Stone Hunter; Skipper, one of the finest young intelligence operations analysts in the business and practically my little sister; my wife Penny; and me.

"He's all tucked in, as snug as a bug," Maebelle said when she joined us at the table.

"How did you manage that?" I asked.

"Dilaudid dissolves nicely in sweet tea."

Singer pointed to the cast on his broken leg. "I like sweet tea."

"I know you do," Maebelle said, "but you're not as stubborn as Clark, so I don't have to roofie you."

When dessert—a chocolate bread pudding homemade by Maebelle—arrived, I decided it was the perfect time for our first official business meeting as a team.

"All right, guys," I began. "We've got a lot to talk about, but first, I'd like to establish some ground rules. Full disclosure and absolute honesty are what you're going to get from me, and that's what I need and expect in return. Don't be afraid to say what's on your mind."

Everyone nodded in agreement, probably because their mouths were full of Maebelle's heavenly dessert.

"It's pretty simple," I said. "We've all worked together before, and we trust each other. If you want to be a part of what we're building, all of you are welcome. If you want to pursue other opportunities, none of us will hold that against you. We all have our skill sets. Some of them overlap, but most of you specialize in something every tactical team needs. Let's start with money. I assume Brinkwater didn't pay any of you for the Khyber Pass job."

Singer and Mongo shook their heads.

"What was your contract daily rate?"

Mongo and Singer shared a look before the sniper said, "We were three hundred a day, and Smoke was four."

I did the math. "So, that's just under three grand apiece for the two of you. I'll cover that. And if you decide you want to stay on with us, I'll pay you an advance against future work to get you by until we're ready to get back in the game."

Mongo protested. "That ain't right, Chase. It wasn't your operation. You shouldn't have to pay us for something Brinkwater owes."

"If that's how you feel, Mongo, consider it a loan. We'll push Brinkwater to pay you guys what you're owed, and if they ever pay, you can pay me back. How's that?"

"All right," he agreed, "but we're not charity cases. We earn what we're paid."

"You absolutely do, Mongo. In fact, you deserve far more than you're paid, but we're going to work on that as well."

That news seemed to please the two operators.

I turned to Hunter. "You have a real job with the Navy, so you have more to think about than the rest of us."

He held up his hand. "Chase, let me stop you right there. I've seen what you guys are capable of doing. I've even worked with some people who know you guys. They all say you're as solid as they come. I'm thankful the Navy gave me a job, but I want to get back in the gunslinging game. This coat-and-tie business is for the birds. I'm a frontline guy, so count me in."

I glanced at Skipper.

She said, "Oh, you know I'm already in."

Maebelle was staring around the table in wide-eyed wonder. "I'm just a chef, but somebody's got to feed you guys."

I pointed to my empty dessert plate. "If you keep feeding us like this, we'll be too fat to work."

Mongo wiped at the corners of his mouth. "Yeah, but we'll sure be happy."

Penny, wearing a somber look, cast her eyes toward her plate.

I leaned toward her. "Are you okay?"

She pressed her lips into a forced half-smile. "Yeah, I'm just not feeling great. I think I'm going to walk down to the boat and lie down for a while. It's been a long day."

The feeling started somewhere beneath my stomach and slowly crawled its way into my throat. Nothing about Penny's look or words led me to believe she was all right.

I tossed my napkin beside my plate. "Maebelle, thank you for another wonderful meal. Is there anything I can do to help you clean up?"

"Oh, no, Chase. I've got this. You should probably…." She motioned with her head, indicating I should follow Penny.

Mongo unfolded himself from the two-hundred-year-old oak chair. "I'll help Miss Maebelle, Chase."

"Thanks, Mongo. Penny and I are going away for a couple of weeks. I'll get you and Singer paid before we leave. You're welcome to stay here as long as you'd like, but if you need or want to go someplace else, I'll call you when we get back."

He extended his enormous hand and engulfed mine. "I haven't had a chance to thank you...."

I slapped him on the arm. "It's not necessary, Mongo. You would've done the same for me if the roles were reversed."

"Just the same," he said, "it means a lot to me, and to Singer, too. You're a good man, Chase, and I'm glad to have you on our side. After what I saw you do in Russia and up on the Pass, I'd much rather be shooting beside you than shooting back at you."

"I feel the same way, my friend."

By the time I walked the three hundred feet down the sloping yard to *Aegis*, my fifty-foot custom sailing catamaran, Penny was already in the shower with the door bolted closed. I pulled enough cash from the safe to pay Singer and Mongo and jogged back to the house.

Mongo loomed over the sink with Maebelle looking like a tiny schoolgirl next to him, and Singer hobbled toward the door on his single crutch. I tossed a banded stack of cash onto the countertop beside the giant, and he stared down at the money.

"Thank you, Chase. I mean it."

"Don't thank me, Mongo. You earned every penny and more. I'll call you in a couple of weeks if you're not still hanging around."

He nodded and turned back to his soapy task.

Singer caught my eye. "Let's walk out back and talk for a minute."

I motioned toward his cast. "I'll walk, but I'm not sure what you call that thing you're doing."

We made it to the back porch, and Singer wasted no time. "All macho crap aside, Chase, are you doing okay?"

"What do you mean?"

He lowered his chin. "You've got a lot on you, and now you've got me and Mongo. I get the feeling this isn't what you signed up for."

I watched a pair of pelicans glide across the glassy surface of the North River, their wings spread to their limits. "Look at those birds, Singer. They look like they have everything under control, and life is one long, smooth glide over the water. When they get where they're going, they'll dive on bait for two hours. If they catch five fish with a hundred dives, that's good enough. People like you and me, we don't have that luxury. We never get to miss. We have to catch a fish on every dive, or the fish get us."

We watched until the birds disappeared into the marsh, and Singer put his hand on my shoulder. "I lay up there in that cave, waiting for my leg to rot off, and for my friend, Clark, to die. And I asked God every day to send us an angel. Do you know who showed up? You, Chase. I've learned a lot of things in my life, but the most valuable lesson I've ever learned is that God knows what I need, even when I ask for the wrong stuff. He knew we didn't need an angel to fly us off that mountain. He sent you instead."

What was I supposed to say?

"I know you've got a lot going on in that head of yours, Chase, but I want you to know—"

I looked away, maybe because I was uncomfortable with the discussion, or perhaps because I didn't want to admit I was over-whelmed.

He hobbled around me on his crutch and broken leg until we were once again face-to-face. "Listen to me. This would be a lot for anybody to deal with, but you need to understand you're not alone. The burden of leadership is heavy, but we're not boots."

I lowered my brow. "What's a boot?"

For the first time in days, he laughed, but only a short, two-second chuckle. "It's easy to forget you're a civilian. A boot is someone fresh out of training with no combat experience. This team of yours is anything but a gang of boots. We've been there, done that, and you can count the bullet holes in us to prove it. But that's not my point."

"So, what is the point?"

A look of stern sincerity overtook him. "Chase, I know you were raised to have a certain faith. It's easy to doubt that faith in the world we live in, but there's a power greater than any of us, and He's got his eye on you. Believe what you want, or doubt what you want, but make no mistake—you belong to the angels, and they've got your back. Don't you forget that. I'm sure your daddy never did."

Chapter 3
Fine

Singer's words rang in my head as I descended the steps and crossed the yard toward *Aegis*. I'd known since the moment I met the Southern Baptist sniper that he was a man of enormous faith, but I never expected him to become my priest. Perhaps that was a role he took upon himself as part of the responsibility he felt to God. I'd never question another man's faith, but I couldn't claim the same confidence in the angels as Singer had.

I double-checked the dock lines securing my boat and cast a cursory glance across the deck. Everything appeared shipshape on the exterior, but what awaited me inside was another story.

I found Penny pretending to be asleep in our bed, and I crawled in behind her. Gently drawing her hair from her face and letting it fall behind her ear, I whispered, "Do you want to talk about what's bothering you?"

She pulled the blanket tightly beneath her chin and mumbled, "I'm fine."

Maybe those words don't qualify as a lie when a woman uses them to prevent—or delay—an argument, but Penny Fulton was anything but fine.

"Okay," I said. "I'm going to check the weather and tides. I'll come to bed in a few minutes."

"Whatever."

It was worse than I thought. I knew what to do when bullets started flying through the air. I knew how to deal with an engine failure in my airplane. I even knew how to disarm underwater explosives at the Panama Canal, but I had no clue how to deal with *whatever*.

According to the prediction, the morning high tide would be a few minutes before eight, and the weather guessers were prophesying southwesterly winds at ten to fifteen knots. I couldn't have designed a better combination for a morning departure for our honeymoon, but the dark cloud looming in the air wasn't as promising as the wind forecast.

This time, when I crawled into bed with Penny, she wasn't faking sleep. Her breathing was deep, regular, and peaceful. I envied her condition but not her tortured mindset. I lay silently behind her, playing out endless scenarios in wasted attempts to determine what was troubling her so badly. I couldn't think of anything I'd done wrong, but that didn't mean I was innocent. I'd likely committed some act of stupidity without realizing I'd missed something meaningful to her.

There would never be anyone more important to me than Penny. She'd filled a void in my life I hadn't known was there. She made everything that was already good so much better, and everything bad, she made tolerable. Her beautiful outlook on life taught me that things were rarely as bad as they seemed, and that often, difficulties were merely thinly veiled opportunities. I loved her then and would never stop. Whatever the problem was, we'd find a way around, over, or through it.

Sleep finally waved its merciful hand, and I drifted off into dreams of never coming home from our honeymoon. In my dream, we found an island carved from the sea that welcomed us as if it had been waiting eons for our arrival. Time melted away, and gunfights, assassinations, political turmoil, and the world of responsibility dissolved into mist.

Dreams are the subconscious mind trying to make sense of reality. Often, that's not only impossible, but also a ridiculous effort. The dreams of that night were anything but ridiculous and left my perspective of Penny's concern crystal clear.

When I awoke and found myself alone, my watch told me it was ten minutes before seven, and my nose told me Penny was frying bacon.

After a brief trip to the head to scrub off the carpet that had grown on my teeth overnight, I climbed the stairs into the galley and main salon. Standing at the stove, wearing yoga pants and a University of Georgia Bulldogs baseball jersey with the number twenty-one and my last name emblazoned across the back, was the woman who made up the core of my world. I slid my hands around her waist and pulled her against my chest, her perfect smile reflecting in the stainless-steel backsplash behind the cook-top. A warm sound of surrender escaped her lips as she pressed her body against mine.

I whispered, "If you want me to quit, I'll never pull another trigger or disappear into the night ever again."

I felt her body relax and her chest rise with a long, deep inhalation.

She slid the frying pan from the burner and spun in my arms until she was facing me with her hands laced around my neck. "I can't ask you to quit. It's what you are. Asking you to walk away from what you are would be like asking you to stop breathing."

I gently kissed her forehead, then her nose, and finally, her lips. "What I am is your husband. As long as you don't ask me to stop being that, I can walk away from everything else in my life."

"I can't do that to you, Chase. I can't. I have to learn to cope with the fear. It's always been hard, but now that we're married, it's different. I'm so scared you're going to go away and never come home. I couldn't bear to take the flag, Chase."

I focused on her pained expression. "What do you mean, you couldn't bear to take the flag?"

"At the funeral...." she said. "They gave Smoke's sister the flag from his coffin. I can't do that."

I almost explained to her I wouldn't receive military honors, and there would be no flag on my coffin, but instead, I said, "High tide is in forty-five minutes."

She pecked at my lips and pulled away. "I'll plate the breakfast while you make ready for sail."

Computers weren't a strength of mine, but I opened the laptop Skipper left aboard and connected to the satellite uplink. When Penny put the plates on the table, I turned the screen to face her.

"What's this?" she asked as she leaned in. Her eyes widened, and she drew even closer to the computer. "What is this, Chase?"

"It's the reason I can walk away from anything except you. Those are two of our investment accounts in the Cayman Islands."

The color drained from her face. "Chase, there's over six million dollars here. Is this your money?"

"Yes. Actually, no. It's not mine. It's ours. What I do pays well, and I got lucky early on when I first started doing this. Some friends recommended a couple of financial advisors in the Caymans, and I made a few good investments with the money I earned from my first mission."

Her eyes were frozen on the screen, and she appeared to be lost somewhere between disbelief and a thousand questions.

I loaded a fork with scrambled eggs and washed it down with the day's first sip of coffee. Waiting for her next question, I continued enjoying the fruits of her early-morning efforts in the galley.

She eased the laptop closed and pressed her lips together. Pulling her hair into a tight ponytail, she found her voice. "I knew, well, I assumed you had enough money to live without worrying too much, but I never wanted to ask."

"Why didn't you want to ask?"

She sipped her coffee. "I was afraid you'd think I was a gold digger. I mean, when you met me, I was mooching off Teri and Kip, and then I fell in love with you, and...."

I laughed. "Penny, stop it. I would never think that of you. You've never mooched off anyone. You worked your butt off on

Teri and Kip's boat, and you've done the same since the minute you came aboard *Aegis*."

She raised her eyebrows. "What about Clark?"

"What about him?"

"Does he...I mean, is he..."

I interrupted. "I have no idea. I've never asked. He's been doing this a lot longer than me, so I assume he's comfortable financially, but I don't know how much he made on the missions he worked before I met him."

"And the others.... Singer and Mongo?"

"They've not been so fortunate," I said. "They're contractors. They only work when they're needed, and they make a few hundred bucks a day while they're working. I imagine they probably live paycheck to paycheck. That's part of the reason I'm so concerned about them and why I offered to put them to work."

She seemed to silently ponder what I'd said and then bowed her head. "Chase, I'm sorry about last night. I shouldn't have been so cold. I didn't know how to tell you what I was feeling."

I took her hands in mine. "Listen to me. You can always tell me anything. It doesn't have to be well thought out. We're a team, and as you saw yesterday, people like me take the word *team* pretty seriously."

"I wasn't going to ask you to quit."

I squeezed her hands. "I know you weren't, but I always want to know what bothers you, even when you can't explain it completely."

She nodded and allowed a warm smile to form. "I love you, Chase."

"Of course you do. Why else would you be wearing a jersey with my name on it?"

She tugged at the shirt and grinned. "It's my name, too."

"Yes, I suppose it is."

We finished our breakfast and went in search of our dog, Charlie.

We found him in the kitchen at Maebelle's feet. He squirmed and wagged his tail when he saw Penny, but he ignored me.

She knelt and scratched behind his ears. "I should've known you'd be in here with Maebelle. She doesn't play fair. She bribes you with food."

Maebelle feigned innocence. "We all have to eat, be us man or beast."

"Yes," I admitted, "but no beast, especially that one, deserves what you create."

She leaned down, offering Charlie a morsel of whatever she was concocting, and he gobbled it up as if he hadn't eaten in days.

"So," Maebelle said, "you two are off on your honeymoon, huh?"

Penny scratched at Charlie's neck again, stood, and squeezed my arm. "Yes, we are, but he won't tell me where we're going."

"Well…" Maebelle let the word drag out longer than necessary. "If you're going somewhere that would require Charlie to be quarantined, he could stay here with me. I can keep him fed and loved while you two are off feeding and loving each other."

I hadn't considered the necessity of quarantining Charlie if we left the country, but Maebelle was right.

"You wouldn't mind?" I asked.

"Of course not," she squealed. "He's no trouble at all, and I love having him around as a taste tester."

"You've got a house full of taste testers," I said.

"Yeah, but they don't wag their tails when I feed them."

Penny said, "I think Clark does."

Maebelle blushed. "I hope so."

"I don't want to be in the middle of your girl party, so I'm going up to check on my partner."

Maebelle glanced toward the stairwell. "Tell him I'll be up with his breakfast soon. Okay?"

"You're going to spoil that man," I said.

"That's my plan," she whispered conspiratorially.

When I tapped on his bedroom door, I heard Clark groan from inside. I pushed the door open to find him sitting on the edge of his bed, gingerly pulling on a T-shirt.

"What's wrong, old man? Are you getting soft in your old age?"

He glared at me. "You just wait. When these ribs heal up, I'll show you what an old man can do."

"Yeah, sure you will," I laughed. "I just came up to tell you Penny and I are going away for a couple of weeks. I owe her a honeymoon."

He finished the arduous task of dressing himself. "You've never taken me on a honeymoon."

"What do you mean?" I argued. "I took you on a whirlwind tour of Eastern Europe and then a fabulous Caribbean dream vacation."

"You dragged me to Moscow and got me shot, then you abducted me and forced me into a gunfight with Italian mobsters. I hardly call that a dream vacation."

"You loved every minute of it."

"Well, maybe, but either way, I hope you guys have a great time. I should be back on my feet by the time you get back."

I picked up a dirty sock from the floor and threw it at him. "You're a slob. You know that?"

"Hey, I'm wounded."

"You're a slob even when you're not wounded. Maebelle's on her way up with your breakfast. Try not to break her heart. Can you do that?"

In typical Clark Johnson style, he put on the crooked half-smile. "I've told you before. It's a curse."

"Yeah, whatever. Feel better. We'll see you in a couple of weeks."

"See ya," he groaned.

* * *

With Penny at the helm, *Aegis* cut her way across Cumberland Sound and through Saint Marys inlet into the North Atlantic. We unfurled the sails, and the boat sighed as if she'd been released from a thousand years of captivity. As the diesels fell silent and the rising sun beckoned, we slid through the waves under full sail on a broad reach.

Chapter 4
Is That Her?

Lying facedown on the surface of the crystal clear water off the coast of Bimini, I watched Penny fin around a coral head twenty-five feet below as if she were a mermaid never wishing to emerge from the sea.

I was mesmerized by her graceful movement through the underwater world, her elegance belied the deadly nature of her mission. On that day—I think it was a Friday in March of 2002—Penny Fulton was no mermaid. She was an assassin in pursuit of prey that would never survive the coming encounter. Her weapon of choice was a 54-inch, custom-made mahogany speargun, with which I'd never seen my wife miss a shot. Penny's prey, some two dozen feet beneath the tranquil surface, was a four-pound grouper. It was destined to be our dinner on the first official night of our vacation in Honeymoon Harbour, an appropriately named anchorage just north of Cat Cay.

Spearfishing while freediving isn't a sport for the faint of heart. Aside from the necessity of holding one's breath for up to four minutes, a free diver must possess the nerve to fire a bolt into her prey, and then swim that prey to the surface, leaving a trail of shark-luring blood in her wake. Penny had few, if any, fears, and sharks weren't on the list.

My watch reported she'd been underwater for slightly over two minutes when she took aim and squeezed the trigger. Less than a second later, the grouper became her most recent victim. Line played out from the spool and left a telltale stream between her gun and the bolt as the grouper fought in vain to make his escape. Penny soon had the fish in her hands and her beautiful face pointed toward the surface. I loved watching her spearfish, but even more, I loved eating the catch of the day.

Back aboard *Aegis*, Penny stood on the swim platform and rinsed the salt water from her body with the freshwater shower. If the photographers from *Sports Illustrated Swimsuit Edition* had been on board, their camera lenses would have melted.

Squeezing the water from her hair, she grinned. "I like how you do that."

"Do what?" I asked.

"Stare at me every time I come out of the water."

"There's not a man on Earth who wouldn't stare at you showering on the stern of a boat."

She aimed the showerhead at me and laughed. "You're silly, but thank you."

An hour later, we watched the sun dissolve across the western horizon and enjoyed the grouper she'd stalked.

"What a perfect day." She sighed and lifted the glass of chardonnay to her lips.

"I can't remember a better one."

She reached for my hand. "Thank you for this. This place, this life, all of it."

"You never have to thank me, Penny. We're in this together…"

Before I could finish, she spun in her seat and focused her attention to the south. "Did you hear that?"

I followed her gaze to see a motor yacht powering into the small anchorage.

The twilight left the surface of the crystal clear water appearing deep purple as the yacht continued ever closer. Instinctually, I glanced up to make sure I'd turned on our anchor light. The bright white LED shone three hundred sixty degrees around the top of the mast, but the yacht kept coming at high speed. A wave of white roiling water cascaded from either side of the bow, and the dark hull grew increasingly larger and menacing as it closed on us.

"Chase, they're going to hit us!"

"Get on the radio, and start the engines. I'll cut the anchor!"

Penny leapt to the helm and yanked the microphone from its clip. "Motor yacht entering Honeymoon Harbour from the southwest, this is the Sailing Vessel *Aegis* at anchor off your bow. Heave to and bear away, immediately!" She blew the horn in repeated, prolonged blasts to warn the oncoming vessel, but the skipper made no effort to either slow down or turn away.

I yanked the snubber lines from the anchor chain and opened the lock on the windlass, allowing all of our anchor chain to play out.

"All back full!" I yelled from the bow.

There was no time to retrieve the anchor. Our only hope to save ourselves and *Aegis* was to back away before the yacht plowed into our starboard hull. Motoring forward would only send our propellers spinning into our anchor chain.

I heard the engines rev to full rpms, and *Aegis* began to back away from the anchor. The yacht was less than a hundred feet away and still coming fast. It was going to be close. If she missed us, it would only be by inches, but it looked as if the bow of the massive vessel would impact our starboard hull just forward of amidships.

I yelled, "Hard to starboard!" and Penny spun the wheel.

Turning *Aegis* to take a glancing blow instead of a full-on collision seemed like the best way to save our boat. The stern swung sharply to the right at the same instant the last inch of our anchor chain played out. The anchor rode came taut as the sky filled with the enormous hull of the speeding yacht.

"Jump!" I ordered the instant it became clear there was no way to avoid or survive the coming collision. I ran aft on the portside hull and dived across the lifeline just as Penny plunged into the water at the stern.

The water enveloped us as the horrible roar of the crash above filled my ears. I struggled to remain submerged while desperately search for Penny. She would be well astern of what remained of *Aegis*, but I'd leapt from the portside hull amidships. The sun was beyond the horizon, leaving me in near darkness, uncertain of my depth, and with lungs burning, almost empty of air.

Searching for Penny in the darkness beneath the surface was futile, so I lifted my head in a direction I hoped was skyward and kicked for the surface. I was disoriented and terrified to see how badly my beloved boat had been damaged. I expected to see her sinking by the starboard bow when I broke the surface, but what I saw left me even more shocked.

"Chase! Are you okay? Chase! Answer me!"

It took all of my will to turn from *Aegis* to see Penny swimming toward me. Just as I'd known she would be, she was unhurt and darting across the surface like an Olympic swimmer.

"Yeah, I'm okay," I managed to force past my lips.

"Good. Me, too," she said through strained breaths. "We've got to get over there!"

She threw her face back into the water and powered across the surface. I followed, but I couldn't keep up with her. When we reached the site where *Aegis* and the yacht had come to rest, entangled and twisted, the scene was utter chaos. The motor yacht was listing to starboard by forty-five degrees. Her port screw was protruding from the water and still spinning at full rpm, with *Aegis's* anchor chain thudding and growing more tightly bound with every revolution of the propeller shaft.

We climbed the sugar-scoop boarding steps at *Aegis's* stern, and I ran through the cockpit into the main salon. "Keep an eye on the hatches for anyone coming out of the yacht. I'll be right back."

Seconds later, I returned with a pair of rifles, a satellite phone, a handheld VHF radio, and two pairs of latex gloves. "Let's go check it out. If anyone's still alive on board, they've got to be badly hurt."

We ran forward, surveying *Aegis* as we went. Surprisingly, she wasn't badly damaged. The yacht hadn't hit the hull, but it had picked up our anchor chain as it passed inches off our bow. The inertia of the yacht carried *Aegis* forward like a thirty-thousand-pound skier until striking the shallow reef and listing horribly onto her side.

"Come on," I said. "We've got to get on board and shut down the engines. Keep your eyes open for anything that moves, and stay on my heels."

We climbed the portside hull and leapt over the rail. There was no sign of life on deck, but it was a big boat with plenty of places to hide. We continued our climb toward the bridge with rifles at the ready. The portside hatch to the bridge deck was secured, and nothing I did could budge it.

Penny pressed her hands to the glass and peered inside. "Chase, there's a woman at the helm, and she's hurt."

I pounded on the glass with the butt of my rifle, but it was wasted effort. Finally, I made my way astern, hoping to make entry from the back on a lower deck and climb to the bridge deck from the interior. Penny stayed on my heels and seemed as anxious as I was to find another route to the woman inside.

The yacht's once-opulent furnishings, glassware, and fixtures lay strewn about the space as if tossed by a hurricane.

Penny said, "I can make my way to the engine room and shut down the engines from there if you want to check on the woman on the bridge."

"No!" I demanded. "We stay together. I've got a bad feeling about this."

There were no signs of life anywhere we looked, and the awkward angle of the yacht made the space disorienting and difficult to traverse. The narrow, semi-spiral stairs leading from the galley to the bridge would make a perfect choke point for an ambush if someone were waiting for me to poke my head around the corner. I had no choice. Shutting down the engines and helping the woman at the helm were essential, so I wedged my six-and-a-half-foot frame into the stairwell and inched my way upward, with the muzzle of my rifle leading the way.

The top step came into view without a hint of an aggressor lying in wait, so I slowly pressed on, creeping upward at the uncomfortable angle. As I reached the bridge, the sickening feeling in my gut was reinforced. There was nothing we could do for the woman lying across the wheel. She hadn't felt any pain for hours. Her long, blonde hair, matted with dried blood, lay across her shoulder. The crimson evidence of her death originated from a bullet hole at the base of her skull.

The complex panel of the yacht left me searching for a way to shut down the engines. Penny beat me to the punch as she pulled the woman's corpse from its position across the wheel and pulled the throttles to idle before hitting both engine kill switches.

When the woman's body came to rest faceup in the captain's chair, my gut wrenched as if it were on the verge of turning itself inside out. The woman was no stranger. It was far from the first time I'd seen her flawless Eastern European skin and hypnotic blue-gray eyes.

A shiver ran the length of my spine as I looked into the face of the woman who'd almost cost me everything.

Penny stood inches behind me, peering across my shoulder. "Chase, is that Anya?"

Anya Burinkova had been a Russian SVR officer dispatched to seduce me and infiltrate my organization on my first official mission as an American covert operative. I'd fallen in love with her, and she'd played her part to perfection.

"There's only one way to know for sure," I said as I tugged at her shirt, untucking it from her belt and pulling it up her back.

"You're going to undress her?"

Penny's question was reasonable, but I wasn't undressing the woman…at least not completely.

"If this is Anya, she'll have a scar from an entry wound at her shoulder blade. I watched her take the bullet in the back."

I held my breath as the smooth, perfect skin of her body revealed itself from beneath the bloodstained material of the shirt. The farther I pulled the cloth, the more the body looked like Anya's. Visions of that skin pressed against mine in moments of passionate abandon raced through my mind.

Finally, with the shirt pulled up to her neck, the woman's pale skin revealed no scars.

I let out a breath. "She's not Anya. She's Ekaterina Norikova, Anya's half sister."

Penny's eyes grew wide. "Is there any chance it's *not* her?"

Before answering, I slipped off the dead woman's right shoe to reveal the absence of her pinky toe. "Nope, no chance of that. It's definitely her."

"Gross! What happened to her toe?" Penny obviously wanted to look away but couldn't. The grotesque scar where the toe had been spoke volumes about the horrors Norikova had been willing to endure to serve the Kremlin.

Penny didn't want to hear details about the relationship I'd had with Anya, but she needed to understand the mindset of the people who'd obviously chosen to force their way back into my life.

"I shot Anya's right pinky toe off during a fight in Saint Thomas shortly after my first mission. This woman"—I pointed toward the corpse—"had her toe cut off, or shot off, to fool me into believing she was Anya."

"My God. Is there anything these people *won't* do?"

"If there is, I haven't found it yet."

Her face flashed pale. "If she is Norikova, that means they were trying to kill you. No, not just you...us."

Chapter 5
Compass, Clock, and Sextant

"So, what do we do now?"

Penny's question was a good one, but I didn't have a good answer. Of the thousand possibilities pouring through my mind, none of them ended with us walking away unscathed.

"Obviously, we can't stay here. Somebody will discover this boat tomorrow and call the authorities. We don't need to get tangled up in any Bahamian investigation. They'll never figure out what happened here, and we're the only living witnesses."

"We have to make sure nobody else is on board," Penny said. "We can't just let it sink without knowing if she was the only passenger."

"Normally, I'd agree with you, but we don't have time to waste. We've got to get *Aegis* out of here."

The reluctance on her face gave way to acceptance, and we forced open the hatch and climbed over the rail. On the descent back to *Aegis*, I hastily assessed the damage. Our anchor and chain were hopelessly entangled in the prop shaft of the yacht and completely irretrievable. There were no unique markings on the anchor or chain to tie to them *Aegis*, so I felt comfortable leaving them behind.

"I have to go in the water to make sure we're not fouled on anything. Start the engines, but don't engage the transmissions until I'm back aboard."

Penny did as I instructed, and I stepped from the swim platform with a mask, snorkel, fins, dive knife, and underwater torch. To my surprise and delight, *Aegis* was floating high and dry with no damage below the waterline. The reef was shallow but still deep enough to allow our hulls to float over it without grounding.

"Get us out of here," I said, shaking the salt water from my skin.

Penny pulled the transmissions into reverse and slowly backed away from the wreck.

"As soon as you're in deep water, turn north with the Gulf Stream. I've got a plan."

The look on Penny's face said she wanted to know what was going on in my head.

"Keep us off the bottom and headed north. I'll be right back."

She acknowledged with a nod, and I bounded down the stairs to the equipment room.

The portside hull of my boat has one cabin with a queen bed and private head. If the boat were a typical cruising catamaran, she would have a second cabin aft on the portside, but nothing about *Aegis* was typical. Instead of an additional cabin, she boasted a workshop and equipment room second to none. After finding what I needed, I returned topside.

"Okay, it's time to do some of that captain stuff you're so good at. We're changing course, but we're going old school."

Penny scowled. "What are you talking about?"

"I'm talking about blinding our enemy."

Penny rolled her eyes. "Have you forgotten that I'm not a spy like the rest of your friends? I have no idea what you're talking about."

I held up two metal boxes the size of bricks. "These are jammers. The only way the Russians could've known where we were was by using a tracking device. These babies will put that device to bed, but it'll do the same to everything else on the boat with a transmitter."

I could almost see the light come on in Penny's head.

"Ah, I get it now. You're going to let the Russians think we're running north, but we're turning for home as soon as you turn those things on."

"Well, not exactly home, but we're turning for Miami, so plot a course and let me know when you're ready to go dark."

Two minutes later, Penny said, "Give me a compass, a clock, and a sextant, and I'll show you the world."

I struggled to remember which famous explorer first uttered those words. "Was it Magellan or Captain Cook who said that?"

"Neither," Penny boasted, assuming the perfect Captain Morgan pose. "It was Captain Penny Fulton. Now, fire those babies up so I can make my turn for the mainland."

The jammers came online, sending every broadcasting device aboard my boat into chaos, including, hopefully, the Russian tracking device.

"All right, Captain. Give me thirty seconds to get the radar reflectors down, and you may turn at will."

As soon as I had the aluminum discs—designed to make us easy to see on the surface radar—down from the rigging, she spun the wheel, and the big boat obediently came about. Our new course put the wind thirty degrees off our starboard bow. That wind angle wasn't enough for *Aegis* to sail well, but it was enough to produce at least a little thrust, easing the load on the engines as we crossed the Gulf Stream. With the sails trimmed close-hauled and the engines purring like lion cubs, we made twelve knots into the wind. It wasn't a pleasant ride—crossing the Gulf Stream rarely is—but *Aegis* took it in stride.

Penny marked our position and time on the chart. Having someone aboard with her seamanship skill made my life immeasurably simpler.

"I have us pointed at Miami, but that's a big target," she said. "Do you have a marina in mind?"

I pointed toward Key Biscayne on her chart. "There. It's a tiny little anchorage called No Name Harbor. We'll tuck in there and get Dominic to send someone out to determine how the Russians were tracking us."

Penny checked her watch. "It'll still be dark when we get there. Do you know the harbor well enough to motor in before sunrise?"

I stared into the dark night sky. "I wish we had a full moon, but as long as the tide isn't running out of control, I think I can do it. If we have any doubts when we get there, though, we'll anchor out and motor in when the sun comes up."

She put her hands on her hips and stared as if I'd lost my mind. "Anchor out, huh? Just which anchor and chain do you plan to use for that? I hope you're not thinking of using the one we left wrapped around the prop shaft of that yacht back there."

"Oh, yeah. Good point. In that case, the answer is yes, I feel confident I can motor into No Name Harbor in the dark."

She rolled her eyes. "We do have a couple small spare anchors on board, but no more chain. We could anchor in calm conditions with line if we have to, but picking up a mooring ball in the harbor sounds much safer."

We sailed on in silence, neither of us thinking of sleep. My thoughts were consumed with identifying who'd killed Ekaterina Norikova and sent that yacht careening toward us.

"Hey! Was there a tender aboard the yacht that tried to kill us?"

Penny stared down at me from her perch at the helm. "Come to think of it, I don't remember seeing one."

"I didn't, either. That probably means whoever shot Norikova set the autopilot and then jumped ship in the tender."

Penny watched my wheels turning and continued listening.

"That most likely means whoever tried to kill us is still on Bimini."

Her eyes widened. "That means they probably know we got away."

"You're right," I said.

"So they're still looking for us. What are we going to do? Even if we figure out how they were tracking us and remedy it, that's not going to stop them."

Penny was right, as usual, and we needed a plan.

I peered over the bow. "How much time do we have?"

"Ninety minutes, maybe a little longer. Fowey Rocks Light should be coming into view soon. Why?"

"I have a lot to tell you, and once I get started, I don't want to stop."

"If an hour and a half isn't long enough, I suggest you save it for another time or give me the *Reader's Digest* version."

"It'll have to do. This can't wait. It's time you knew everything."

She took a long, deep breath. "Okay, let's hear it."

"When I finished the initial training to become what I am, one of my trainers took me on a field trip to New York to protect a racehorse in the Belmont Stakes. That's the first time I saw Anya. I once thought that was a coincidence, but I can't be sure anymore. She was there specifically to get my attention."

Penny narrowed her eyes but didn't interrupt.

"So, anyway, after that mission with the racehorse, I was sent to Havana to kill a Russian hitman whose real name was Anatoly Parchinkov, but everyone called him Suslik. That means *gopher* in Russian. He was badly bucktoothed and looked a lot like a gopher. So, I did it. I killed him. But he wasn't alone. It turned out he was a triplet. When it was all over, all three of them—or him —were dead, and I got a big fat payday on my first real assignment. That's where most of our money came from."

She bit her lip. "Why are you telling me this?"

"To understand why the Russians are trying to kill me, you have to know the backstory. Just listen. It's important."

She scanned the ocean around us before settling her attention back on me.

"After that, Anya got shot in Miami while we were rescuing Skipper. You know about that, but what you don't know is what happened in the wake of all of that. Anya obviously didn't die from the gunshot, and she was taken to a CIA safe house for interrogation. The Russians even pulled a pair of illegals out of hiding to find Anya. They wanted their girl back…badly."

Penny's mouth hung open. "This sounds like a James Bond movie. I can't believe this stuff really happens."

"Trust me, it happens. But we're a long way from getting you caught up. Clark and I stole a Russian spy sub from Havana Harbor to lure an SVR colonel out of Russia. His name was Victor Tornovich. He's the one who trained Anya and planned the mission to infiltrate my organization by using her as a honey trap."

Penny squinted. "Honey trap?"

"Yes, that's what we call it when a foreign operative seduces one of ours to gain access. Anya was a honey trap."

Penny huffed. "It sounds to me like she was a good one."

If I'd responded to that statement, I would've slept alone for several nights to come, so I ignored it. "Tornovich came out to play, and he lost. Clark and I killed him in Virginia. That's when I met you."

"Yeah, I remember. That's when the saboteurs put the explosives on Kip and Teri's boat instead of this one."

"Exactly," I said. "So, now you're pretty much caught up. I killed all three Susliks. Well, really only two—Anya killed the third. But that doesn't matter. Oh, I almost forgot. Along the way, we killed a Russian billionaire named Dmitri Barkov, the Kremlin lost two embedded illegals, Mike and Sara Anderson, plus, we barbequed Colonel Tornovich. There's just one little tidbit that ties all of this together."

She sighed. "Oh, I can't wait to hear this."

"Actually, you already know most of this one. Anya was thrown in the Black Dolphin Prison when they exchanged her half sister—the dead girl on the yacht—for her. We broke Anya out of the prison and stuck Ekaterina Norikova in her place. So, needless to say, I've stepped on a lot of Russian toes over the past few years. I guess it was foolish to think they'd leave me alone.

I'm sure Norikova caught the bullet in the brain as punishment for getting caught, and they wanted to make sure I knew."

Penny held up a finger. "What if they wanted you to *think* she was Anya? Wouldn't that be a bigger kick in the, well, I'll just leave it at that."

I considered her thought. "Surely, they knew I'd check for the bullet wound in her back."

She shook her head. "Not if you only caught a glimpse of her while she was running over you with a yacht."

"You've got a good point. Maybe that was it. Either way, that's why the Russians are after me. It was stupid to believe they'd let me get away with all of that."

The reality of the moment struck me squarely in the chest. "And, once again, I've put you right in the middle of a life-threatening situation. I don't know why I keep doing that."

She ran her fingers through my hair. "Chase, stop it. I volunteered. If I wasn't willing to accept the risks, I wouldn't have married you. We're in this together, and we'll get out of it together, but you're going to have to tell me what to do. I can run a boat and shoot fish, but I don't know anything about killing Russians…although there's one I'd like to get my hands on."

I pulled her hand from my hair and held it against my chest. "There's no way she has anything to do with this. She's gone, and we'll never see her again."

Penny narrowed her eyes in a look that left no room for interpretation. "As long as she's alive, she's not gone."

Chapter 6
She's a Spy

We motored through the Cape of Florida until No Name Harbor came into sight. A few working lights illuminated the entrance just enough for me to believe it was safe.

I stepped to the wheel. "Okay, Captain, I have the helm."

Good nautical decision-making dictated that no sailor should attempt to enter a harbor after dark if he isn't intimately familiar with every detail of the area. Good nautical manners dictated I shouldn't shine my spotlights into a harbor where other boaters were trying to sleep in the middle of the night. I ignored both.

At idle speed, I crept into the narrow inlet, carefully watching the depth-sounder. After what felt like too many minutes holding my breath, the inlet opened up into the postcard-sized harbor, and I eased *Aegis* alongside the seawall.

Penny stepped from the starboard hull onto the concrete seawall. "Nicely done."

"You may be the better driver," I said, "but I can park."

"Yes, my love. You can park. Shore power or not?"

I tossed the heavy, yellow cords onto the seawall. "Sure, let's plug them up."

Penny had the shore power connected and *Aegis* tied securely to three cleats in no time. After climbing back aboard, she pecked me on the cheek, then headed downstairs. "I'm going to rinse off and hit the sack. I'll see you when you come down."

I finished the few remaining tasks of securing the boat from our trip across the Gulf Stream, and everything seemed to be shipshape.

"I'm sorry the first night of your honeymoon ended with somebody trying to kill us," I said as I climbed into bed.

She rolled over and slid her body against mine. "That's not how the first night of our honeymoon ended. That's how it began. *This* is how it ends."

Her idea of an ending was much better than being targeted by a rogue Russian yacht.

Five hours later, the sun broke over the eastern horizon, and the smell of coffee roused me from sleep. I climbed the stairs to find Penny in plaid pajama pants and a Baylor Bears sweatshirt, pouring coffee into a pair of mugs.

"Good morning, sleepyhead. I wondered if you were ever going to get up."

I nabbed a rolled-up chart from the counter and swatted at her like a drunken swordsman. She yanked the chart from my hand. "Stop it before I have to hurt you. Now, let's go up top and have our coffee."

I gave in, accepted a mug, and headed for the upper deck. The sunrise was spectacular, and I was happy to see only three other boats in the anchorage. Hopefully, no one from Moscow knew where we were.

A jogger came trotting by and waved up at us. "Good morning. That must've been you who came in late last night."

"That was us," I replied. "I hope we didn't wake you."

"Oh, no. I was just surprised to see anyone try that inlet in the dark."

"We didn't have much choice," Penny called down. "My husband"—she motioned toward me—"lost our anchor, so it was motor in or drift around all night."

The jogger glanced toward *Aegis*'s bow and let out a low whistle. "Ouch. How'd that happen?"

I held up my palms in surrender. "Some people should never be allowed to have any responsibility on a boat...and I'm one of those people. She's the sailor. I'm just here to make her life difficult."

Still focusing on where our anchor should've been, he said, "Hey, I'm going into town later. I could give you a lift if you want. You can pick up a new anchor."

"Thanks, I really appreciate the offer, but we'll be okay. If it's not too much trouble, though, I'd love to use your cell phone. Mine sort of went the way of the anchor."

He pulled a phone from his pocket and tossed it up. "Sure, no problem. Just lay it at the helm station on that Sea Ray. I'm going to grab a shower."

"Thanks. I'll have it back to you in a few minutes."

With a wave, he was gone, and I was left with the man's phone, but not his name. I climbed down the ladder and took a stroll toward the tree line where Clark had taken his position when we tried to lure Loui Giordano, the mafia hitman, into No Name Harbor only weeks before. The memory of how badly that night ended would haunt me for the rest of my life.

When I was a sufficient distance from the jammers still humming away aboard my boat, I dialed the borrowed cell phone. "Dominic, it's Chase. I'm sorry to call so early, but I'm in a little pinch."

My handler cleared his throat. "Imagine that. You in a pinch. What have you done now?"

"It's not what I've done. It's what was almost done to me."

I filled him in on the near-miss in Honeymoon Harbour and how we'd activated the jammers and run home.

"It does sound as though you've gotten yourself into another mess. Where are you now?"

"We're in No Name Harbor on Key Biscayne."

"I'll come get you and bring a tech who can find the bugs. Give me an hour."

After returning the cell phone to our neighbor, I discovered Penny had made omelettes and French toast in my absence.

"It's good to be me. Not only can you drive a boat like nobody I know, but you're also a world-class omelette chef."

She struck a pose by the sink. "I'm a lot more than just a pretty face."

"That's exactly what Clark says, but he's never made me breakfast."

"Yeah, but he *is* pretty," she said.

We ate breakfast on the upper deck as the world around us yawned to life. Pelicans dived on baitfish near the entrance to the harbor while a pod of dolphins feasted at the same buffet. The contrast of the tranquility of our morning against the previous night's chaos was astonishing.

Penny finally asked the question she must've been holding back for hours. "What happens next?"

It'd become so easy to forget she wasn't an operator. She had no idea how my world worked. The training Clark and I had endured was as foreign to her as life in North Texas was to me.

"This is an oversimplification," I began, "but basically, we'll find out who's trying to kill us, and we'll kill them first."

"But won't that make everything worse? I mean, the reason they're trying to kill you, or us, is because you killed or embarrassed them in the first place. If you, or we, kill more of them, won't they just send more until they finally win?"

"Maybe," I admitted, "but what other option do we have? If I, or we, kill enough of them, maybe they'll finally decide killing me isn't worth what it costs them."

She stared into her coffee cup. "What if you stop?"

"Stop what?"

"All of it," she said. "What if you stop doing this? All of it. If you retire or quit or whatever spies do, will they stop trying to kill you then?"

"First, I'm not a spy. Second, that's not how it works. I don't have the option of telling the Russians, 'Hey, guys, I'm not playing anymore,' and expect them to stop coming."

Penny didn't look up. "What about her?"

"Who?"

"Anya, or whatever her name really is. Can she make them stop?"

Hearing Penny say Anya's name sent a shiver down my spine. I didn't like the woman I love having to think about the woman before her. Loving Anya wasn't real, but to Penny, there was nothing truer and more concrete than the way I'd felt about the Russian seductress.

"I'm not sure what you're suggesting, but I have no way to contact her, and even if I did, what would I tell her?"

Penny licked her lips and placed the cup on the table. "You'd say something like, 'Hey, Anya, it's Chase. Remember me? Some of your countrymen are trying to kill me. Is there anything you can do about that?'"

I foolishly let the sound of Anya's Russian-accented English play through my head.

"Yes, of course I remember you, Chasechka, but I cannot stop SVR from trying to kill you. I am only one girl out in cold in Siberia. I can do nothing to help you."

I gathered my wits, and my courage, as I downed the last sip of coffee. "Even if I could find her, she's not inside the Russian government anymore. She's on the run, probably living somewhere in Siberia, or maybe not even in Russia at all. Anya is definitely *not* the answer."

Penny winked. "That may be the smartest thing you've ever said, Chasechka."

Relieved to hear my wife laugh about Anya, I said, "Texas twang doesn't play well with Russian pet names."

She lifted my mug from the table. "Texas girls don't play well with Russian girls who are after their man, either. Remember that. I'll be right back with more coffee for the spy who loves me."

I watched her descend the ladder and thought about how much better my life was with the beautiful and vivacious Penny Fulton than it ever could've been with Anastasia Burinkova.

When Penny topped the ladder, instead of carrying a pair of coffee mugs, she was holding a baseball in her right hand. "Hey, catcher... Catch!"

With that, she tossed the ball toward me, and I instinctually stuck out my left hand to make the grab. Looking down at the brilliantly white ball in my palm, I read, "We sure wish you could've been here." It was signed by general manager John Schuerholz and manager Bobby Cox of the 1998 Atlanta Braves.

If my baseball career hadn't been demolished, along with my right hand and wrist, in the 1996 College World Series, I may have been a member of that 1998 Atlanta Braves team, though probably in the minor leagues.

"How did you get this?"

Penny smiled. "Happy honeymoon!"

I couldn't stop staring at the ball. "But seriously, how did you get John Schuerholz and Bobby Cox to sign a ball for me?"

She performed a little happy dance. "Do you have any idea how hard it is to surprise a spy? I had to do a lot of sneaking around while you were out saving the world."

I stood and took her in my arms. "Penny, you're amazing. This is amazing, and I can't believe you pulled it off. I love the ball, and I love you."

She leaned back and looked up at me. "I love you, too, Chase, and I really like surprising you."

"You surprise me every day, Penny. I don't know what I'd do without you. Oh, and I'm not a spy."

She gave me the stink eye. "Oh, I'm pretty sure I know what you'd do without me. Or at least *who* you'd do. And I know for a fact she's a spy."

I stood on the upper deck of my boat, bouncing the auto-graphed baseball in my right hand and thinking about what Penny had said. "You know, you may be onto something. What if we threw the Russians a curve they never saw coming...with their own ball?"

She backed away and cocked her head to the side. "I'm not following."

"I need some time to work it out, but you're right. She *was* a spy."

Chapter 7
Bad-Ass Angels

Dominic pulled up in his Land Rover with a pair of particularly geeky looking minions in his wake. The two men wore cargo shorts and tattered black T-shirts, one boasting AC/DC, and the other, Metallica. Each man carried a matching plastic case.

Dominic gave us a quick wave. "Good morning, Chase. Permission to come aboard?"

"Of course," I said. "We'll be right down."

Penny and I descended the ladder and met the three men in the cockpit.

"Good morning, Dominic. Thanks for coming out so soon. Would you like some coffee?"

"I'd love a cup, but these guys"—he motioned toward his two minions—"they're anxious to get to work."

I pointed toward the interior of the boat. "Make yourselves at home. I still have the jammers running. I can show you how to turn them off if you'd like."

The two men shot a look at each other and laughed like hyenas. One of them said, "We installed the jammers, so I'm pretty sure we can turn them off."

Dominic grinned. "Techs aren't like normal humans, Chase. They're odd little creatures."

Penny materialized with three cups of coffee, and Dominic took one from her hand. "Thank you, Penny, and congratulations on the new last name."

She smiled. "Thank you. It was a spur of the minute thing, but I couldn't be happier."

He blew across the surface of the steaming coffee. "So, tell me about the near-miss."

I motioned for the settees, and the three of us took a seat. "Well, we were having dinner in Honeymoon Harbour when a yacht—at least a hundred fifty footer—came plowing into the anchorage at full steam. She was bearing directly on us. I cut the snubbers and opened the windlass while Penny backed us away from the anchor. The yacht missed us by inches but picked up our anchor chain and dragged us onto a shallow reef. When the dust settled, we boarded her and found Captain Ekaterina Norikova dead at the helm. She was the only one aboard."

"Let me guess. She was already dead before the yacht entered the anchorage."

"You got it. A bullet to the base of her skull did the trick."

He sipped his coffee. "Interesting. And you're sure no one else was aboard?"

"We didn't tear the yacht apart, but we did a cursory search, and there were no signs of anyone else."

Dominic pulled a photograph from his leather binder and slid it across the cockpit table. It was an aerial shot of Honeymoon Harbour without a boat in sight.

He motioned toward the picture with his coffee cup. "That was taken as soon as the sun came up this morning."

Penny jerked her attention toward him. "That's not possible. When the sun went down last night, there was a yacht on her side right here." She stabbed the upper edge of the picture with her index finger.

Dominic shrugged. "Well, that may be, but there isn't one there now. In fact, there isn't a yacht matching the description you gave within fifty miles of that spot."

I locked eyes with Dominic. "So, what are you saying?"

"I'm saying either it never happened, or someone towed a two-hundred-ton yacht off that reef and out of that harbor and then sank her overnight."

"Oh, it happened," Penny and I said in unison.

"I believe you, but unless we can find that yacht on the bottom, you're going to have a hard time convincing anyone else. Did you take pictures?"

I slowly shook my head. "No, all I could think of was getting out of there and jamming any signal *Aegis* was broadcasting."

"Unless you caused the chaos, always take pictures."

Even though I'd been in the covert ops game for over half a decade, I still had a lot to learn.

Penny examined the photo. "The ocean is almost three thousand feet deep just five miles west of where it happened, so there's no chance of finding that yacht if the Russians sank it out there."

"That's not what concerns me," Dominic said. "The problem is the Russians obviously have a ship capable of dragging a yacht off a reef, and a crew capable of sinking that yacht in a few hours. In the dark. Less than sixty miles off Miami."

I closed my eyes and sighed. "That means they had a team close enough to see us run."

Penny said, "Yeah, they might've seen us run north out of Honeymoon Harbour, but you set the jammers and took down the radar reflectors before we turned west. There's no way they could've tracked us all the way home."

"Unless they followed us."

Penny shook her head. "We were watching all night with night vision. We would've seen a tail."

"Maybe," I admitted, "but it's still possible they followed us."

"Here's my recommendation," Dominic said. "I think you two should take a long vacation somewhere inland. You can take my Porsche or the King Air. It doesn't matter. Just get away from the water for a while so we can sort this out."

I swallowed my last drop of coffee. "I've got a better idea."

Penny and Dominic immediately focused on me. "I think we should let them kill me."

"What?" came Penny and Dominic's shocked replies.

"Okay, I don't mean literally kill me, but I have an idea that'll make them *believe* they've killed me."

Dominic leaned in. "Let's hear it."

"I don't have all the details worked out yet, and it relies on something Penny suggested earlier, but if we can find Anya, there's definitely a chance. It's going to take a knuckleball to pull it off, though."

Dominic didn't flinch, but Penny's eyebrows raised. "What are you talking about?"

"You said it earlier, Penny. You said maybe Anya could help. I didn't think it was possible at the time, but it just might work."

I outlined my plan for them until the pair of technicians reemerged from *Aegis*'s interior. Without a word, the tech in the Metallica shirt tossed my fluorescent green emergency position indicating radio beacon onto the table in front of us.

I looked up at him. "So what? That's my EPIRB."

The tech shook his head. "No, it's not. It *looks* like your EPIRB, but it wouldn't have done you a bit of good if you'd set it off in the middle of the ocean."

"What are you talking about?" I demanded.

"Somebody replaced your EPIRB with this device that looks identical on the outside, but the electronics inside transmit only on one frequency, and that frequency isn't used by the Coast Guard."

I gritted my teeth. "It was hidden right under my nose."

"That's right," the tech said. "It's brilliant. If only we had a way to use it to our advantage...."

I slapped the geeky little man on his shoulder. "You're a genius. I've got just the guy."

The two techs glimpsed at each other with confusion as I pulled my cell phone from my pocket. "So, are you saying it's safe to use my phone?"

"Sure. The only culprit on this boat is that thing. Your phone is fine."

Thirty seconds later, NCIS Special Agent Stone Hunter answered. "Agent Hunter."

"Hunter, it's Chase." I watched for a reaction from the technicians. "How are things at Kings Bay Naval Submarine Base?"

As I expected, the technicians' eyes lit up.

"Things are fine up here, Chase, but why are you calling me on your honeymoon?"

"We had an unexpected visitor, and I think you can help."

I spent the next few minutes detailing my plan. When I finished, his response was all the confirmation I could want.

"I can be there with Singer and Mongo in less than three hours if you want security on the northbound leg."

"Hang on a second, Hunter." I covered the phone with my palm and turned to Dominic. "Do you have any trigger pullers who don't get seasick?"

"I've got Clay," he said. "You met him on that thing in Bimini."

Pressing the phone back to my cheek, I said, "Bring Mongo, but Singer's broken leg makes him a liability. I've got another good man down here, and he worked with Penny on board a job in the Keys."

"We'll be there ASAP, but you need to talk to the Navy brass about using one of their boats. That's way above my paygrade."

"I'll take care of that. You heard the president when he told me I had a blank check and the Navy's full cooperation."

Hunter chuckled. "Yeah, but when was the last time you heard of a politician keeping his word?"

"We're about to find out."

Dominic was already on the phone activating Clay, the operator who'd kept Penny and Skipper alive during the Mario Righetti job when *Aegis* got herself shot to hell. He'd proved his mettle under fire as far as I was concerned, and his familiarity with my boat was a definite asset.

Dominic hung up. "Clay will be here in less than an hour, but what did you say about the president writing you a blank check?"

"Oh, yeah," I said. "That's something we need to talk about."

He raised his eyebrows but didn't speak.

"While I was in D.C. settling a few scores with Brinkwater, the Secret Service scooped me up and dropped me off in the Oval Office for a chat with the commander in chief." I paused, waiting for Dominic to open his mouth, but he sat in impatient silence. "So, anyway, the president asked me to build a tactical team—Team Twenty-One, he called it—in Saint Marys, Georgia, and said I'd have all the budget I needed and the full cooperation of the Navy just across the fence at Kings Bay Naval Submarine Base."

I thought Dominic would surely have a comment by that point, but still nothing.

"The chief of naval operations, Admiral Gene Galloway, was in the meeting, as well as General Tommy Beaufour, the DCI."

That did it. Dominic reached the limit of his patience. "Yeah, Chase. I know who Tommy Beaufour is. What I don't know is why you'd be in a room with the president, the DCI, and the CNO making deals I've not authorized. You're a twenty-eight-year-old rookie with half a dozen ops under your belt. What makes you think you have the authority to do something like that?"

It was time for my eyebrows to go up. "Look, Dominic. I didn't stroll up to the White House and knock on the door. The president sent for me. He offered the deal. I didn't—"

Dominic's face glowed like coal embers. "You didn't! I'll tell you what you didn't do. You didn't follow protocol. You work for me. You've gone way off the reservation on this one, scout."

I drove my fist into the tabletop. "Listen very closely. Next time you plan to yell at me, no matter how few ops I have under my belt, you won't do it on my boat."

"Your boat?" he belted. "You wouldn't have this boat if it weren't for me, and I've never asked you for a penny for it!"

My teeth ground together as I tried to control my rage. "Is that what this is about, Dominic? Huh? You want me to write you a check for this boat? Fine! Name the price."

He sat stewing in his anger, then pounded his fingertip into the settee. "This is a two-million-dollar boat, dammit."

I stormed from the table and returned moments later with a checkbook. After writing the check, I slammed my coffee cup on top of it. "There you go. There's your check for this two-million-dollar boat. Now it's your turn to write me one for the two-hundred-fifty-million-dollar yacht I handed you the day you brought this one to me. Is that what you want, Dominic? Do you want to start keeping score with dollar signs?"

Dominic closed his eyes and took several long breaths. "Okay, Chase. I'm sorry. You're right. But you're my responsibility. When you make deals—especially deals with the president of the United States—that affects operations you can't understand."

I gathered my thoughts. "So teach me. I've been doing this since ninety-seven, and I've never met anyone above you in this organization. I don't even know what this organization is. I don't know who funds it, who manages it, who decides what missions we take. A bunch of old guys I barely knew recruited me and sent me off to a training camp straight out of a James Bond movie. You tell me where to go, who to kill, when to run, and when to fight. I've never signed a contract. I've never even negotiated a rate of pay. I've let you lead me around by the nose for five years. If I've gone off the reservation, as you put it, then show me the fences of that reservation. Let me meet the chief. And for God's sake, stop expecting me to know the rules that everyone seems to be making up as we go along."

"You're right. I have kept you in the dark, and everyone, especially me, knew this day would come. You're the best young operative to ever come out of The Ranch. You've got instincts like no one I've ever seen. Hell, even Clark says you're the best he's ever seen, and he never has anything good to say about anybody younger than him. When Dr. Richter recruited you, he knew exactly what he was doing, and thanks to him, three of the world's deadliest assassins are dead…by your hands. We know more about Chinese spy technology than we've learned in the fifty years prior to what you did in Panama. And thanks to you, my son is alive. He would've died on that mountain if you hadn't saved him and the team. You're not a baseball player anymore, Chase. You're a force in the world. You're changing the geopolitical landscape of the planet, and none of us knows what the hell to do with you."

I was speechless, and as usual, when I don't know what else to do, I turned to Penny. My beautiful, North Texas, wild-haired wife sat with her mouth agape, obviously as dumbfounded as me. She'd never seen me lose my cool like that, and she certainly had no idea I was the man my handler had just described.

Dominic cleared his throat. "The president wasn't rewarding you, Chase. He was putting his thumb on you because he's afraid of you. Everybody on Earth who has a brain is afraid of you. You've proven time after time that the only way you can be stopped is to kill you. That's why the Russians want you dead. If you take on a mission, regardless of it coming from me or if you dream it up yourself, you don't stop until it's complete, no matter how many bodies pile up in the process."

I couldn't tell if he was sincere or if he was playing a psychological game of flattery with me. "Dominic, I'm what *you* created. The trainers at The Ranch turned me into what I am."

He squeezed his tongue between his lips and clenched his eyelids as if he were deciding what to say next. "No, that's not true. We could send a hundred thousand kids through The Ranch and never get another Chase Fulton. We didn't create you—we discovered you. Just like a diamond miner doesn't create the gems. He digs them out of the earth and hands them off to someone else for polishing. No, Chase, we didn't create you. We just polished you."

I dismissed his flattery as simply that. "Okay, the question still remains. What *should* I have told the president?"

"You should've never been in that meeting."

"So, who do I...who do *we* work for?"

A look of surrender came over his face. "We work for a board of directors with no name. We're funded, sometimes, by the federal government, but not always. Sometimes our funding comes from overseas sources, but everything we do—and I do mean everything—is always done for the preservation of the way of life America has come to expect and deserve. If it doesn't directly benefit Americans or our allies, we don't do it."

"Who makes those decisions? Who decides when I'm going to be sent to Panama to screw with the Chinese?"

He nodded almost imperceptibly. "The board. They decide when a mission needs to happen, and then they talk to handlers like me to decide who is best suited to complete the mission. Invariably, you get the nod when the job would kill everyone else. We all believe you've got one bad-ass guardian angel who's claimed you as his own."

I cast another glance toward Penny, who'd become a sponge, sitting in silence and absorbing everything around her.

"Okay, so let's say everything you're telling me is true. What's wrong with working directly for the president with a bottomless pit of money at my disposal to keep doing exactly what I've been doing for you?"

"That's a great question, and the answer is...nothing. There's absolutely nothing wrong with doing what you're describing under *this* president, but what happens in a few years when the country changes its collective mind and elects a president who doesn't think the American way is the best way? We don't need a president like that having full control over people like you. We don't need a president like that knowing people like you even exist."

He was right. In fact, I can't remember a time when he was wrong, and I'd just learned a valuable lesson about the wisdom of experience versus the exuberance of youth.

Dominic watched my wheels turning. "What did you tell the president?"

I let the meeting in the Oval Office replay through my mind. "I didn't commit, but the president acted and spoke as if I had."

He huffed. "That's what he does. No matter what answer he gets, he pretends it's the one he wanted and congratulates you on making a great decision. He's one of the good guys, but he's a politician through and through."

Resigned to accept his advice, I asked, "So, what do I do now?"

"You tell the president no," came his oversimplified reply.

I tried not to laugh. "I'm not sure that's how this works."

Dominic gave in and made no effort to stifle his laughter. "No, you're right, but you have to find a way to tell him no and make him believe it was his idea to withdraw the offer. I think it's time for you to put a little of that psychological education to work."

Chapter 8
Mission Brief

"Permission to come aboard?" came a booming voice from ashore.

I peered over the rail to see Clay, the knuckle-dragging trigger-puller who'd defended Penny, Skipper, and my beloved boat against an attack in the Western Caribbean, and nearly lost his life doing so.

"You never have to ask. Come aboard anytime, Clay. How are you?"

The fireplug of a man climbed the sugar-scoop boarding ladder and immediately hugged Penny. When she'd finally let him go, he turned to me and stuck out his hand. "I'm great, Chase. Oh, and Dominic, thanks for calling me. I appreciate the work, and I'll never pass up a shot at a mission with Chase."

I glanced down at my watch. "It's too early for cocktails, but we've still got coffee if you'd like a cup."

Clay waved a dismissive hand. "No, thanks. I'd rather have a mission brief."

"Well," I began, "you'll be glad to know we're not dealing with the mob on this one."

"Been there, done that," Clay said. "But who is it this time?"

"I'm pretty sure it's the *Sluzhba vneshney razvedki Rossiyskoy Federatsii*."

Clay pursed his lips. "Ooh, the Ruskies. You don't mess around, do you?"

I held up my hands in mock surrender. "Hey, they started it."

He laughed. "Somehow, I doubt that."

"Okay, maybe I poked the bear a little, but I'm glad you're on board."

Clay offered an exaggerated salute. "Oh, I'm in, but it'd be nice to know what we're doing."

I met Dominic's warning glance. "Well, until just moments ago, it was my plan to sail *Aegis* up the east coast of Florida to Saint Marys, Georgia, pass this EPIRB..."—I pointed to the bright green device lying on the table—"...off to the deck of a naval warship, then watch the fireworks."

Clay stared at the EPIRB. "I've never claimed to be the honor student, but I'm completely lost."

I lifted the device from the table and tossed it between my hands. "Last night, Penny and I narrowly escaped an attempt on our lives in Honeymoon Harbour off Bimini. It seems the Russians have been using this device disguised as an EPIRB to track my boat."

Clay's face lit up. "Ah, now it's coming together for me. You were going to let the Russians believe the EPIRB was still on your boat and let 'em deal with the big guns of the U.S. Navy next time they made a run at you."

"Exactly," I said, "but Dominic put the kibosh on that plan because I have to turn down an offer from the—"

Dominic cleared his throat and sent his shoe crashing into my left shin. I got the message.

"Dominic says I have to decline an offer from some people I don't necessarily want to be in bed with, and that'll eliminate the Navy's willingness to play along with my little game of peek-a-boo with a warship."

"So, what's the plan now?" Clay asked.

"It's not as sexy as watching a Navy destroyer unload on an unsuspecting Russian hit squad, but it'll be exciting if we can stay alive long enough to pull it off."

Penny smiled for the first time in hours. "Did he scare you off yet, Clay?"

"Are you kidding? I don't scare that easy, and besides, whatever it is sounds like a lot more fun than executive protection or convoy ops. I'd wade through Hell in gasoline underwear to fight a buzz saw with you and Chase, so count me in."

Penny's question surprised me. I'd never questioned her bravery or commitment to me, but this mission had the potential to push our relationship beyond any limits either of us could imagine. I still wasn't ready to tell her all the details.

My phone trilled, and I stuck it to my ear. "Chase here."

"It's Hunter. We'll be wheels up in two minutes. A dude name Crip from Saint Marys is bringing us down. He scored a Cessna Four-Fourteen while his Baron is down for annual inspection. You'll cover his gas and fee, won't you?"

I covered the phone and grinned at Penny. "Your boyfriend, Crip, the pilot who took us to Charleston, is bringing the guys down."

She rolled her eyes.

"Yeah, I know Crip," I said. "Tell him Penny says hi, and I'll be glad to pay him."

"Wilco. Are we going to need anything heavier than a three-oh-eight?"

"We will, but there's no need to haul the cannons down on the airplane. Dominic will set us up with what we need down here. I'll see you guys in a couple of hours."

As I hung up the phone, I realized my mouth had written a stack of checks my butt may not be able to cash. I'd promised Hunter, Mongo, and Singer jobs on Tactical Team 21, relying on the president's promised budget to cover their salaries. Since Dominic had gotten my head straight about dealing with politicians, I had inherited three employees. The board—whoever they were—would foot the bill for getting the Russians off my back, but after that, I'd be on the hook for payroll. All of a sudden, my stress level headed for the stars.

"Hunter and Mongo are airborne and should be here in a couple of hours. I'll brief the whole team when they arrive instead of duplicating briefings. Are you guys okay with that?"

Penny nodded.

"Sure," Clay said. "Whatever. But do you realize there's a two-million-dollar check lying on this table?"

Dominic slid the check from beneath the coffee cup, folded it in half, and slid it into his shirt pocket. "Yes, it's a little insurance policy to keep Chase from making deals with politicians without my approval. If he pulls that stunt again, I'll cash his check."

I glared at him, unsure if he was serious. "Are your techno-geeks still around?"

Dominic whistled as if he were summoning a hunting dog, and the pair of wizards materialized.

I held up the EPIRB. "Can you guys emulate the signal this thing emits and broadcast it from somewhere else?"

The two men stared at each other as if they shared a brain…a very big brain. Finally, the one in the AC/DC shirt said, "No, we can't do that, but we can lie to the transmitter, and that's almost as good."

"I don't understand," I said. "Can you explain that a little better?"

AC/DC said, "Sure. We can't make the transmitter emit a signal from anywhere else, but we can reprogram it to make it think it's someplace else. That way, when you turn off the jammers, the transmitter will tell whoever is listening that it's in coastal Africa or wherever you want."

"That could come in handy," I said, "but for now, let's leave it dark while we're waiting for Hunter and while I find a new anchor and chain."

Dominic spoke up. "I think I can help with that. Bring *your* boat around to the yard, and I'll have the shipwrights install new ground tackle. We'll stow a spare aboard as well, just in case."

The techs' eyes suddenly danced wildly, and that made me nervous.

"Are you guys okay?" I asked.

Metallica offered a sheepish grin. "Are you going to sail to the shipyard?"

I glanced at the wind vane at the top of the mast. "Yeah, we'll sail if there's enough wind. Why?"

He shot a look back at AC/DC, and the man nodded furiously. He then turned back to me. "If you wouldn't mind...I mean, if it's okay... Or maybe if..."

I shook my head. "Come on, man, spit it out. What are you trying to say?"

Penny giggled. "Do you two want to sail with us to the yard?"

AC/DC said, "Oh, that'd be great. We've done a lot of work on sailboats, but neither of us has ever left the dock."

Penny didn't wait for me to respond. "Yes, of course, you can sail with us."

Dominic tried not to laugh. "Okay, Clay, come on. You can follow me back and leave your car at the shipyard. We'll see you guys back there." He turned his attention to me. "If you let my two best techs fall overboard and drown, you'll owe me a lot more than two million dollars."

Penny had the engines warming up before I could get ashore to cast off the lines, and the techs were in awe of every move she made. Most men were in awe of Penny, but the nerdy gadget guys were especially smitten.

I climbed back aboard as Penny brought *Aegis* about and motored through the narrow inlet. The channel was far less ominous in the light of day, and she made the task look easy. To everyone's delight, especially the techs, the wind was blowing sixteen knots on Biscayne Bay.

Penny stuck the bow in the wind, and I called for AC/DC and Metallica to help me hoist the mainsail.

"Heave-ho! Heave-ho!" I called as the two men pulled on the mainsail halyard with every ounce of strength they possessed.

"Chase, cut it out. That's not nice," Penny chided from the helm.

"Okay, okay," I said as I wrapped the halyard around the motorized winch and pressed the button. The halyard came taut, and the mainsail slid effortlessly up the mast under the power of the winch. The techs stared aloft as the enormous white sail billowed in the wind.

Penny allowed *Aegis* to fall off the wind, and the mainsail filled, taking over the job previously belonging to the diesels. The engines fell silent, and the headsail unfurled, adding its strength to the efforts of the main. My boat danced across the one-foot waves and settled into the wind at ten knots.

Penny made a come-hither motion with her finger and called, "Oh, boys! Who wants to drive?"

After a five-minute training session from Penny, the men took turns at the helm like giddy schoolboys fighting over a new toy.

When she was confident the techs could handle the boat without hitting anything, she joined me on the trampoline at the bow.

"This is nice," I said.

"What's nice? Having someone else drive or hanging out with your wife on the trampoline?"

"Both. Definitely both."

Twenty minutes later, a voice came from the helm. "Uh, could you maybe tell us where we're going?"

Penny cupped her hands around her mouth and yelled. "Look at the chart plotter! I programmed the shipyard as our destination. Follow the magenta line."

Half an hour later, the boat turned into the wind and stalled. Penny and I sat up to watch the techs try to figure it out. The pair stared up at the rigging and traced lines through blocks, clutches, and winches.

I stood to help them resolve the issue the turn had caused, but Penny grabbed my arm. "No, give them a minute. I think they can figure it out. They *are* supposed to be geniuses."

I returned to her side and watched the circus. Finally, the light came on for Metallica, and he turned the wheel, allowing the boat to fall off the wind and pick up speed again.

"I think they're figuring it out," Penny whispered.

As *Aegis* accelerated through seven or eight knots, the tech turned the wheel and began to haul in on the headsail sheet, trimming the sail for the new wind angle. The mainsail traveler proved a little more challenging for the pair, but they finally figured it out, and soon we were sailing close-hauled, straight toward Dominic's shipyard.

Penny and I returned to the cockpit. The utter joy glowing on the techs' faces was amazing, but it was time for Penny to take over.

"I'm sorry to kick you off the helm, but I think I'd better take it from here."

They begrudgingly surrendered the wheel, and Penny expertly reclaimed her rightful place. Soon the diesels were purring again, and the sails were furled. Dominic and Clay helped us tie up alongside the seawall, and the techs took turns hugging Penny and gushing appreciation as if it were her boat. Perhaps they understood far more about the reality of things than me.

What I knew better than anyone was that over the coming days, reality for a great many people was going to change in ways few of them could predict. I only hoped the core of my reality could withstand the strain and remain intact.

Chapter 9
Ground Tackle

"Your ground tackle is rigged, Mr. Fulton. We installed three hundred feet of chain and two new anchors. We also made a few repairs. There was some damage that wasn't easy to see on the surface, but when we got into the job, it was obvious it needed a little more attention."

The shipwright was rugged-looking and in his fifties, with the skin of a man who'd spent his life in the sun.

I shook his hand and slipped two hundred bucks into his palm. "Thank you. I appreciate you taking such good care of *Aegis*. She's a good boat."

"She sure is," he said. "And thanks, but this isn't necessary. Mr. Fontana pays us well."

"I'm sure he does, but that boat means a lot to me."

The man looked over his shoulder at *Aegis*. "Yeah, she means a lot to me, too. I'm the one who rebuilt her."

"Rebuilt her?" I said.

"Yeah, don't you know your boat's history?"

I saw Penny leaning toward the shipwright as he spoke.

"No, I don't know her history. I just know I got her from Dominic, and he pocketed a big check from me."

"I'm Tommy Adkins," the man said, sticking out his calloused bear paw.

"Nice to meet you, Tommy. I'm Chase, and this is my wife, Penny."

He nodded toward Penny. "Ma'am. Anyway, we pulled that boat off the bottom near Cabo and stuck her on a cargo hauler in ninety-seven. They hauled her through the ditch and dropped her here, and she became my pet project. I worked on that boat for over a year. New everything—engines, generators, wiring, electronics. You name it, she got it. Those two characters you brought in with you today, they pulled every inch of wire and installed everything that makes a spark on that baby. She's a heck of a boat."

"How did she sink?" Penny asked, suddenly more intrigued than before.

"Oh, she was built to sink. That was her job. I figured you knew."

Penny gasped, and I cocked my head. "Built to sink? What do you mean by that?"

Tommy turned to Dominic. "You didn't tell 'em?"

Dominic smiled. "No, it never came up. But go ahead and tell the story. Chase and Penny are with us."

Tommy pulled his handkerchief from his back pocket and wiped his hands as he apparently considered where to start his story. "I guess you're gonna need a little background. There was this cartel guy on the Baja." He glanced at Penny. "You know, the Baja California—the peninsula in western Mexico."

Penny smiled. "Yes, I know."

"So, anyway, there was this guy. He had every politician on the West Coast in his pocket. Or a better description would be that he was shoving paper money into the pockets of every lawmaker, judge, and top cop in California to look the other way when his *product*"—he made air quotes around the word—"magically found its way across the border at Tijuana."

I was losing patience. "This is a great story, but I'm having trouble figuring out how it has anything to do with my boat."

"Keep your shirt on. I'm getting to that part. So, we built this boat and arranged for it to fall into this guy's hands—you know, like a gift. This dude was flashy and arrogant, so he wanted the biggest, fastest, most extravagant catamaran in the Pacific. Man, we decked it out with all the trimmings. If it shimmered, shined, or glittered, we stuck it on that boat. We also designed a major defect in the hulls and water-activated locking mechanisms on the hatches."

Penny said, "You mean you drowned the guy intentionally?"

Tommy shot a look at Dominic and then back at me, obviously unsure how to answer her question. "Well, um…yes, ma'am. That's sort of what we do. He was a bad dude, and the crap he was sending across the border by the truckload was killing a hundred kids on the street a day. Nobody was willing to stop him because he was making every one of them rich."

Penny leapt to her feet, threw her right hand in the air, and gave the man an exuberant high five. "Well done, Tommy!"

The man appeared a little uncertain about what to make of Penny. I knew exactly how he felt.

"I love it," I said, "but I really appreciate you getting all that glitter and bling off the boat when you rebuilt her. We're a little less flashy than your run-of-the-mill cartel kingpin."

"Yeah, so that's the story of your boat. She's been to the bottom once for a good cause, but I hope she never has to suffer that fate again."

I sighed in appreciation for his affection toward *Aegis*. "I'll do my best to keep her on top for the rest of her life, Tommy. Thanks again for the ground tackle and repairs."

He shrugged. "It was my pleasure, and it was good seeing the old girl again."

When Tommy made his exit, Dominic pulled the two-million-dollar check from his pocket and fed it to the shredder beside his desk. "Quite a story, huh, Chase?"

"Nothing is as it appears," I said.

Dominic glanced at his watch. "Speaking of appearances, it's about time for your friends from up north to touch down."

As if on cue, my phone trilled, and Hunter's voice came through the speaker. "Chase, we're on deck at Opa-Locka, and we can't exactly climb in a cab with our, um…equipment."

I covered the speaker and looked up at Dominic.

He spoke before I could ask my question. "Have them see Mario in the FBO. He has a van for them under my name."

I passed the word, and thirty-five minutes later, I watched Hunter step from behind the wheel, Mongo peel his enormous frame through the passenger door, and Singer—the Southern Baptist sniper—hobble from the back seat with his leg still in a full-length cast.

Hunter spoke before I could protest. "Don't blame me. He said he'd shoot any vehicle out from under us if we didn't bring him, and you've seen him shoot. I wasn't going to take the chance."

"Singer," I began, "what use are you going to be on a boat with a broken leg?"

He grinned his always-infectious grin. "Nobody's gonna sneak up on us if I'm on board. If I can see 'em, I can shoot 'em. Who else is gonna snipe for you if I'm not around?"

"I can't argue with that," I admitted. "Let's get inside and talk about what's going to happen."

On the walk—well, the hobble for Singer—back into Dominic's office, I pulled Penny aside. "Listen, I should've told you this earlier, but my plan involves finding Anya. I know you're not completely cool with that, but please save your objections until you've heard the whole plan, okay?"

She grabbed two fistfuls of my shirt and pulled me toward her. "Chase Fulton, listen to me. I know enough about you to know you get what you want. If Anya is who you wanted, she'd be the one making your coffee and frying your bacon every morning. And I think you know what I mean by *frying your bacon*. You chose me, and that means I'm who you want. If using Anya to get you out of the Russians' sights is what it takes, I'll help you find her. Oh, and I'll also gut her like pig if she makes any moves on my man."

I kissed her forehead. "I never want my bacon fried by anyone else but you."

I was the last one into Dominic's office. Singer was situating his broken leg in a position that must've hurt less than any other position he tried.

"Okay, so here's what's going on." I retold the story of what happened in Honeymoon Harbour and how the techs found the dummy EPIRB broadcasting *Aegis's* position to the Russians. "This is the plan. I'm going to contact the SVR—heck, I may stroll right up the steps to the Kremlin and knock on the door— and cut a deal with them. They want Anya. They probably want to behead her. I don't know, and I don't care. It really doesn't matter because they're never going to get her, but I'm going to cut a deal with them to leave me alone if I deliver Anya to them. We know they've been hunting her down since the day we broke her out of the Black Dolphin Prison, and so far, they've not found her."

Mongo stared at the ceiling. "If the whole Russian government can't find her, what makes you think you can?"

"That's the beauty of my plan," I said. "I don't have to find her. She just needs to know that I'm trying to find her. If that happens, she'll find me."

Mongo huffed. "This sounds like a terrible plan already, and that's my favorite kind of plan. Keep talking."

"The other advantage we have that the Russians don't is Skipper. She's the best operational analyst I know."

The team didn't need to know that I really only knew one operational analyst.

Hunter stuck his finger in the air. "Forgive me for stating the obvious, but how do you plan to get this Anya person to surrender herself to the Russians after she finds you?"

I pointed directly at him. "Bingo. That's the right question, Hunter, and I'm glad you asked. The answer is simple. I'm going to convince Anya to kill me and let the Russians watch. You see, the Russians want me dead more than they want Anya back in prison, so if she kills me—and if they get to watch—they'll slowly accept her back into the loving arms of Mother Russia. It's a win-win. Anya comes in out of the cold, and the SVR gets that pesky American wiped off the face of the planet."

Singer let his cast leg fall to the floor. "Am I the only one who isn't a fan of the part about you getting killed?"

I folded my hands together. "Thank you for caring, Singer. Of course, I'm not really going to let her kill me, but we're going to put on the performance of a lifetime. A performance fit for the Bolshoi Theater." I stopped talking and sat in silence while the room pondered my idea.

Singer was first. "I don't like it, Chase. There's too much that can go wrong."

Mongo agreed. "You know I'll follow you anywhere, but Singer's right—this plan has a lot of holes in it."

Hunter stared me down. "What if she takes you up on the offer before the Russians show up to watch? Can you stop her from killing you and dragging your body into Red Square?"

Dominic had been silent throughout the briefing but obviously couldn't hold his tongue any longer. "It's a logistical nightmare, Chase, and there's a thousand moving parts. I'm with these guys. I don't love it."

The last person I could've imagined coming to the defense of my plan spoke up, and her words rang through the room like a bell. "He's my husband, and he's the bravest, smartest man I know. I was there last night when they tried to kill us. They're not going to stop coming. You don't have to love Chase's plan, but unless you've got a better one, please figure out how to make this one work. You all know that's exactly what he'd do for you."

Chapter 10
Loose Lips Sink Ships

Silence has a way of turning seconds into hours and minutes into days in the psyches of men and women of action. The people in Dominic's office fell well into that category, and the heaviness in the air felt like anvils on our shoulders.

A knock at the door pulled the five of us from our anxious need for a better plan.

The voice of Tommy, the shipwright, came pouring through the door. "I'm sorry to interrupt, but I need to talk to Chase for a minute."

I stood, thankful to have an excuse to do anything other than stew the shallow broth of the worst plan I'd ever concocted. "I'll be right back."

I met Tommy at the door and saw *Aegis* suspended ten feet in the air, hanging from the cradles of a massive boat lift.

"What's my boat doing out of the water?"

"That's what I need to talk to you about," Tommy said. "I sent a diver in to inspect the hull, you know, just in case there was some damage we couldn't see from above the waterline. Anyway, he found a little issue. Come on. I'll show you."

He led me beneath the thirty-thousand-pound behemoth and slid his hand along the starboard keel as we walked. "See this?"

I studied the fiberglass hull covered in marine growth. "I don't see what you're talking about, but she looks like she could use a bottom job since you've got her out of the water."

"Oh, she's definitely getting a bottom job, but run your hand along the fiberglass right here." He motioned toward a seam in the hull.

I followed his instruction.

"Do you feel that?"

"I feel a little bit of a seam, but it doesn't feel bad. What do you think it is?" I asked, still sliding my hand back and forth across the slick fiberglass.

"That's where one of the flooding ports was when this hull was originally molded. It feels like it's coming apart to me. We'll x-ray it, but I want to sand it down and make sure it's still solid. The stress the boat was under when she got yanked around by her anchor chain was pretty dramatic. I think it's better safe than sorry."

I stopped listening after *flooding ports*. "Tell me how you made the original hulls sink."

He frowned as if he couldn't understand why I'd ask the question. "We did it the same way you make anything sink. We flooded them with seawater by opening a pair of ports formed into the fiberglass."

I stared at the hull. "Tell me exactly how you did it."

"It was a simple mechanical valve in a four-inch port. When we opened the valves, there was a simultaneous system that latched the hatches, trapping the SOB in his cabin. The same system opened four vents in the topsides of the hulls, allowing air to escape as water rushed in. It took about eight minutes to sink the thing."

I wiped my hand on my pants. "How long would it take to build a near replica of this boat, but with those flooding ports and vents you described?"

He glowered at me. "Why?"

"How long?" I demanded. "No interior. Just the exterior to make it look identical to this boat on the outside. And all we'll need on the inside is a pair of engines and transmissions. I don't even think we'll need electronics. All I want is a bare-bones, sink-able hull that would pass for *Aegis*'s twin from five hundred feet away. How long would that take?"

He shook his head and held up his hands. "I don't know. We still have the molds for the hulls. Maybe six weeks. Two months, maybe."

"How much?"

"How much what?"

I grabbed his shoulders and gave him a shake. "How much would it cost me?"

He pulled himself from my grasp. "I don't know. You'd have to talk to Dominic about that. I'm a mechanic, not an accountant."

I patted him on the chest. "You're a genius is what you are." Pointing to my hull, I said, "Do whatever you need to make sure that's fixed. And get ready to break out those molds. We're build-ing a boat, my friend."

I sprinted back into Dominic's office, bursting through the door.

Penny looked up. "We've got some ideas, Chase."

I waved her off. "Ideas are great, but I've got a plan. Dominic, how much will it cost to build another original, sinkable *Aegis* with no interior, just a pair of engines and the exterior to match my boat?"

His eyes widened in instant recognition and approval of my plan. "Not a penny. We'll eat the cost to keep you alive. You brief the crew. I'll have Tommy dust off the molds."

I held up a hand. "He's checking out something he doesn't like in *Aegis*'s hull right now, but as soon as he's finished, I want him on the new build."

"Done," was all he said as he headed out the door and across the shipyard.

"The plan just got exponentially better," I began. "We're going to build *Aegis* a twin with one huge difference. She'll be empty hulls on the inside and designed specifically to sink."

A broad smile appeared on Penny's face. "Does this mean you aren't going to have to involve...*her*?"

Her obvious and understandable desire to leave Anya as far out of the operation as possible made perfect sense, but I had to burst her bubble.

"Unfortunately, the new plan relies even more heavily on *her* involvement."

She rolled her eyes. "You're determined to find a way to see your old girlfriend, aren't you?"

"She was never my girlfriend," I protested.

"Maybe to her she wasn't, but to you, there was no doubt. You can deny it all you want, but I know you, Chase Fulton. When you're in, you're in one hundred percent, and you were definitely in with...*her*."

Penny had a way of reminding me she knew more about me than I'd ever know about myself. I loved that about her, but in many ways, it terrified me as well.

"Not that I'd ever dare change the subject when my wife wants to talk about an old girlfriend, but I'm changing the subject."

My clumsy effort to deflect and redirect was met with nervous laughter from everyone except Penny. Instead of laughing, she suppressed a smile by pressing her lips together and shaking off my comment.

"Here's the revised plan in a nutshell. I'll approach the SVR and offer them Anya in return for letting me live. They'll take the deal. There's no question they want her far worse than they want me. While I'm brokering that deal, Skipper will be at work making sure Anya knows I'm looking for her. Once we find her —or, more likely, she finds us—I'll sell her on the idea that delivering me up to the SVR will put her back in their good graces. Hopefully, she'll agree to create the ruse with me. "

Penny cleared her throat loud enough for everyone to hear. "I'm pretty sure you mean she'll agree to create the ruse with *us*, and not just you."

"Well, yes, of course that's what I said. You must have misheard."

The previous nervous laughter morphed into full-blown belly laughs at my expense.

"Okay, okay. You guys are having way too much fun with this. Let's get on to the good part. When the dummy *Aegis* is ready, we'll ship both boats across the Atlantic into the Mediterranean and all the way into the Black Sea if we can pull it off. If my memory of world geography is correct, the Black Sea is over seven thousand feet deep in places. That sounds like the perfect spot to send dummy *Aegis* to the bottom while the Russians watch. The likelihood of them spending the money and time required to send an ROV to the bottom of the Black Sea to verify my body is aboard is extremely low."

I could see Hunter's wheels turning as I met his gaze. "What is it, Hunter?"

He grimaced. "It all sounds too neat and tidy to me. I don't know this Anya character everyone else seems to find so amusing, but am I wrong in assuming she was SVR?"

"No, you're not wrong. She was an SVR officer sent as a honey trap for me several years ago."

"Oh," he said, "so, she's trained and skilled in deception."

"Yes," I admitted.

"And the Russians have a nice track record of playing fair and keeping their word with American operatives, right?"

"I get your point, Hunter, but—"

"No buts," he interrupted. "You're planning an op around the assumption that you can make a deal with arguably the most lethal and deceptive intelligence agency on Earth. And you're planning it with faith in a former spy who happens to be a red sparrow and has already trapped you at least once with her honey pot."

"You're right about all of that, but my life, as well as Penny's life, is on the line. If we do nothing, one or both of us won't survive. Do *you* have a better plan?"

"I know I'm the new guy here," Hunter said, "and my background as a combat controller doesn't exactly make me the expert in this sort of thing. I don't want you to think I'm not on board. I'm in, but I'd like to know we're going to have some backup if this whole thing blows up in our face."

A collective chuckle erupted from the room.

Mongo said, "We're glad you're with us, Hunter, but you ain't in the Air Force no more, and there ain't no fighter jets waiting for you to call in an airstrike. When we go out, we're out. If we don't take it with us, we don't have it when the lead starts flying. Chase's plan, as risky as it is, looks like a piece of art compared to most of the crap we call plans when we lock-and-load and hit the road."

Hunter shrugged. "All right. In that case, get the Russians on the phone. Let's see if loose lips really do sink ships."

Dominic came through the door just as we were wrapping up the planning session. "I think we can do it in less than a month."

"Do what in less than a month?" I asked.

"Have the sinking *Aegis* ready to go. Without an interior, the build is a piece of cake."

"That's great news, Dominic. Should we take *Aegis* back to Saint Marys or leave her here during the build?"

He looked at the ceiling as he considered my question. "Take her back up north since you have the team here, but leave the EPIRB with me. I have an idea."

"Whatever you say. When will *Aegis* be ready to sail?"

Dominic glanced at his watch. "Midday tomorrow."

"Perfect," I said. "I'll call Skipper while you arrange for a ride."

"A ride to where?" he asked.

"South Beach. If we've got twenty hours to kill, we might as well do it in style."

Chapter 11
Follow the Money

Skipper answered on the second ring. "Hey, Chase. How's the honeymoon?"

"Interrupted. That's why I'm calling. I need you to find Anya."

"What? Why?"

"It's a long story," I said, "but I need her to know I'm looking for her. I doubt you'll actually be able to find her, but if you can figure out a way for her to learn I want to talk with her, that's good enough, and she'll find me."

"Chase, I'm not sure this is a good idea. What does Penny—"

"Penny's in on the whole thing. I'll fill you in on the details as soon as I can, but for now, just put out some feelers for her. Oh, and get me a personal contact number for whoever's in charge of the Directorate KR: External Counter-Intelligence. I want to wake him up in the middle of the night. Can you do that?"

Skipper scoffed. "Can I do that? What do you think?"

"Okay," I said. "That was the wrong question. How *quickly* can you do that?"

"Finding Anya isn't so easy, but Colonel Nicholai Sokolov is in charge of Directorate KR, and I'll text you his contact information as soon as we hang up because I know you don't have a pen and paper handy."

"I don't know what I'd do without you, Skipper."

"You'd get shot in the head sniffing around where you and your nose don't have any business. That's what you'd do without me."

"You're probably right," I admitted. "Call me as soon as you make any progress on Anya."

"Are you going to tell me what's going on?"

"Yes, I'll tell you in Saint Marys. Meet me at Bonaventure in two or three days, and bring your computer."

"Chase, telling me to bring my computer is like reminding Clark Johnson to bring a gun."

I laughed. "I know, but it makes me feel good to see you do something I've told you to do...even if you would've done it anyway."

"Bye, Chase."

* * *

We spent the evening and night on a different planet. South Beach is like nowhere else. Ocean Drive looks out over a recreational beach where thousands of people of every description stroll, play, dance, and strut. The flawless bodies of chiseled gods and goddesses are as common as the seventy-five-year-old tank top and Bermuda-shorts-wearing tribes. The music is Cuban and hip-hop. The food is some of the best in the world. And the people-watching is a master class in the life-eccentric.

My merry band of misfits didn't stand out at all. Penny, of course, put any other wannabe goddess to shame with her natural perfection. Hunter disappeared in the crowd with his ability to blend in almost anywhere. Mongo's massive size gave him a vantage point a foot above everyone else on the street. Singer silently took it all in, his sniper's eye collecting and cataloging every potential target and firing position. I wondered how his immense faith perceived the debauchery around him. His broken leg slowed him down only slightly and even drew the attention of the Swedish bikini team who all wanted to sign his cast.

A team of killers lurked, awaiting the perfect time to put a bullet through my skull, so I was obsessed with every face that bore the sharp features of an Eastern European heritage. I made every effort to pretend I wasn't in the sights of any trigger pullers on South Beach, but knowing I was being hunted made it difficult to see anything other than an assassin's glare in every pair of eyes on the street.

"Dance with me, Chase!"

I looked away from a pair of tracksuit-clad, pale-white twenty-five-year-olds to see my beautiful wife biting her bottom lip and moving in time with the Cuban beat pouring from a street band.

Mongo bumped me with his hip. "You'd better dance with the lady, or I'm going to start thumpin' the heads of the dudes lining up to take your place.

"No head-thumpin' tonight, Mongo. I'm going."

Dancing with Penny was like painting with Michelangelo. No one noticed me, but no one could look away from the wild-haired beauty at my fingertips. I loved her ability to become completely absorbed by the world around her. Diving on a coral reef off Key Largo, she became a mermaid. In the cockpit of a flying machine, she was a soaring angel. At the helm of *Aegis*, she was the wind dancing on the waves. On Ocean Drive, with Cuban drums pounding in the air, she became the music. Everything about her was beautiful to see, hear, and know.

Beads of sweat glistened on her flawless skin as she peered around me and giggled. I turned to see what she'd found so amusing. The scene playing out behind me was pure South Beach. Mongo danced his version of the salsa with two of the tiniest women on the street. Perhaps the appearance of their size was more a statement of contrast than a perception of reality. Hunter moved like a pro with a dark-haired beauty who would have been several inches taller than him even if she weren't wearing the five-inch heels. Clay was doing something that looked a lot more like a two-step than a salsa, but he was having fun. The most amusing sight, by far, was Singer, the broken-legged,

Southern Baptist sniper. He hopped about on one foot with a sunburned brunette who wore a brilliant pink cast on her broken left arm. I laughed out loud at the sight, and he yelled, "Hey, even King David danced. Don't judge me."

"I'm not judging," I yelled back. "I'm celebrating!"

Penny fell into my arms. "I'm starving. Where's that little Cuban place we loved so much?"

I inventoried my team, who were still doing what they defined as dancing. I pretended to spoon imaginary food into my mouth, and they fell in lockstep behind Penny and me as we made our way to one of the best Cuban restaurants north of Havana.

They served us family style, and we ate for two hours, just as a family should. I had known from the moment I first laid eyes on Penny that she'd always be my home, but I was also quickly coming to perceive the men around me as my family. I missed Clark and Skipper, but we'd see them soon enough.

* * *

Just as promised, *Aegis* was back in the water and anxiously awaiting our departure. Dominic took the Russian tracker disguised as an EPIRB and replaced it with a real beacon. I didn't know what his plan was, but I'd learn in time. Even when we did disagree, he never led me astray.

Dominic patted me on the back. "The wind and tide are in your favor, Chase, so you'd better get underway. We'll have the sinker ready in less than a month, and you've got plenty to do before then."

"Keep me posted on the progress, and I'll do the same," I said, offering him my hand. "Thanks for taking care of us, Dominic. I'm sorry about…. Well, you know."

He almost smiled. "Don't be sorry, Chase. We all have to learn. That's what keeps us alive—our willingness to learn from our mistakes. Now, get on the boat. You've got a long trip ahead of you."

"I'll let you know when we make it home."

He bounced the fake EPIRB in his palm. "And I'll let you know when we turn this thing back on."

An hour later, we were under full sail on a beam reach and surfing the northward current of the Gulf Stream. *Aegis* made fourteen knots across the ground with the help of the four-knot current. Singer lay on the upper deck with his rifle by his side and a spotter's scope on a short tripod in front of him. Overwatch had become his life, and I'd never met anyone better at it. Mongo lounged on the trampoline with his two-acre shirt wadded up as a pillow. Of course, Penny was at the helm, and I was on the phone with Skipper.

"Have you made any progress?"

Skipper sounded almost offended at my question. "Of course I have, but you're not going to like what I learned."

"Is she dead?" When the words left my tongue, I felt a knot form in the pit of my stomach. I tried to tell myself it was only because she was a major hinge pin in the operation, but I knew the truth. What I'd felt for her had been based on a lie, but the feeling was real. Although I'd never consider trading Penny for a thousand Anyas, there would always be a part of me that wanted Anastasia Burinkova to be happy and free.

"Yeah, she's alive…or at least I think it's her. But she's a long way from Moscow. In fact, she's closer to America than the Kremlin."

I pressed the phone tighter to my ear. "What are you talking about?"

"If I'm right—and I usually am—she's in extreme Eastern Siberia in a place called Ust-Kamchatsk."

I drew a mental map of Siberia, but nothing resembling Ust-Kamchatsk appeared. "I've never heard of it."

"Nobody's ever heard of it. It's a tiny godforsaken place on the Bering Sea at the mouth of the Kamchatka River."

"I've heard of the river," I said, "but what makes you think that's where she is?"

"I followed the money. That's how you find everything. When you gave her the money she inherited from Dr. Richter, your favorite analyst—that's me—was smart enough to put a tracker on the account."

"You're the best. I'm on my way home now. We'll be back at Bonaventure in a couple of days, and I need to know everything you can find out about Ust-Kamchatsk."

She sighed. "Don't get too excited, Chase. I can't guarantee she's still there. All I know for sure is she spent a lot of money there last fall."

"How much money?"

"A little over a hundred grand."

"What on Earth would you spend a hundred thousand dollars on in Siberia?"

"I don't know," she said, "but I intend to find out."

"You do that. I'll see you in a couple of days."

I hung up and tried to imagine why Anya would be so far from civilization and what could possibly be worth a hundred grand on the shores of the Bering Sea.

"Are you okay? Hey, Chase. Is everything all right?" Penny's voice shook me from my trance.

"Sorry. Yeah, I'm fine. Skipper thinks she's found Anya."

She motioned for me to come out on deck. "That's great, but you've got to see this."

I followed her through the cockpit and up to the helm. She pointed toward the bow. "Look at Mongo."

I could only see the lower half of the giant hanging over the bow and reaching toward the surface of the water.

I laughed. "What's he doing?"

"He's playing with a pod of dolphins. They've been running with us for ten minutes or so, and he's like a little boy."

I watched the big man as the dolphins continued to mesmerize him. He was one of the deadliest warriors I'd ever know, but inside the giant beat the heart of an innocent child. I hoped the terrible things I'd see in my life would never rob me of the ability to become completely lost in the beauty around me, but the nature of evil is to devour everything and everyone in its path. Only the strongest—like Mongo and Singer—were capable of clinging to the good when the darkness beckoned with such a mighty voice.

Chapter 12
Dead-On

If I'm in command, watches aboard a sailboat are four hours long. Penny agreed. Any longer than that tends to breed complacency born of boredom. Complacency was not a luxury I could afford with the whole of the Russian Foreign Intelligence Service gunning for me. Perhaps believing the entire SVR was chasing me was a bit arrogant, but in matters of self-preservation, cockiness isn't always a bad thing.

Penny scanned the panel in front of her. "The wind is holding steady at eighteen knots out of the west southwest. All rigging and systems shipshape. Autopilot has the steering. You have the helm."

"I have the helm," I said with confidence.

"You have the helm," Penny restated.

Every exchange of command aboard both our boat and every airplane I flew happened in precisely that manner. There could never be a question who was in command and had responsibility for the ship and all aboard. The formality and respect for the inherent responsibilities of command are part of what made the British Navy the world's greatest seaborne fighting force for hundreds of years. If it worked for the redcoats, I believed it would work for me.

A cruise of three hundred fifty nautical miles would take *Aegis* less than thirty-two hours to complete. That would put us alongside the dock at Bonaventure Plantation before sunset the following day if my gambit with the tracker worked. If it didn't, and the Russians were tailing me, I may never see the plantation again. If that were the case, I was confident we had enough firepower and skill aboard to drag several Russian souls from this world if they were dumb enough to start a gunfight.

As I sat at the helm wishing I had some way to see across the horizon, I remembered Skipper's ability to do exactly that.

She answered on the first ring. "Chase?"

"Yes. How did you pick up so fast?"

"I didn't pick up," she said. "I was calling you."

"GMTA, I guess."

"GMTA? What's that supposed to mean?"

I laughed. "If you're going to hang on to the title of world's greatest operational analyst, you'll need to get a lot better at acronyms. GMTA means great minds think alike."

She huffed. "Ha! Don't flatter yourself, operator. I'm the only great mind in this operation."

"What about Clark and Penny?"

"Well, maybe Penny," she admitted, "but definitely not Clark. He's too busy chasing skirts and getting himself blown up."

"You may have a point there. But I need your help."

"I was calling to offer you some help, actually. There just happens to be a whole flock of satellites with nothing to do for the next couple of days. I could see about tasking one or two of them to check your six…and your nine, and three, and twelve."

"It's like you're living in my cerebral cortex, Skipper. That's what I was going to ask you to do."

"Give me twenty minutes. Fire up the laptop I left for you on the boat, and make sure you're connected to the secure uplink. I'll send you the data ASAP. What time do you think you'll be here?"

"Here?" I asked.

"Yeah, here. I'm at Bonaventure, playing with Charlie and waiting for your slow butt."

"We'll be there tomorrow afternoon, and my butt isn't slow."

She made a sound as if she knew something I didn't know. "Well, it's slower than mine, apparently. See you tomorrow."

She was gone before I could return a salvo, and I put Penny to work bringing the laptop online.

In less than half an hour, we saw a live satellite image of *Aegis* and every boat within two hundred miles. Penny tagged eleven boats that appeared to be on the same course as us and making similar speed. They could've been other sailboats coincidentally cruising up the east coast of Florida on a perfect spring afternoon, but just like the redcoats, better safe than sorry.

An hour later, only four tagged boats remained, the others having changed course or headed inland.

"It's time for an SDR," I declared.

I could see Penny's wheels turning as she tried to decipher SDR, so I ended her mental misery. "Surveillance detection route. I'm going to make a dramatic turn and see who follows. Keep an eye on the four suspects, and see what they do."

After scanning the deck to account for everyone on board, I gave the command, "Prepare to gybe!"

No one answered since *Aegis* was designed to be a single-handed boat, meaning I could manage both the steering and the sails without the aid of a deckhand. Regardless of that detail, I stuck to British naval tradition. With the touch of a button, the mainsheet winch centered the mainsail boom, and I gave the command of execution. "Gybe-ho!"

Aegis, as spirited as she is on the wind, tends to get a little sloppy when bringing her stern through the wind, so I disengaged the autopilot and hand-steered her through the easterly turn. I rolled out of the turn heading southeast, straight toward the four boats that had been paralleling our course and matching our speed. Easing the mainsail sheet put the boat back in a starboard beam reach against the flow of the Gulf Stream.

Her bow bucked as we cut into the turbulent sea and settled on eight knots of boat speed. The ride was far less pleasant than the northbound course had been, but we hoped we'd only be on that course long enough to watch our tail either match our turn or stand fast.

I couldn't see the laptop from the helm, so Penny relayed what she saw. "Targets one, two, and four are holding course, but target three turned dead-on."

Mongo came scampering—as much as a three-hundred-pound man can scamper—across the deck to the helm station. "What was that all about?"

"Just doing a little SDR," I said. "We've got four boats that appear to be tracking our course and speed about twenty-five miles southeast of us."

"I've got two questions," he said as he stared over the bow.

"Let's hear them."

"First, how do you know? And second, did they turn with us?"

I pointed toward the main salon. "You've heard of the Mother of Dragons, the mythical queen who could command an army of airborne fire-breathers. Well, Skipper is the mother of satellites. They may not be able to breathe fire, but they can see over every horizon."

He grinned. "I've played cowboys and Indians my whole career, and that girl's playing *Star Wars*. You're lucky to have her."

"Don't I know it?" I said.

"How about my second question?"

"So far, three held fast, and one turned directly toward us."

He squinted as if he could see twenty-five miles across the North Atlantic. "That doesn't sound good."

I leaned down from the helm, trying to see into the main salon. "Any changes?"

"No, number three is on a collision course with us. He should be visible on radar by now."

My radar dome was mounted forty-eight feet above the waterline, about halfway up my mast. That gave me the ability to see twenty miles with pretty good accuracy. I switched the chart plotter to the radar screen and scanned the area dead ahead. Several targets appeared, but there was nothing directly on our nose.

"Keep watching," I yelled. "I can't see it yet."

I held the course as *Aegis* bucked in protest at the pounding from the waves of the Gulf Stream, but still no radar target.

Penny emerged from the salon and climbed into the cockpit with me. "Are you sure you've got the radar turned out? She's eighteen miles and closing."

I stepped aside and motioned toward the screen. "Feel free to double-check me, but I'm pretty sure it's looking out to thirty miles for surface targets."

She pressed several buttons on the screen, completely shutting down the radar system and restarting it. The same targets I'd seen were still there and tracking as they had before, but there was nothing on our nose.

"That's bizarre," she whispered, then disappeared back inside the boat.

"Chase, whatever she is, she's not a sailboat. She's increasing speed and making over thirty knots. That'll put us nose-to-nose in twenty minutes."

"Get Singer out here!"

I'd insisted Singer get some rest instead of lying behind his rifle all day and night, but things were about to get exciting, and I wanted my sniper in position when it started hitting the fan—especially if I was going to be the fan.

"What is it?" Singer asked, sticking his head through the companionway.

"Get your broken-legged butt out here. We've got a potential bad guy on our bow, closing fast."

Seconds later, he was poised like a cat ready to pounce. Well, perhaps he wouldn't be doing any pouncing with his leg in a cast, but his trigger finger was more than capable. He peered through his spotter's scope. "Range to target?"

Penny answered, "Fourteen miles and closing."

Neither his spotter's scope nor the ten-thousand-dollar optics on his rifle could see fourteen miles. I watched him slowly allow his eyelids to close and his lips to whisper a nearly silent prayer.

His ability to marry his faith with his duty fascinated and bewildered me, and I wondered what a devout Christian sniper prayed for when he was on the verge of sending another human soul to the promised land. I wondered if his prayers sounded more like "…deliver my enemies into my hands…" or "…Thy will be done…"

What faith I had, although I longed for more, leaned toward the "deliver my enemies" variety.

Would the British Navy have started a fight with their sails aloft if they had twin diesels below deck? Me thinks not.

The engines answered at the touch of my fingertips, and I yelled into the salon. "All hands on deck! Battle stations!"

Clay and Hunter poured through the companionway, a rifle slung across each of their chests. Penny leapt from the cockpit to the helm. "Do you want the helm or the mainsail?"

I winked at my beautiful wife, who just happened to be the most competent helmsman I'd ever seen. "You have the helm. Put us in the wind."

She smiled. "Aye, Captain. I have the helm. Coming about."

"You have the helm," I said as I climbed the ladder to assist the mainsail into the lazyjacks.

The instant *Aegis's* bow pointed into the wind, Penny opened the clutch and sent the enormous mainsail cascading down the mast. Just as it'd been designed to do, the enormous sail stacked perfectly on top of the boom. I had it securely stowed seconds later. *Aegis* turned beneath me, returning to her southeasterly course as the headsail furled neatly around the forestay.

Leaning against the telephone-pole-sized mast, I squinted into the afternoon haze, hoping to catch a glimpse of the aggressor on our bow. But there was nothing to see.

I considered how to get Singer to the upper deck where he'd have a much better sniper's position, but the only idea that came to mind was having Mongo throw him up the ladder. As amusing as that would've been to watch, I decided to leave him where he was.

Sliding down the ladder, I scanned the deck. Everyone was in position. A quick glance at Skipper's computer screen showed the aggressor still coming hard at just ten miles.

"Do you see anything on radar yet?"

Penny yelled back, "Nothing. It's like she's invisible."

Nothing's invisible, I thought as I watched the aggressor grow closer with every passing minute. The data tag Penny had placed on the screen to track the target showed the vessel making forty-two knots.

I climbed back to the helm station and laid my hand on Penny's arm. "Listen. I have no idea what's about to happen, but it's coming quick, and I can't think of any way it's going to be good news when that thing gets on top of us. I'd like for you to go below and let us fight this out. When it's over and the smoke clears, you can call the Coast Guard."

She lowered her chin, glared at me, and declared through gritted teeth, "I have the helm."

With my fifty-caliber Barrett slung across my back, I climbed the ladder to the position I wished Singer occupied, and nestled behind the massive weapon. The coming battle pitted one of the world's deadliest—and holiest—snipers, one Barrett fifty-cal in my hands, and two AR-10s in the arms of Clay and Hunter against an unknown force that was apparently invisible to radar and capable of mind-blowing speed.

The seconds ticked by like hours as we waited to see our opponent. Penny set the autopilot and ran between the helm and the computer, constantly checking the bandit's position.

Singer looked up at me, several feet above his head. "What's the ROE, Chase?"

His question drove home the terrifying fact that I was far from ready to command a force of men who'd placed their trust in me. I hadn't briefed the rules of engagement. "Identify friend or foe. If foe, execute with extreme prejudice, and send her to the bottom."

"And if they're friendlies?" he said.

"If they were friendlies, they would've identified themselves by now."

Singer glanced over his shoulder at the rest of the team. "Did you guys copy that? If they ain't good guys, kill 'em when you see 'em."

"Two miles!" came Penny's shout.

Why the hell can't I see a boat two miles away?

I watched Singer roll away from his spotter's scope and pull his rifle snug against his shoulder. Through the scope of my Barrett, I scanned the surface of the gray water and caught a white flash.

Are they shooting at us?

No, the white flash turned into a prolonged, rolling white line.

"Tally-ho! Bow wake, twelve o'clock, three thousand yards!"

"I got 'em," Singer answered. "Whatever she is, she's haze gray and on her way."

"Identify!" I yelled.

"Still nothing on radar," came Penny's report.

I can see it with my own eyes. Why can't my radar see it?

As the screaming vessel kept coming, my heart rate crept toward triple digits.

"Identify!" I yelled again, but no one spoke. I peered down to see Singer's clear fan of fire to his left. "Bear away hard to starboard!"

Penny's wordless reply came in the form of a ninety-degree turn to the right, and I never took my eyes from the closing bandit.

"Identify!"

I put the crosshairs of my scope ten meters off the bow of the charging vessel and slowly began pressing the trigger. I could feel the pulse in my index finger as the tension in the trigger grew stronger with every millimeter of movement. Ten rounds of armor-piercing fifty caliber in her hull would stop the aggressor dead in the water but wouldn't sink her. We'd be in the fight of our lives if she had deck guns and in a nasty shootout even if they only had rifles. The North Atlantic was about to turn bloody.

"Hold your fire! Hold your fire! She's American!"

It was Singer's voice, but it was too late. The Barrett recoiled and sent a projectile the size of my thumb through the salt air toward the bow of an American warship. My heart plummeted into my stomach as I prepared for the ramifications of opening fire on an American military vessel.

I'll never know if the helmsman of the boat reacted to the muzzle flash from my Barrett or to Penny's turn hard to starboard, but he cut the throttles and brought the Navy Mark V fast patrol boat to a stop ten feet off our port bow with my fifty-caliber round bouncing harmlessly across the surface of the Gulf Stream.

Chapter 13

The Sniper's Prayer

"Ahoy, *Aegis*. I'm Lieutenant Schauble, SEAL Team Four out of Little Creek. Lower your weapons, please." The loud hailer mounted on the cabin top of the patrol boat crackled as the SEAL commander identified himself.

I rested my Barrett on the deck and stood, cupping my hands around my mouth in an improvised megaphone. "Lieutenant Schauble, you and your boat crew almost got blown to hell. Why didn't you announce yourselves instead of closing on us like that?"

"Permission to come alongside?" came his reply.

I yelled down to Penny. "Come about on course, and deploy the fenders. They're coming alongside."

"We're coming about," I yelled toward the SEAL's boat. "Stand off until we're underway on course."

The helmsman of the patrol boat motored away to the north, giving my much larger boat room to maneuver. Penny brought us about with the wind, once again, across our port beam, and I slid down the ladder with my Barrett in tow. When we were established on course and making nine knots, the Navy helmsman laid his patrol boat alongside our starboard hull as gently as a baby's kiss, and Lieutenant Schauble said, "Permission to come aboard?"

"Come aboard," I yelled over the droning of his engines.

The SEAL commander removed his combat boots and socks and stepped from the gunwale of his boat onto *Aegis*'s deck as if he'd done it a thousand times. The Navy helmsman powered away and paralleled our course, matching our speed twenty feet off our beam.

"Welcome aboard, Lieutenant, but I still want to know why you didn't announce yourself when you charged us from forty miles out."

The young officer lowered his chin. "How did you know we were closing on you? You shouldn't have been able to see us."

"Your little tug there must have some radar-absorbing stealth capability. My radar couldn't see you, but it's hard to hide from the satellites."

Instinctually, he looked toward the sky, and I continued my questions. "Why were you pacing us, and what caused you to make a run at us?"

"I was pacing you because that's what my orders told me to do. I was to identify you and provide silent escort for you from Miami to Kings Bay. You must have some powerful friends, sir. The orders came directly from the CNO."

I glanced back at the patrol boat. "The chief of naval operations ordered a SEAL platoon to shadow me up the east coast of Florida? Is that what you're saying, Lieutenant?"

"No, sir. We're not a platoon. Just an element. But otherwise, you got it right. We were ordered to pace you and intervene if any vessels made to intercept you. When you pulled that Crazy Ivan turn, we had a moment of disagreement on board. Some of us thought you were just trying to shake a tail if you had one, and the others—me included—thought you might be turning to run from an aggressor. Either way, we needed to step in to either eliminate your tail for you or play a little game of sniff-and-fetch with your aggressor."

"So, you could see me from forty miles?" I said.

"We can task a satellite, too, you know. So, like I said, you must have some friends in high places."

I scoffed. "I'd say they're temporary friends, at best."

He cocked his head and eyed me as he considered my odd response. "Well, you're certainly well armed for a civilian-cruising yacht."

I glanced down at the nearly thirty-pound Barrett at my feet. "You can never be too careful out here. You never know when you're going to get charged by a stealth gunboat full of frogmen."

The lieutenant motioned toward his crew, and the helmsman laid the patrol boat alongside even more gently than before.

The officer stuck out his hand. "Well, it's nice to meet you. We'll be just over there if you need us."

I shook the offered hand and motioned toward his bare feet. "Thanks for taking off your boots before coming aboard."

He almost smiled. "This is a nice boat, and I've swabbed enough decks to know combat boots and white fiberglass don't mix."

He offered a quick salute and leapt back aboard his stealthy magic carpet. The boat and the SEALs were gone as quickly as they'd arrived.

Clay laid his rifle on the deck and spat overboard. "You wanna tell me what that was all about?"

"It was just an element of SEALs ordered by the highest-ranking officer in the Navy to keep an eye on us. Don't you get a Special Forces escort when you travel?"

He pulled the wad of tobacco from his cheek and tossed it overboard. "Ha! I don't even have Triple A. I need to step up my game if I'm gonna hang with you big dogs."

With the tension of the moment over, my team relaxed. Singer climbed down from the cabin top and cleared his rifle.

"How's the leg?" I asked, motioning toward his cast that still bore the signatures of the girls from South Beach.

He shrugged. "Annoying. I'm ready to get this thing off."

I perched on the settee beside the sniper. "Do you mind if I ask you a question?"

He squinted against the afternoon sun. "You just did."

"What?"

He chuckled. "You asked if you could ask me a question. That was asking me a question. I'm starting to think Clark was right about you not learning much at that fancy college of yours."

"There's nothing fancy about UGA," I said. "It's just a fine Southern university with a long and storied history of educating bright young men and women like me."

"Man, I hope that ain't true," he said, suddenly serious.

"What do you mean?"

He grinned again. "I hope there's not a whole flock like you in Athens with diplomas in their hands."

"You're a funny guy. You know that, Singer?"

"Yeah, it's all part of being a sniper. We're a funny bunch. Now, what's your question?"

I took a long, deep breath, carefully forming the question. "I noticed you were praying when we thought we were about to get into a gunfight. Do you mind telling me what you ask God in moments like that?"

He put his arm around my shoulder. "I ask him to look after my friends and let my enemies die quickly so they don't have to suffer."

I initially thought he was joking, but the look on his face said he was deadly serious.

"You don't ask Him to look after you?"

He wrinkled his nose. "Nah. If He wants me to live through it, He'll protect me. And if not, I've got a fine place to go when I die where I won't never have to send another bullet downrange in anger, and I get all the milk and honey I want. Sounds like a pretty good place, doesn't it?"

I swallowed hard. "It sure does, my friend."

He patted me on the back. "Don't you worry, Chase. Like I told you before, you belong to the angels, and they'll look after you. That's what they do. Just like you and me look after people who aren't strong enough to take care of themselves, those guardian angels of yours, they're working 'round the clock to keep you doing exactly what you're meant to do 'til you get called home."

What an incredible solace that must be to have a belief so strong. Why couldn't I have the faith of my father and Singer? Why was everything so easy for them to believe and so tough for me to swallow?

"If you boys are finished with whatever ritual you're having down there, I'd like some help getting the sails back in the air. Diesel fuel is expensive."

Singer elbowed me. "I think the captain's talking to you, cabin boy."

With a little effort on my part and a lot of skill from Penny, *Aegis* was soon making twelve knots under full sail, and all hands aboard rested a little easier knowing we had a silent-but-deadly element of some of the world's most elite warriors playing guardian angel. Who said angels had to have wings and halos instead of deck guns and body armor?

Sunset is a time of reverence at sea. Ignoring the golden orange, red, and purple hues claiming the western sky is all but impossible when our nearest star melts into the calling depths. Darkness doesn't come quickly; instead, it creeps over the waves from east to west, and the wind softens while the cool night air makes everything heavier, deeper, and somehow endless. Even for seasoned operators with more scars on their flesh than fingers on their hands, the failing light and all-consuming darkness reminds them of their own imminent mortality. My team was not immune to those feelings, and even the air aboard my boat took on a taste and feel somehow more ominous and introspective than that of the daylight hours.

Night watch is lonely aboard a vessel of any size, but when at the helm of a fifty-foot catamaran, well out of sight of land, with no other living soul awake, all sounds and sensations are magnified. Every ripple of a luffing sail, every creak in the rigging, and every slap of the waves against the hull sounds like the melodious roar of a symphony. The sounds can be hypnotic when they become a melody. Fighting the beckoning trance becomes the arduous task of the four-hour midnight watch. That watch was mine. I claim it as if it were my birthright, not because I don't trust others to stand the watch, but because it's my church, my temple, my confessional. I had demons to face and dragons to slay, and like the medieval knights who knelt in prayer beneath the dancing flames of the priest's candles in the hours before riding off in defense of their king and country, so I knelt behind the wheel of *Aegis* and beneath the flickering lights of a billion stars and offered myself, my soul, to what I believed, praying for the strength to face what the coming dawn and days would stand in front of me. I would look into the eyes of the man who wanted my head on a pike, and I would offer him the only thing he wanted more than my life. I'd offer him the woman who would've been my undoing, the woman who reached into my chest and held my beating heart in her grip, the woman who could've taken my life at will. I would promise to deliver Anastasia Burinkova into Colonel Nicholai Sokolov's hands in exchange for my life, and he would grind his teeth to the roots in the agony of accepting my terms.

Facing Colonel Sokolov didn't frighten me, but knowing in the days to come I would stand in front of Anya again sent daggers of frozen fire into my spine. Skipper had found her—a task I hadn't believed possible—but she'd done it. When my plan spawned in the far reaches of my mind, I believed Anya would come to me, but instead, thanks to the skill and brilliance of a young girl I'd known as a sister, I would knock on Anya's door and look into her eyes of blue-gray ice and remember how I'd loved her, and how I'd almost lost everything to her. I would do to her what she had devoted years of her life in doing to me. I would deliver her to the masters of the Kremlin, and I would do it only to save my life. Would I have the strength to pray the sniper's prayer and ask God for her death to come quickly so she wouldn't have to suffer, or would the shame of my deed force me to hide my face from the God of my father?

Chapter 14
The Russian Porch Light

The next afternoon, I laid *Aegis* against the plantation dock at twenty minutes after three and saw my partner, Clark Johnson, propped up. He was pretending to be comfortable in an oak rocking chair on what the rest of the country calls a *porch*, though in the Deep South, it's a *gallery*.

"Sorry for not running down to help you tie up," he said, pressing his palms against the arms to push himself to his feet.

The plastic clamshell brace he wore around his chest and abdomen made him look like a child's action figure.

"It's good to see you, old man. How's the back?"

I took his hand, a formality we'd continued since the day we met, even though our relationship was anything but formal. We'd bled, nearly died, fought, escaped, lost, and won a dozen battles since our first meeting. We'd do it all again, I hoped, but until his back was fully healed and he'd worked himself back into fighting shape, he was relegated to the rear echelon and a supporting role. Clark was a man of action. Relegation of any kind soured on his stomach and left him hungry for the fight.

Knocking on the plastic shell, he said, "I just need to rub a little dirt on it and embrace the suck."

Maebelle, master chef, dog sitter, and chief nursemaid to my partner came prancing through the kitchen door, her apron covered in flour. "You'll be doing no such thing, mister, and I'm here to make darn sure of it, too."

I motioned toward the beautiful young woman. "I think she's got your number, Clark."

He produced the half-smile he'd perfected over the years. "Yeah, she's quite the whip-cracker. It's all I can do to negotiate my way into a couple of hours a day on the porch."

"*Gallery*," Maebelle said. "And I'll have you know it was my idea for you to get some fresh air."

Penny and Clay came bounding up the steps, laughing like children. "Chase, you've got to see this. Look!"

It was the last thing I could've expected. Mongo had Singer—broken leg and all—tossed over his shoulder as he strolled up the path from the dock.

Singer pounded on the big man's back with both fists as if beating a drum. "Put me down, you big ape."

Mongo laughed and continued up the steps until he finally gave Singer his wish and deposited the man gently on the weathered deck. "I'm tired of watching you hobble around on those crutches. It's easier on you, and way easier on me if I just carry you wherever we go."

Maebelle giggled and hugged Penny. "Welcome home, girl. I don't know how you put up with this bunch of crazy boys. Who's this one?"

Penny hugged her back in spite of the dusting of flour. "Maebelle, meet Clay. Clay, this is Maebelle, the finest chef you'll ever meet. You'll see soon enough."

Clay stuck out his hand, but Maebelle slapped it away. "I'm a hugger. Come here, big boy. It's nice to meet you. They flatter me, but I do think you'll like what I've thrown together for supper."

Clay leaned back after the hug with a white powder imprint of Maebelle's apron on his chest. "It's nice to meet you, too, Miss Maebelle. I'm looking forward to supper."

"Is the Judge back yet?" I asked as Penny and Maebelle headed for the kitchen.

"No, but he'll be back in a couple of days. His lady friend in Atlanta is slow to let him get away when he goes up to visit."

The door had barely closed when Skipper came bouncing through it and straight to Clay. She threw her arms around him. "Hey, Clay! I didn't know you were coming."

"Hey, Skipper. It's good to see you again."

She leaned back, appraising him. "You look like you healed up nicely after that...*thing* in Mexico."

Clay had fought off a team of pirates during an attack on *Aegis* off the Yucatan Peninsula, saving the boat, Penny, and Skipper's lives. For his trouble, he'd been awarded an all-expenses-paid tour of duty in the hospital ward of the Research Vessel *Lori Dannielle*, commanded by retired CIA Agent Captain Stinnett. Clay's wounds had healed well, but he hadn't seen Skipper since the attack.

I gave them a few minutes to catch up and then claimed her for myself. "Let's take a look at what you've got, Skipper."

"I'll see you later, Clay. The boss says it's time to go to work."

We climbed the stairs of the antebellum mansion and then entered Skipper's lair. Everywhere she set up shop became her lair. Not only was she the best operational analyst I knew, she was also the most adaptive when it came to work environs. She was equally at home in a locked vault in Silver Spring, Maryland, as she was on the deck of my boat or an upstairs bedroom on a pecan plantation.

Skipper had the astonishing ability to switch from twenty-three-year-old playful socialite to all-business analyst in a snap. "Here's a map of Eastern Siberia, and here's that town nobody's ever heard of."

A topo map filled the left screen of her computer setup.

I reached for the mouse and zoomed in and out, carefully studying the terrain of the easternmost reaches of Mother Russia. "What is she doing all the way out there?"

Skipper pulled the mouse from my hand and went to work on a second screen. Soon, a poor-quality photograph of columns of Cyrillic script appeared.

"I can't read Russian, and the quality isn't good enough for me to grab the text and translate it, but the part I have been able to translate is here." She highlighted a section, but I didn't need to read what her software believed the script said.

Serdtse Kateriny. 4,436,744 rubl'.

"Oh, this is not good."

"What is it?"

My head landed in my palms, and my heart pounded as if it were on the verge of exploding. When I finally caught my breath, I whispered, "*Katerina's Heart.* Four point four million rubles."

"Yeah, that's the one," Skipper sighed.

I looked up. "And you're sure this purchase was made with the card from the Cayman bank?"

"Yeah, Chase, I'm sure."

"In that case, we didn't find her. We simply discovered the porch light she left on for me."

"I don't know," Skipper argued. "That seems awful risky. If she left the light on for you, what would keep the Russians from seeing the light, too?"

"Because the Russians don't know about the Cayman account, so they'd never look for it. But she knows that's the first place I'd look if I were trying to find her."

Skipper closed her eyes and slowly shook her head. "So, that means she knows you're coming."

"No, that's not what it means. It means she knows I have a way to find her if I ever try. She has no way to know I'm trying, and that gives us the upper hand."

I leaned back and pursed my lips as Skipper considered what I'd said.

"You're doing that thing again, and it freaks me out. Tell me what's happening in your head."

I pretended not to hear her while I allowed the ideas to march around the seats in my head. When the needle came off the record and ideas lunged for seats, catch-him-on-vacation was left standing.

"Find Sokolov's dacha and his *lyubovnitsa's* schedule."

"Speak English," Skipper said.

"*Dacha* is a vacation home, and *lyubovnista* is a mistress. All senior Russian officials have both, and I'm sure Colonel Sokolov is no exception."

Soon an aerial view of a small house on a rocky beach appeared on the screen in front of Skipper. "There it is. Sokolov's dacha on Allée des Sternes, in Hyères in the South of France. The mistress is going to take a little longer."

I leaned in, memorizing the map and wondering how an SVR colonel could afford a place like that on the French coast. "You're amazing, Skipper. Let me know when you have something on the mistress…or even the wife. Essentially, I need to know when Sokolov will be at the dacha."

"I'm on it," she said as her fingers flew across the keys.

Back downstairs, Maebelle was setting the table as the rest of the team loitered impatiently in the kitchen.

"Okay, listen up, everybody. Skipper found Anya, or at least she found the town where she was last fall. It's a little town in Eastern Siberia called Ust-Kamchatsk, one of the most remote spots on the continent. That's a great start. She also found Colonel Sokolov's dacha in the South of France. Hopefully, she'll have an itinerary for his next visit soon. If the timing works out, having Sokolov on the French coast is perfect."

"Perfect for what, exactly?" Penny asked.

"Perfect for me to look him in the eye and offer up Anya."

"I thought you were going to do that over the phone," she said.

"I was, but it'll be far more effective in person."

"And far more dangerous," she added.

Hunter spoke up. "That all depends on who he takes with him. I believe it was Winston Churchill who said, 'With careful consideration in choice of allies, victory is assured in any conflict,' but maybe I just made that up. I really can't remember, but you get my point."

Every eye in the room focused immediately on me, awaiting my response to Hunter's comment. Clark would naturally be my first choice. I trusted him more than I trusted myself, but his broken back took him out of the running. Singer was out. That broken leg limited his ability to run if things got out of hand. I could see the desire in Penny's eyes, but regardless of how much I'd love to give her exactly what she wanted, I needed a seasoned operator who'd been under fire and wouldn't flinch in the face of a Russian bully. I didn't know Clay well enough to anticipate his next move if bullets started flying, and Mongo was simply too big. That left only one man.

"Are you volunteering, Hunter?"

"Do you really have to ask?"

I smiled. "*Parlez-vous français?*"

He chuckled. "I'm not much of a talker when I'm overseas, but I have a way of getting my point across. I've learned just about everybody understands getting their ass kicked."

Penny's expression relaxed, and she almost smiled. "I think you may've just found the next best thing to Clark Johnson."

Hunter pulled at the hairs of his beard. "I think I'll take that as a grand compliment."

"Supper's ready!" Maebelle declared, and suddenly, our meeting was adjourned.

Or at least I thought it was adjourned until Skipper called it back to order. She flew down the stairs waving a handful of papers. "I've got Sokolov's itinerary, and you're gonna love it!"

"Let's hear it."

"He won't be with his mistress because it's his anniversary, and he always spends his anniversary at the dacha the last week of April."

I kissed her with great flamboyance squarely on the forehead. "That's the best news I've heard all year. The timing couldn't be better. The sinking *Aegis* will be ready by then, and that gives us plenty of time to find Anya."

Skipper shoved me away. "Yeah, the timing is perfect, but I'm not so sure about finding Anya. I think that's going to be a boots-on-the-ground operation. We don't have any assets in Siberia, and I don't have access to a satellite that's capable of identifying a particular person, especially in a place where every-one is wearing hooded parkas."

I glanced at Hunter.

"I don't speak Russian, either," he said, "but the same rule ap-plies, and yes, I'm volunteering."

"In that case, it's settled. Hunter, pack your parka. Skipper, figure out how to get the two of us into Siberia. Other than that, all that's left to do right now is tear into this feast Maebelle's created."

Chapter 15
One Way

March in the Georgia low country is as close to perfect as weather can be anywhere on the planet. I sat on *Aegis*'s upper deck with my favorite cocktail—Penny's old-fashioned. It was the perfect complement to a gorgeous afternoon. I don't know if it had anything to do with her secret recipe or if I was simply in love with everything that woman did for me, but either way, I hoped she never stopped making me that drink.

Penny put on a mischievous smirk. "Do you remember the first time you had an old-fashioned with me?"

"How could I forget? It was at the Peninsula Grill in Charleston where you pretended to have never tried one. Then you set about seducing every man in the room with the way you savored what you wanted me to believe was your first taste."

Feigned innocence replaced mischief as she batted her eyelashes. "Why, I'd never do any such thing. I was only trying to seduce *you*. And I do believe it worked."

"Oh, it worked, all right. And it still does."

Quiet moments alone with Penny were becoming rare, so I treasured them more every day.

Her affectionate stare turned sullen. "I can't go, can I?"

"That's no place for you. It won't be safe, but I'll have Hunter with me."

Part of a smile returned to her face. "Yeah, but he better not try to seduce you if you let him sip your old-fashioned."

I pulled an ice cube from my drink and tossed it toward her. She slapped it out of the air, sending it over the rail and splashing into the North River. The ripples from the floating ice cube played across the water.

"Please don't let her do it again."

"Who?" I asked, genuinely confused.

"Anya," she said. "Please don't fall for her again. Chase, I love you, and we have this wonderful life together. I don't want...."

Her voice trailed off, and I knelt at her feet, taking her hands in mine.

"Penny, you're the woman I love, and the only woman I want. Anya's true colors shone through when she made it clear where her loyalties lie. Even though the Kremlin turned its back on her since then, when she was faced with the decision of loving me or serving the Rodina, I was just a mark."

She bit her bottom lip. "But you loved *her*, and maybe you still do."

"No! You're wrong about that. I *thought* I loved her. I loved who and what I *thought* she was, but that's not the same thing as loving her. She's a spy, trained in the art of seduction and manipulation. An actress playing a role. That's all."

She stared at me, her eyes glistening with what could become tears. "Can you honestly tell me you wouldn't be attracted to her if she tried to seduce you again?"

"Attraction isn't the same thing as willingness. We have no power to decide if we're physically attracted to someone. That happens deep inside some of the oldest parts of our brain. What we *can* control is how we react to that attraction. Just because a dozen chocolate glazed donuts look inviting, I choose not to eat them because I know they're terrible for me. It's the same with Anya. She's even worse for me than the donuts."

Her smile wouldn't come. "Just promise me you won't—"

I pressed my finger to her lips. "Penny, I'm not going to do anything to risk losing what we have together. Nothing is worth hurting you."

She wrapped her arms around my neck and pulled me against her body. "I'm sorry for being so...."

"Never be sorry. Never."

"But you've got enough to worry about without me nagging you over an old girlfriend."

"You're not nagging. You're loving me, and that's the best thing anyone's ever done for me. I'm not going to screw this up."

She kissed me softly, and I could feel her warm breath against my skin as if her very soul was playing against my flesh. Nothing, especially not a Russian spy, could compete with that.

"Hey, Chase! Are you up there?" Skipper yelled from the dock below.

I leaned back, brushed Penny's unruly hair from her face, and tucked it behind her ears. "I'm all yours, Mrs. Fulton."

She grinned and kissed me on the tip of my nose. "Go see what Skipper needs."

"Yeah, Skipper. We're up here."

"Can I come up?"

I started for the ladder. "Come aboard. I'm coming down."

She climbed into the cockpit with a pair of manila folders in her hand. "I hope I'm not interrupting anything, but I think I've found a way you can get into and out of Eastern Siberia without getting caught and killed."

"Let's hear it," I said as I settled into the settee.

She opened the first folder and pulled out a map and satellite imagery of the North Pacific. "Ust-Kamchatsk is here on the western edge of the Bering Sea. There's nothing pleasant about it...at all. It's a terrible place—isolated, desolate, and cold. And I know how much you hate the cold."

I studied her map and photos. "It definitely looks cold, but we don't have any choice. We have to go."

"I know, and I'm getting to that part. Look at this long arcing line of islands. Those are called the Aleutians."

"Yeah, Skipper. I took world geography."

"Hey, give me a break. I'm usually the smartest person in the room, so I've learned not to expect everyone to know the things I know."

"You really need to hang out in larger rooms," I said.

That earned me a slap with a folder, but it was worth it.

"Okay, so tell me more about the Aleutians, smart girl."

"Adak is the last American outpost in the chain. Getting you there is pretty simple. Either we can charter a flight out there, or, and this is my suggestion, you can take Dominic's Cessna Caravan. If you take the Caravan, that opens up a nice little avenue to get you onto the eastern coast of Siberia, low and slow. You could stash the plane and hike in."

"What if somebody finds the plane and decides to claim it for themselves while we're inland?"

She held up one finger. "I think I've found a solution for that potential issue. Look at this."

She pulled out another satellite image. It showed a relative close-up of the coastline with several dilapidated buildings and part of a boat dock.

"What and where is that?" I asked.

"Keep your shirt on, impatient boy. I'm getting to that part."

She pulled out a wider-angle photo. "*Where* is more important than what. Here's Ust-Kamchatsk, and here's the site from the smaller picture. What it is will make you happy. It's a former Soviet-era military floatplane training facility. These buildings were built to house the floatplanes. Now the site is completely abandoned."

"Completely?" I questioned.

"Well, as far as we know," she admitted.

"How far is that from the town?"

"It's a little over three miles to the northern edge of the town. The other option is a lake about twenty miles west."

"That's out of the question," I said. "Three miles is possible, but hiking twenty miles in the wilds of Siberia isn't something I'm interested in doing. Hunter and I can run three miles if necessary, but definitely not twenty. The lake is out. The abandoned base—if it's truly abandoned—looks good."

"I thought you'd say that, so I've requested aerial photos every time a satellite flies overhead so I can watch for movement."

"How often does that happen?"

"Once every ninety-four minutes."

"All of that sounds good. There's just one problem."

"Oh, there are lot more problems than just one," she said, "but which *one* are you talking about?"

"I don't have a seaplane rating."

Her mouth fell open. "What? I thought Clark—"

I shook my head. "Nope. Clark's not a seaplane instructor."

She closed her eyes, and I could see her wheels turning. "Okay, that's not such a problem. We'll get Dominic to find someone to get your rating done. I've already okayed it with him for you to use the plane."

"Just tell me when and where."

She made a note on a pad she pulled from her pocket. "Okay, I will. There's one more issue. Ice."

"Oh yeah," I sighed. "Everything liquid in that part of the world is frozen this time of year, isn't it?"

"Yep, it sure is, but it's thawing as we speak. The ice on the southern peninsula and the mouth of the Kamchatka River is already breaking up. In another week, most of the ice should be gone."

"*Most* of the ice?" I asked.

"Well, yeah, there might be flow from the north bringing down some chunks, but it'll be mostly thawed."

I grimaced. "Do you have any idea what a fifty-pound chunk of floating ice will do to one of the floats on the Caravan? It'll be like reenacting the Titanic."

"Okay, then. I have another idea. What if you go meet Sokolov before you find Anya? That'll give the ice an opportunity to fully melt, and it'll buy you some time before the Russians try to kill you."

I gave her idea some thought. "I like it. I like it a lot, actually. The only thing I don't like is waiting a month for him to show up in France."

"I know you suck at waiting, but a little patience might be necessary. Besides, don't you have a conversation with the president that needs to happen?"

I took a long breath and let it out slowly. "Yeah, but I'm not looking forward to it."

She shrugged. "According to Dominic, you have to do it."

"I know. I'll make the call tomorrow, but I think we need to be ready for some fallout."

"We'll deal with that if it comes," she said, "but we can't let that stop this mission. We have to keep you alive, and just like getting in and out of Ust-Kamchatsk, there's only one way."

Chapter 16
Presidential New Deal

I lay awake all night planning and dreading the phone call to Washington D.C. People like the president of the United States aren't accustomed to being told no.

After mustering the courage and practicing my speech half a dozen times, I dialed the number the president had written on the small blue card in the Oval Office. I had no idea who'd answer, and suddenly, I had no idea what I'd say.

The phone rang twice, and a no-nonsense voice answered. "Command post. Say authorization code."

I didn't have an authorization code. I didn't even know what that meant. As I squeezed the card between my thumb and index finger, I was consumed by the thought that I was in so far over my head, I'd never claw my way out. With no other ideas, I shot a glance at the card and saw an alphanumeric code in tiny script across the bottom.

Blurting out the series of numbers and letters must've done the trick because the voice on the line said, "Stand by, sir."

I tried to control my breathing and practice my speech again, but I didn't have time. A booming voice came on the line. "Good morning, Chase. How are you? How'd you like the SEAL escort?"

"Uh, good morning, Mr. President. I, um…I mean, I appreciate the escort. I didn't expect…I mean, it wasn't necessar—"

"I wasn't expecting to hear from you, Chase. This must be important, so let's have it."

I couldn't believe I was talking to the president of the United States. My lungs filled with air, and I prepared to break the bad news. "Sir, I don't think I can do what you asked."

"Don't be preposterous. Of course you can do what I asked. What has you so shaken up, Chase? I'm sure we can solve whatever you think the problem is."

"No, sir, I don't think you can. I have to handle this one on my own, but that's not why I called. I can't build the team you want, Mr. President.

"Of course you can. I have every faith in you, and your country needs you. You can't turn your back on your country, son."

"It's not that, Mr. President. It's that you won't always be president. I generally agree with your policies, and I have enormous respect for your military service. My fear is when your second term is over, we may elect some jackass who doesn't share our way of thinking about the world."

"You can't think like that, Chase. You have to keep your eye on the ball. I think you know that term, don't you?"

"Yes, of course, Mr. President, but in my opinion, the ball is protecting the America you and I love so dearly. If I agree to build Team-Twenty-One, I become an official entity and a name the next president will need to know. If his politics are contrary to what you and I believe is important, he'll shut me down at best—and have me shot down at worst.

"Chase, you're being overly dramatic. We need you. We need to call on you when there's no one else we can send. I want—no, I need—to be able to pick up the phone and call you. America needs me to have that option."

I wasn't willing to push the president any further, so I chose to compromise. "Mr. President, I'm not willing to write a blank check to the White House, but I am willing to write one to you. I have a team. I have a home for that team, and I have the means to train, support, and deploy them. Pending approval from my handler, I'll make the commitment to you that I'll answer the phone when you call, and when you run out of other options, I'll do what has to be done. But this is a deal between you and me, man-to-man, nontransferable, no matter who takes your place in that big house."

The president cleared his throat. "What if this handler of yours vetoes the deal you're offering just like he shot down our previous deal?"

"We didn't have a deal, Mr. President. We had an offer from you, but we never closed the deal. The truth is, I never had the authority to close the deal."

"What sort of obligation are you under to this handler, Chase?"

I didn't hesitate. "A moral obligation, Mr. President. I looked him in the eye, shook his hand, and gave him my word. In my opinion, that's the only obligation that has any real meaning."

"I knew I liked you the second I laid eyes on you. Talk this out with the man to whom you have this moral obligation, and you get back to me."

"I will, sir."

"And one more thing, son. Be careful over there. It's mighty cold that far from home. If you get yourself in a pickle, somebody answers that number you called around the clock, even on Christmas Day."

Before I could respond, the line went dead.

* * *

Hunter and I spent the next several days shooting, running, and learning how each other moved. If lead started flying—and it would—I wanted to know exactly what he would do, and I wanted him to know what to expect of me. Clark and I had danced our way through enough gunfights to move as a single unit, completely confident in each other. Developing that level of connection can't be done in training; it only happens under fire. But I was determined to come as close as possible to recreating that action on the banks of the North River with my new partner.

Mongo, Clay, and Singer played opposing force. Singer's broken leg kept him from chasing us, but his sniper's eye never missed a detail of our training. He'd served as overwatch on more missions than anyone I knew, and that made his experienced eye one of the best tools we had in the arsenal.

Clark drilled Hunter's head full of everything he knew about me. The more time they spent together, the cleaner our drills became. Hunter was hungry for action and devoted to learning my habits and quirks, and Clark's wisdom and experience fell on his welcoming ears. It'd been a few years since he'd been under fire, but the warrior's heart beating inside his chest showed itself in self-discipline and drive. I don't know if I'd chosen him as a partner or if he'd been a gift from above, but either way, I was thankful to have him at my side while Clark was healing.

Mongo put us through our hand-to-hand paces. Fighting with a giant is an exhausting endeavor, but Hunter seemed to thrive on the challenge. He'd lost ten pounds, and I gained four. We shot at least a hundred thousand rounds. And most importantly, we finally started anticipating each other's movement and communicating with glances and nods. If a recon mission turned into a gunfight, I believed Hunter and I were as capable as any two-man tactical team of surviving and thriving. If it turned to fisticuffs, I liked our chances even more.

As Hunter and I stumbled up the back steps of the plantation house after a twelve-mile run—a race I'd easily won by at least two strides—Clark said, "Are you ready to trade me in on a younger model with fewer miles?"

I tried to catch my breath. "Ah, I think you're faking a broken back because you're scared, so I'm just grooming your replacement in case you never get your courage back."

Clark closed one eye and stared me down. "As soon as I get out of this medieval torture device, I'll show you how it feels to be scared." He pounded on his clamshell.

I laughed. "That thing makes you look like a middle-aged mutant ninja turtle."

"Go ahead, College Boy. Laugh it up while you can. You know I'm coming back, and I'll show you how middle-aged I am when I run your butt into the ground."

"Since you're on the disabled list, I'll let that go for now, pa-paw, but I'll be sure to keep the tennis balls changed on your walker."

After my shower and some much-needed calories, Skipper announced, "I just got off the phone with Dominic. He's arranged a seaplane instructor for you, and he wants you to see the progress of what he's calling 'the dunker.'"

"Perfect. I'll give him a call and let him know we'll be there tomorrow. Do you and Penny want a couple days in South Beach while I'm learning to land on the water?"

Her eyes lit up. "If it includes your credit card, you bet we do."

"They're Penny's cards now that we have the same last name, but you've earned a break, so consider this one an all-expenses-paid getaway."

Skipper's grin turned into a hug. "Thank you, Chase. Not that I didn't earn it, but I do appreciate it. My brain could use a little retail therapy, and hot guys on the beach are a bonus."

"Speaking of hot guys on the beach," I said, "where's Hunter?"

"He's outside with Clark. I think they're talking about you."

Even though I'd never admit to being a spy, I wasn't above a little eavesdropping when required. From the kitchen door, I listened as Clark laid out the truth about me.

"He's the best instinctual operator I've ever seen. He shoots on-time every time and never pulls the trigger when he shouldn't. He'll sometimes second-guess his planning, but when his boots hit the dirt and gunpowder starts burning, he'll fight 'til he's out of bullets and then beat you to death with his pistol. He's fast, strong, deadly, and fearless...completely fearless."

Hunter said, "I'd expect nothing less from any tier-one operator, but I need to know his kryptonite. What sends him off the rails?"

Clark glanced over his shoulder as if searching for a curious ear. I leaned back out of his line of sight. I knew my weaknesses, but I was anxious to hear his opinion.

"He's only got one I've ever seen. Anya Burinkova. You'll understand when you see her. She's enough to make any red-blooded guy weak in the knees, but it runs a little deeper with Chase. Just keep an eye on him, and don't let her get in his head. Or his pants."

Hunter didn't react, but I did. It felt like a kick in the crotch... from Mongo. Maybe Clark was right. Maybe Anya was my kryptonite, but I didn't have to like it. I just had to overcome it.

I made a show of approaching and opening the door. "Hey, Hunter, you don't happen to have a pilot's license, do you?"

He looked up as I approached. "Well, I've got a single-engine private ticket, but nothing beyond that. I've not flown in a couple of years, though. I'll need a biennial flight review and medical to get current. Why?"

"Pack a bag. We're going back to Miami tomorrow for some seaplane training. If it's going to be you and me over the Bering Sea, I don't want to be the only one who can land that thing."

"Are you taking the one-eighty-two?" Clark asked.

"Yeah, I thought I would. I'm taking Penny and Skipper so they can get a little beach time while we're flying."

He pointed toward Hunter. "Let him do the flying on the way down and back. It'll be good for him to get a little stick time before he jumps in the Caravan. That thing's a handful if you've not flown in a while."

"That's a good idea," I said, "and we'll get the seaplane instructor to do his BFR in the one-eighty-two while we're down there."

"There's no need for that," Clark said. "If he can get a medical certificate before you go, the seaplane rating will satisfy the BFR requirement."

Hunter glanced at his watch. "Doc Campbell is a flight doc. If I can get in to see him, he can write me a medical this afternoon."

"You get on that. I need to talk to Clark."

Hunter turned back to Clark as he stood. "Thanks, man. I really appreciate you taking the time."

Clark grinned. "No problem. Besides, somebody's gotta keep my boy alive. God knows he can't do it on his own."

I slid into Hunter's chair and wasted no time. "Do you really think Anya is my kryptonite?"

Clark stared at the river. "You heard that, did you?"

"I did."

"You know, I'd never say anything behind your back that I wouldn't say to your face, right?"

"Yeah, I know that."

He adjusted his clamshell. "I've seen you fight and live when most people would've died, and that girl's the only thing I've ever seen that makes you stumble. Do you disagree with me?"

My gaze fixed on a weathered crab trap float, standing like a sentry in the ever-changing tide of the relentless brine, where the river had become an ocean for eons. I relived the first time I saw Anya half a mile away on top of a water tower in Elmont, New York, and the last time I saw her in a farmer's barn outside Sol-Iletsk on the Russian-Kazak border after we'd pulled off the first successful escape from the Black Dolphin Prison.

"No, I don't disagree, and the truth is, I'm glad I heard you say it out loud. I guess admitting our weaknesses is the only way to overcome them."

Clark tapped his shoe against the gallery railing. "Don't go getting all philosophical. Just keep your head on straight and your zipper up tight. You'll be fine. Hunter's top-notch. He'll take care of you, but remember, he's an Air Force combat controller at his core. Those guys are used to being alone in a bunker and calling down hell from above. Don't get me wrong. He's an operator, but don't let him forget it's just you and him when you jump off. There's nobody to answer the radio."

"Thanks, Clark. Even when I'm picking on you, I appreciate you always teaching me the important stuff and keeping me out of trouble. I know Hunter's strong, and I'm glad to have him, but it won't be the same without you."

"Things change, Chase. I'm almost forty years old, and you're right—I'm on the disabled list. I've been shot up before, but never like this, and never at this age. You've got to remember, unlike you, this is all I've got. Kicking down doors is all I know."

I grabbed a handful of his shirt just above his collar. "Look at me. You're coming back. You've got too much experience, knowledge, and way too much skill to throw in the towel. You're coming back even if I have to drag you back."

He brushed my hand away. "Go get packed. You need some sleep. You've got a big day tomorrow. Besides, nobody drags Clark Johnson anywhere."

Making my best effort to mimic his trademark half-smile, I said, "I dragged your broken ass off the Khyber Pass."

He shook his head. "I don't remember that, so it didn't happen. But just in case it did…. Thanks."

"Just in case it did," I said, "you're welcome."

Chapter 17
Gear Down and Welded

Hunter was a little rusty in the cockpit, but by the time we reached our cruising altitude, it was all coming back to him. With her new engine, N682CF performed flawlessly, even with the four of us and a couple of bags aboard.

I pulled the mic to my lips. "We'll do some stalls, slow flight, and a few landings on the way home, but it's obvious you know how to fly."

Hunter set the autopilot. "Thanks. It's nice to get back in the saddle."

"Clark's an instrument instructor, so we'll get you an instrument ticket and more flight time, but for now, I'm glad to have somebody else who can find an airport and get us back on the ground if something happens to me."

We flew the rest of the trip without incident, and Hunter made an acceptable landing at Opa-Locka, although I did have to remind him to put down the landing gear.

"Most of my flight time is in a one-seventy-two with the gear down and welded," he said in his defense.

"That's why we use the checklists," I reminded him.

Dominic picked us up in the Land Rover, and we dropped Penny and Skipper off on South Beach before heading to the seaplane base.

After two hours of academics in the trailer and a careful pre-flight inspection of the Caravan, we headed inland over the Everglades where we practiced landings, takeoffs, step-taxiing, docking, sailing, and emergency procedures for the remainder of the afternoon. Hunter's learning curve was steep since he'd never flown a turbine, but by the end of the day, he was keeping his head above water, even if he was feeling a little overwhelmed.

Day two on the water left me feeling confident after a few hours of additional practice, so I spent the rest of the day at the shipyard while the instructor and Hunter continued without me.

* * *

"Well, there she is," Tommy said as he ran his hand along the dunker's hull.

I watched the shipwright admire his handiwork as I followed him through the tour.

"We'll put new sails on your boat and move yours onto the dunker," he explained. "That way, anyone who sees this one will believe she's *Aegis*, even if they've got pictures."

"That sounds like a good idea, but my sails are almost new. We had them installed after the little mishap off the coast of Mexico."

"Yeah, I know, but they're not as good as the ones I'm having made. I think you'll be happy with the upgrade."

"I'm sure I will. Can we go aboard?"

Tommy pulled a ladder to the stern of the dunker. "Absolutely. After you."

He followed me up the ladder and into the cockpit that made me feel right at home. It was an exact copy of *Aegis,* right down to the smallest detail.

Tommy slid open the hatch to the main salon. "This is where it gets a little rough."

The interior of the boat was as he'd described: rough, with no finishes. We descended the stairs past a panel full of valves.

"Don't worry about those," he said. "It's all automated, so you won't be messing with the valves."

Everything was raw fiberglass and wood, and in each engine room was a diesel that had seen better days.

"They're old, but there's no sense in sinking a pair of brand-new engines."

"I guess you're right, but it seems weird to see old engines in a new boat."

He opened a watertight compartment to reveal an array of impressive electronics I didn't recognize. "This is the heart and soul of the dunker. For lack of a better term, this is the remote control. It's all run through a secure satellite uplink. It can steer, navigate, and avoid other boats, but the best thing is its suicidal tendency. Every other system is secondary to the self-destruct mechanism. It's specifically designed to open the thru-hull valves and flood the interior in minutes. This one will be even better at sinking itself than yours was originally. There's concrete in the hulls to make her waterline identical to yours, and so she won't bob around like a cork without all the weight of the interior."

I continued examining the inside of the hulls. "It looks like you've thought of everything."

"We try to. It's the little details that get you busted when you're dealing with pros like the Russians. They may not make Levi's and Coca-Cola, but they're good at the cloak-and-dagger."

I tried to imagine Tommy's background. Something about him made me believe he'd spent a lot of time nose-to-nose with bad guys.

"When is she going in the water?" I asked.

"That'll be up to Dominic, but I'm sure he'll want you to get your boat down here in the next few days so we can trade out the sails and get this girl started across the pond."

"I'll talk to him about the schedule, but I can have *Aegis* down here whenever you're ready."

He shrugged. "I'm just the hired help. I don't make big decisions."

"Me, too, Tommy. Me, too."

We found Dominic in his office, poring over charts of the Black Sea.

"Come on in, guys. What do you think of the dunker, Chase?"

"Until I walked inside, I couldn't find anything about her that wasn't pure *Aegis*."

He nodded. "Yep, that's the idea. If we can just make the Russians see the same thing, I think our chances of pulling this off are pretty good."

"When do you want *Aegis*?" I asked.

He ran his finger across his calendar. "The sails will be here tomorrow or the next day. If you can have her here by Monday, we can have the dunker in the Med in less than two weeks."

"Two weeks?" I scoffed. "If everything went perfectly, you can't sail that thing across the Atlantic in two weeks."

"Who said anything about sailing her? We're putting her on a cargo ship to Istanbul. The shipyard there will launch her, and Tommy and I'll sail her to Sochi."

"You're going?" I asked. "I didn't know you still…."

"Still what?" he growled. "You didn't think I still knew how to sail?"

"No, not that. I didn't…."

He chuckled. "Yeah, I know. You didn't know I still operated. I don't. Those days are long astern, but I can still ferry a sailboat for young bucks like you who get to have all the fun."

"Oh, yeah. That's what this is. Having the Russian Foreign Intelligence Service trying to kill me…that's fun."

Dominic slapped my shoulder. "You wouldn't have it any other way. Anything less would bore you to tears."

I held my palms up, mimicking a set of scales. "Let's see. In this hand we have me being chased by Russian assassins, and in the other, we have a relaxing honeymoon with my beautiful new wife. Yep, I think I'll take the honeymoon."

"It looks like you get to have your cake and eat it, too, my boy."

I sighed. "I hope so."

* * *

The following morning, I passed my check ride with the FAA-designated pilot examiner and was awarded a seaplane rating on my commercial pilot certificate. Hunter wasn't quite ready for the check ride, but the instructor did endorse his logbook with a successful biennial flight review, making him, once again, legal to fly. The seaplane rating for him wasn't as important as the BFR. The training gave me enough confidence in Hunter's skill to know he could get us safely back to Earth if I couldn't, even in the Caravan.

After my check ride, Dominic met us at the Miami Seaplane Base with his beloved leather-bound folder under his arm. While the examiner was completing my temporary airman certificate containing my new seaplane rating, Dominic slid a stack of papers across the table toward me.

"What's this?"

"It's a contract," he murmured, as if I was supposed to be expecting one.

"For what?"

"For that airplane," he growled.

"What are you talking about?"

He tossed a ballpoint pen onto the table. "Just read the contract."

As I scanned down the first page, I read:

Purchase Agreement: Chase D. Fulton agrees to purchase from Dominic J. Fontana one 1997 Cessna 208 Grand Caravan for LIKE KIND EXCHANGE of one motor yacht "Moscow Mule" formerly of Belarussian registry further identified as...

My jaw fell open, and I met Dominic's gaze. "Do you mean..."

"Yes, Chase. *Aegis* is yours, and the Caravan is yours. Barkov's yacht is mine, and we're square."

I was still in awe. "But I saw that yacht headed into Wilmington. I even talked with her skipper on the radio."

He finally smiled. "Yes, I remember. You seem to have forgotten that I'm a voice guy. I can sound like anybody from anywhere."

I stuck out my hand, and he shook it, cementing a deal we'd never mention again.

Before the ink had time to dry, Dominic shoved the signed contract into his binder. "I'll go pick up the girls and bring them to the airport. You'll probably want Hunter to do a few landings before you send him home in your one-eighty-two."

After a call to the insurance company to add Hunter and the Caravan to my policy and inform them of my new seaplane rating, Hunter and I blasted off for the first time, with me as the pilot in command of my new magic carpet. The versatility of the Caravan with its amphibious floats and incredible useful load was second to none. She would essentially carry anything I could shove through the door and land anywhere I could find a straight enough strip of water or concrete.

By the time Dominic arrived at Opa-Locka Airport with Penny and Skipper and their overflowing bags of booty from their South Beach shopping adventures, Hunter had proven to me he could safely land my Skylane without forgetting to put down the landing gear.

I hugged my wife, who'd been sound asleep when I left the hotel that morning.

"Congratulations on your seaplane rating," she said.

"Thank you, but it wasn't a big deal. Clark prepared me for most of it. I just needed a little practice."

"Well, I'm proud of you, even if you don't think it's a big deal." Penny looked down at the ground and twisted her foot side to side. "Um…"

That made me nervous. "Um…what?"

She looked around at the bags Dominic was unloading from the Land Rover. "I know we were close to max gross weight in the plane, but we bought a lot of stuff. Do you think it'll be okay?"

"As long as you didn't buy more than three thousand pounds, we'll be just fine."

She screwed up her face. "What?"

I decided to have a little fun. "Do you remember when we were in Wilmington and you smelled like a goat because you hadn't showered for three days?"

She slapped my arm. "What's that got to do with buying three thousand pounds of new shoes? And you like it when I smell like a goat."

"Okay, maybe a little," I admitted. "Anyway, do you remember the yacht named *Moscow Mule* we saw as we were leaving Wilmington?"

"Yeah, I remember."

"Well, I didn't tell you everything I knew about it."

The look on her face made it clear she wasn't happy that I'd withheld something, so I quickly continued. "Well, I actually captured that yacht from a Russian billionaire named Dmitri Barkov who, well...let's say he didn't need it anymore."

"Oh, really?" she said, disappointment becoming intrigue.

"Yes, really. I couldn't keep a dead billionaire's yacht for myself, so I gave it to Dominic. Sort of."

"Sort of? What does that mean?"

"It means I traded it to him for *Aegis*, but the yacht was a little more valuable than our sailboat, so he and I have sort of been carrying a balance for a few years. We squared up this morning, though."

"So, that's what you were yelling about when you wrote the two-million-dollar check that nearly made me wet my pants."

I pointed toward the Caravan on the ramp beside my one-eighty-two.

Penny's eyes turned to saucers. "Chase, are you serious? That's ours?"

"It is, and now I have a license to fly it."

"You may have the license," she said, "but I'm flying it home." She sprinted toward Dominic and wrapped him in an excited hug.

I couldn't hear what she was saying, but the look on his face said he was glad to have made my wife so happy.

If possible, Skipper was even more excited about the Caravan than Penny, but she agreed to fly home with Hunter just so she could get some front-seat time.

Skipper and Hunter took off thirty minutes before Penny and me, and we landed only minutes apart at Saint Marys. The Caravan would never be accused of being a speed demon, but it was comfortable, capable, and best of all, it was mine. Well, according to Penny, it was ours.

* * *

The day had come. Hunter and I were booked on a flight from Jacksonville to Marseille, with at least two stops along the way. I wasn't looking forward to being a passenger, but other than sailing *Aegis* across the Atlantic, there were no other options.

Penny and Skipper would sail *Aegis* down the east coast of Florida so the sails could be exchanged, making the dunker look even more authentic.

Penny took my face in her hands and locked eyes with mine. "Chase Daniel Fulton, you've got a wife now. I know you're good at what you do, but you're playing in somebody else's backyard on this one. And you're not exactly dealing with some two-bit hit man. You still owe me a real honeymoon where no one tries to kills us, and I mean to have that honeymoon. Do you hear me?"

I wrapped my arms around her. "I'll be careful, and you'll have that honeymoon. I promise."

We kissed goodbye, and I watched her fight back the tears. Walking away from her got harder every time, and I wondered how much longer I'd be able to do it. If I couldn't pull off the most complex mission of my life, Mrs. Penny Fulton would become the widow Fulton, and I'd never see Honeymoon Harbour or Bonaventure Plantation again.

Chapter 18
Ardeur Française

The private charter boat from Marseille to Hyères turned out to be operated by none other than my old friend, Pierre Arnoult, a former French foreign legionnaire who, the year before, Clark and I worked with during our mission to trade Ekaterina Norikova for Anya.

He spoke only French and behaved as if he'd never met the six-foot-four-inch American and his friend pretending not to be spies. Once we were well offshore, Pierre's French became accented English. "My old friend, Chase. Is so good to see you again. Introduce me to your friend."

"Pierre, this is Hunter. Hunter, meet Pierre Arnoult. He's a bit of an enigma—a Frenchman who loves Americans, guns, and trading mercenary services for stolen helicopters. It's a long story, but suffice it to say, Pierre is one of the good guys."

The two men shook hands, and Hunter said, "It's nice to meet you, Pierre. I've done a little training with the legionnaires in North Africa, and I've even got a pair of French jump wings in a shoebox at home."

Pierre appraised my partner. "You do not look like American paratrooper."

Hunter grinned. "Nope. I was a cook in the Air Force. Or was it a payroll clerk? I can never remember."

Pierre launched into a hearty French laugh. "Oh, *mon ami,* perhaps you were an airborne cooking clerk."

Hunter pointed at the Frenchman. "Yep, that's exactly what I was. How'd you know?"

We all shared a good laugh. Perhaps the last laugh we'd have for a while.

"So, it is time to get down to business as you say in America, no?"

"Yeah, I guess you could say that," I answered. "What do you have for us?"

He pulled a black Pelican case from beneath the console of the boat. "I have for you two of the finest pistols in all of the world."

He opened the case to reveal a pair of FN Five-seven pistols, a stack of fully loaded magazines, and shoulder holster rigs for each. The Five-seven was capable of piercing most Kevlar body armor and packed a nice punch.

I lifted one of the pistols, examined it carefully, and nodded. "Well done, Pierre. Excellent choice."

"*Merci.* I have also for you picks for the locks and throwaway cell phones, completely untraceable. Also inside is five thousand euros. Oh, I almost forgot the best thing I have for you." He removed the false bottom in the Pelican, revealing a dozen syringes. "This will render a man—even a man the size of you—completely unconscious for half an hour or more. You only need to inject him in a large muscle like the leg, arm, or derriere, and in only a few seconds, he will become weak and no longer able to stand."

Hunter let out a low whistle. "I guess it's nice to have friends in French places."

I asked, "What do we owe you for all this, Pierre?"

"I would love to have another helicopter if you happen to find one lying around, but otherwise, your analyst has already paid for everything, including the boat ride. I am number seven on the speed dial when you are ready for a ride back to Marseille."

"Thanks, Pierre. We'll try to give you plenty of lead time for the outbound leg."

The Frenchman smiled mischievously. "Lead time is not necessary. I will not be far away. Having an old legionnaire in the area when you need him can be, as you say in America, just the ticket."

Pierre dropped us off at a resort with a beautiful marina less than a mile from Colonel Sokolov's dacha. He passed us two booklets. "You will check in using these."

Inside the booklets were Canadian passports stamped through customs at Charles De Gaulle Airport the previous day.

Hunter shoved the passport with his picture into his shirt pocket. "It looks like you thought of everything, Pierre."

"No, *mon ami*. It was your analyst who thought of everything. She is very good. Even better than when we worked together last time."

I felt my heart swell with a little pride. "Yes, she's very good and getting better every day."

We checked into the resort and thankfully found a clerk whose English was far better than my French.

"Okay, boss. We're here. Now what?"

"Now we eat, sleep, and let our bodies adjust to whatever time zone we're in. Tomorrow, we'll do a little recon on the good colonel's home away from home."

We slept off the jetlag, ate croissants the size of footballs, and drank coffee as strong as Mongo. The resort provided its guests with bicycles, which made for the perfect recon vehicles.

The house was precisely where Skipper said it would be, and we rode around the property twice without attracting any obvious attention from the three noticeable guards. I motioned for Hunter to follow me as I headed for the beach, where the sound of crashing waves made excellent conversation cover. No one would be able to hear or record our chat.

"What did you see?" I asked as we planted ourselves in a pair of weathered chairs.

"One armed guard on the door, and one at each front corner of the house, with an overwatch in the second-story dormer on the right. There was a trash can in front of the garage door, so they don't have a car, or if they do, they haven't used it lately. Second-story window on the back was open six inches, so that's probably the bedroom. If the house has been closed up all winter, the wife probably wanted some fresh air."

"Good eyes," I said. "I missed the overwatch in the dormer, but I agree with everything else. I caught a glimpse of the staircase through the window to the right of the front door. The doors had new hardware but no deadbolts, which means they've been serviced recently. They didn't look too sophisticated, so we can probably pick the locks without any trouble."

"Why don't they have a man on the back door?"

"I don't know. Maybe they've got a camera we didn't see or a man inside the door."

He glanced over his shoulder. "Or maybe they're sloppy."

"No, the Russians aren't sloppy about anything, especially security for the chief of Directorate KR. I say we make another pass and look for a camera."

"You're the boss," Hunter said, "but how about one of us blowing a tire outside the back gate so we can get a better look?"

"Too risky. They may know my face, and I don't want to take a chance of being ID'd and blowing the whole op before we even get started."

"Yeah, you're probably right," he said, "but they don't know me."

I gave his idea some thought. "Okay, I like it. I'll take up a position in the tree line across the street. You do a little play-acting, but get out of there if it turns ugly. I don't want to have to shoot our way out of France."

"Whatever you say."

I took a circuitous route through the wealthy neighborhood until I made my way into the grove of trees and shrubs directly behind the colonel's love shack. Just as I got settled in, Hunter came pedaling up the street and suddenly spun the handlebars ninety degrees to the left. The rapid turn forced the front tire off the rim and sent my partner flying across the handlebars. Instead of ducking his shoulder and rolling gracefully to his feet, he made a grand show of sprawling onto the street and cursing in believable German.

His acting was so good, for an instant I thought the crash was unintentional, but he never took his eyes off the house throughout the wreck. Before the rear bicycle tire stopped spinning, a young, imposing Russian appeared from out of nowhere with a Makarov pistol pointed at my partner's head. "*Vstat' i uyti!*"

Hunter appeared unfazed and looked up, ignoring the man's insistence that he get up and go away. In excellent German, my partner said, "My bicycle is broken. May I use your telephone?"

"*Ukhodi!*" ordered the Russian.

I didn't know if Hunter understood him, but even if I didn't speak Russian, it was clear he was ordering Hunter to leave.

My partner focused on the gun and slowly stood up, dusting himself off. He slung the bike across his shoulder. "Okay, I'm going. Take it easy."

The Russian clearly didn't understand Hunter's German, but my partner's willingness to leave seemed to satisfy him.

I took one more long, thorough look at the back of the house. A pair of eyes peered through the small window beside the door, and a second gunman showed himself from behind a row of low shrubs.

* * *

When Hunter finally made it back to the resort, we sat around the table in our room, sketching what we'd seen behind the house.

"It looks like you were right," he said. "They aren't sloppy. That guy was on me before I stopped sliding."

Remembering the act, I couldn't suppress a little laugh. "That was some crash, by the way. You almost fooled me."

"Short of shooting out my own tire, that was the only way I could think of to make it look real. I'm glad you liked it. Did you see the guy in the bushes?"

"Yeah, I saw him at the end, but not before you stood up. Where did the gunman come from?"

He shook his head. "I have no idea. I was hoping you saw his hidey-hole."

"He had to be tucked away behind the gate, but he was quick."

Hunter pulled the aerial photos from the file and studied the first one. "It makes me wonder if they have more men up front than we saw on the two passes we made."

I stared at the pictures. "I was thinking the same thing. This isn't going to be as easy as I thought. The colonel must be a little paranoid."

"I'd be paranoid too if you and I were chasing me."

"But he doesn't have any reason to think we're after him."

"Sure he does," Hunter argued. "He knows he missed you in Bimini, and he knows your tracker went dark right after you left the anchorage. He knows you're alive and pissed off. I think he knows you're coming after him, but he probably thinks you're coming to kill him, not strike a deal."

"Killing him would be easy, but that doesn't solve my problem. I need him alive and convinced I can deliver Anya."

"Do you think they've got night vision?"

"I don't know," I said, "but I doubt if they're using it. There's a lot of lights in the area, and I think nods would be more trouble than they're worth."

Hunter lined up several pictures and lifted a pencil from the table to use as a pointer. "If they're not using nods, I think we can hit the corners up front. I believe the three guards we saw are the only ones looking out front. Their presence would send any would-be attackers to the back, right into the hands of the stealthy shooters."

"I think you're right, but how do we get past the overwatch upstairs?"

He spun a picture and slid it toward me. "Look. From a sixty-degree angle from the front, the overwatch is blind to the flanks. If we can slip through the fence and stick a needle in each of the corner guards, we have the front of the house to ourselves. We can stay tight against the front wall and get in the door right under the overwatch's nose."

"It's a solid plan," I said. "Let's make it happen."

"Have you practiced your speech to the colonel yet?" Hunter asked, half-joking.

"No, I thought I'd just wing it and see what comes out. It's more fun that way."

"Right on. Let's get some rest and hit them in the middle of the night when they're nice and complacent."

"Don't kid yourself," I said. "Complacency is the same as sloppiness, and the Russians don't do either."

Sleep came, but it did so reluctantly. I yawned and stretched myself awake around 10:30 and saw Hunter studying the aerial photographs under the bathroom light.

He noticed I wasn't sleeping. "Good, you're awake. I've been thinking, and we're going to need a distraction in the back."

I cleared my throat. "I was thinking the same thing as I was falling asleep. If we can get as many guards as possible looking the wrong way, our chances of getting inside go up substantially."

I pulled my throwaway phone from the nightstand and pushed number seven. "Pierre, it's Chase. I need a favor. We need a distraction behind the colonel's house at one a.m. Have you got any ideas?"

The line was silent long enough for me to believe I'd lost the connection. When I returned the phone to my ear after glancing at the screen, the Frenchman said, "You'll have your distraction at one, and I'll pick you up at the resort marina thirty minutes before sunrise."

"What'd he say?" Hunter asked before I could lay down the phone.

"He said he'll provide the distraction and pick us up just before daylight at the marina."

"Did he say what kind of distraction?"

"I didn't ask. I'm taking him at his word. He's never let me down before."

"There's a first time for everything," Hunter said.

We devoured a loaf of French bread and a block of cheese so our stomachs wouldn't growl at an inopportune moment, then we headed back for Colonel Sokolov's dacha aboard another pair of borrowed bicycles.

At ten minutes before one a.m., I saw a flicker of orange flames through the dense trees behind the dacha. The flicker became a knee-high flame and finally, a fully involved house fire. At twelve fifty-nine, the rear guards showed themselves and stood in wonder of the roaring flames. When the clock struck one, every siren in town whined to life, sending dogs barking and lights switching on all over the neighborhood.

Pierre had definitely come through…and in spades. As the French fire raged, drawing everyone's attention away from the front door, I nodded toward Hunter. We slithered through the fence, beginning our arduous crawl through the yard and toward the two guards on the front corners of the house.

Chapter 19
Goodnight, Colonel

For his version of a distraction, I definitely would've found a way to steal a helicopter and gift it to Pierre. Most people wouldn't burn down a house on the French Riviera, but Pierre wasn't most people. The corner guards showed incredible restraint by keeping their focus on the front of the house, but human curiosity is a phenomenon of remarkable predictability. With a fire raging a quarter mile away and sirens blaring into the night, it would be all but impossible to not have a look. As well trained and dedicated as the guards were, they were still human, and, as such, incapable of ignoring the fire.

Hunter and I crept like sloths through the yard, him on the left, and me on the right. We kept one eye on each other, gauging our progress to coordinate our strike, and one eye on our targets. Sooner or later, the guards would turn to see the fire. It was simply a matter of having enough patience to wait them out. With every inch, I watched Hunter pull himself through the shadows with his body pressed against the earth. I followed suit, drawing ever nearer to our prey. But our prey was proving to be less and less human as the raging fire succumbed to the efforts of the French firefighters drowning the inferno with water hoses.

With every passing minute, it became clearer that our targets were not going to turn. I envied their dedication, but I knew it wasn't a sense of duty that kept them facing forward. It was fear for their lives. Failure to protect their primary wouldn't result in a slap on the wrist or a demotion to office duty. It meant their bodies would find their way into a woodchipper or a dumpster somewhere outside Moscow.

There are few things more important in a multi-operator mission than communication. Hunter and I had no electronic comms, but we'd spent enough time crawling together through the marsh grass of Bonaventure Plantation to anticipate the other's next move based on his previous posture. I saw him draw his left leg up and dig his toe into the grassy lawn. My partner had made the same determination as me. Our targets weren't going to peek. That left us no option other than springing on them and taking them down as quickly and quietly as possible.

I planted my right boot against a bowling-ball-sized rock in the landscape and pressed my fingertips into the sandy soil. Hunter was going to lunge forward in the next few breaths, and I'd be only an instant behind him. With any luck, we'd have our prey on the ground, injected, and silenced in seconds. Hunter had called an audible at the line of scrimmage, and the opening gambit of our game plan changed in the blink of an eye.

Hunter sprang to his feet, making four feet per stride and closing on his man with unimaginable speed. My body, eight inches taller and forty pounds heavier, didn't explode from the prone position as efficiently as his, but I'd hit my target with significantly more force, hopefully more than making up for the deficiency in quickness. Ignoring my partner and focusing every sense on hitting my target with maximum force, I thundered forward, closing the distance like a puma charging the antelope that would soon be his breakfast.

The guard I was charging saw my advance from the darkness and drew his pistol. He was a quarter-second away from putting two 9mm Makarov rounds in my chest when my legionnaire upped the game and earned his second helicopter of the night. An enormous explosion behind the house sent roiling clouds of orange fire and black smoke pouring into the night sky. In that instant, my target proved to be human by flinching just enough to allow me to juke to my left, avoiding the rising pistol.

My shoulder landed an inch beneath his chin, collapsing his trachea and sending his head snapping backward with a sickening snap of his neck. He was likely dead when we hit the ground, but what air remained in his lungs exploded from his mouth when my two-hundred-twenty pounds crushed him into the lawn.

Two fingers against his jugular confirmed my diagnosis. I hadn't meant to break his neck, but putting him down was my only option before he could get off a pair of shots. Leaping to my feet, I heard the telltale whisper and hiss of bullets leaving the muzzle of a suppressed pistol. Our FN Five-sevens weren't suppressed, so the shots had to come from one of the Russian guards. If my theory was correct, my two-man operation had just become a solo mission.

If the other guard was carrying a suppressed weapon, the dead guy at my feet probably had one as well. I scampered around his body, feeling for the cold steel in the grass. When my hand finally felt the familiar Makarov grip, I pulled the weapon against my gut and headed for the front of the house. The man on the front door had heard the shots from the other side of the house, just as I had, and he slowly moved away from me and toward the blasts.

I raised the Russian pistol, squeezed the trigger twice in rapid succession, and watched the guard wither to the ground. With my pistol trained on the corner of the house, I waited for the guard who'd killed my partner to show his head. I'd send him into the next life where Hunter might have a chance to get even.

I stepped over the body of the guard I'd shot and never allowed my eyes to stray from the point where I knew I'd see Hunter's assassin. Continuing my advance, I crept low and slow beneath a pair of windows until I was six feet from the corner of the house. That's when I heard the sweetest words I'd heard all night.

"Pull a gun on me? What were you thinking, you little red commie son of a bitch? That'll teach you to draw on a combat controller."

Relief pouring over me, I snapped my fingers twice—our predetermined signal for "Are you okay?"

A single snap resounded from just around the corner, and I stepped forward, happy to see my partner collecting the dead guard's equipment.

I whispered, "Doing a little shopping, are you?"

Hunter looked over his shoulder, his teeth gritted. "This bastard thought he was going to draw on me and survive. He was wrong."

"Yeah, my guy made a poor life choice as well. I put him and the front-door man down. Let's get inside before this turns into a carnival."

I picked the front-door lock while Hunter covered my back. We made entry in less than a minute, and what we found inside was something on the verge of hitting the proverbial fan. As the back door stood open, we saw all the way through the house and the silhouette of flames dancing in the distance.

On a landing halfway to the top of the stairs was Colonel Nicholai Sokolov in a robe and house shoes, a cigarette dangling precariously from the corner of his mouth. Inches in front of him was a man who could've been the twin to any of the dead men on the front lawn.

Sokolov drove his index finger into the man's chest like a woodpecker pounding at a tree trunk. The man stood like a statue while the colonel whisper-yelled in angry Russian, "I'm on my anniversary. If you wake me again, I swear to you it will be last thing you ever do."

"What's he saying?" Hunter whispered.

I pressed my index finger to my lips as the colonel turned and stomped back up the stairs while the other man descended, rage boiling in his expression. When the man reached the bottom of the stairs and turned for the back of the house, I pointed toward

Hunter and then at the man's back. My partner silently followed the man through the house, matching his footfalls exactly and gaining on him with every exaggerated stride. Two steps from the back door, Hunter laced his arm around the man's neck and lifted him from his feet. In one perfectly smooth motion, he buried the syringe into the man's butt and pressed the plunger. He completed the choke hold, eliminating the possibility of the man yelling out. I wasn't sure if it was Pierre's drugs or Hunter's choke hold that made the man wither into a lifeless heap on the floor, but I was glad he was down.

Hunter slammed the back door with far more force than I liked since I was still trying to maintain a sense of stealth, but my partner's plan turned out to be genius. Ten seconds later, Sokolov came thundering down the stairs, pulling on his robe and yelling in furious Russian with every step. I watched as the spymaster turned the corner toward the rear of the house and came face-to-face with Special Agent Stone W. Hunter and the muzzle of a suppressed Makarov 9mm.

I closed the distance, sandwiching the colonel between Hunter's muzzle and mine.

Hunter said, "Greetings, Colonel Asshole. Do you *sprechen sie* English?"

I slid a pair of flex-cuffs around the Russian's wrists and pressed my muzzle firmly beneath his right ear. In my best menacing Russian, I growled, "My partner wants to know if you speak English."

"What do you want?" the colonel grunted, pulling against the nylon cuffs.

"We just want to have a little chat with you and your blushing bride. That's all. Now let's go before you end up like your chief of security there." Hunter stepped aside, allowing Sokolov a view of the man lying motionless on the floor.

I ripped one of the pockets from Sokolov's robe, wadded it up, and shoved it in his mouth before wrapping the robe's cloth belt twice around his head. This left him entirely incapable of making a sound.

Forcing my knee into the back of Sokolov's, I drove him to the floor. "You take care of the guard in the dormer, and I'll bring our new friend up right behind you."

Hunter nodded and disappeared silently up the stairs. Seconds later, the suppressed pistol hissed twice, and the sound of a body hitting the floor reverberated through the house.

I frog-marched Sokolov up the stairs, meeting my partner at the top. Hunter took control of the colonel as we slipped through the bedroom door, and I moved toward the bed where Tatiana Sokolova lay sleeping like a child. I didn't want to hurt the woman, but as Clark had taught me, never leave room for confusion about who's in charge.

In one rapid movement, I clasped my left hand over Tatiana's mouth and my right hand behind her head. Her eyes shot open and instantly filled with terror.

I spoke in calm, confident Russian. "Do as I say, and I will not hurt you. Do anything other than what I say, and you and your husband will die together. Blink twice if you understand."

Her horror-filled eyes blinked twice in rapid jerks.

"Good. Now, are you going to do as I say?"

Again, two spasmodic blinks.

I pulled the woman from the bed, bound her wrists with flex-cuffs, and put her on her knees a few feet away from her husband.

Motioning toward the colonel's mouth, I said to Hunter, "Ungag him so we can have a little chat."

He did as I said, and when Sokolov spat the cloth out, he immediately began spewing threats. "You have no idea what you've done. My men will tear you to shreds—"

I sent a sharp palm strike to the tip of his nose, causing blood to explode from his face. "I know, I know... And they'll gut me like pig. I've heard it all before. It's just what Colonel Tornovich told me. Remember him? I sent him to Hell in a gasoline tuxedo, and you're next if you don't shut up and listen."

He spat blood and tried to wipe his face on the shoulder of his robe. In English, he said, "You are both dead men, no matter what you do to me."

"Oh, look," said Hunter. "He does *sprechen sie* English."

I yanked a pillow from the bed and tore off the case. Kneeling in front of the colonel, I wiped the blood and spit from his mouth. "Listen very closely, Colonel, and take a good look at my face. My name is Chase Fulton, and you've been trying to kill me." I rolled my eyes. "Well, that isn't entirely true. *You* haven't been trying to kill me because you're a coward, but from the safety of your cushy office at the Kremlin, you ordered your hit squads to try and kill me. News flash, Colonel. They failed."

"Killing me will not save your life, you miserable little—"

It was Hunter's turn to interrupt Sokolov's threat, and he was a little more creative than me. Instead of a palm strike to the nose, he lifted a vodka bottle from the bar and swung it like a baseball bat into the colonel's mouth, sending shards of glass, vodka, broken teeth, and blood in every direction.

Tatiana gasped and shuttered. In quivering Russian, she begged, "Give them whatever they want, Nicholai. Please."

I raised my borrowed pistol to her face and thumb-cocked the hammer. "I'm not here to kill you, Colonel, but I've not ruled out spraying your wife's brain all over this room. After all, that's what your crackpot team tried to do to my wife with that radio-controlled yacht of yours."

Tatiana sobbed. "What is he talking about, Nicholai?"

"Shut up, woman," Sokolov ordered through his broken teeth and blood-gushing lips.

I moved to within inches of what remained of Colonel Sokolov's face. "As I said, I'm not here to kill you. I'm here to give you something you want even worse than you want me dead."

"There is nothing I want more than your head, American spy."

I grinned. "I'm not a spy. I'm an assassin. Just ask your buddy Barkov or the Suslik triplets. Oh, I'm sorry. You can't ask them because I killed them all." I paused for dramatic effect and then pointed my muzzle at Tatiana's head. "And she's next if you open your mouth one more time."

He had to be consumed by the agony of having his nose and several teeth broken, as well as the flesh of his lips sliced to shreds, but that didn't stop Colonel Sokolov from furrowing his brow in anger as I threatened his wife. Obviously convinced I'd pull the trigger, he held his tongue.

"Good. Now we're getting somewhere. As I tried to tell you before, I'm not here to kill you...this time. I'm here to offer you something in return for you calling off the manhunt for me. I'm here, so I'm obviously better than the mouth breathers you keep sending after me. Your guards are dead. Your wife is pissing her pants. And your face is a mess. The little message in a bottle you sent with the yacht in Bimini was a nice touch, but it showed your weakness. Well, one of your many weaknesses."

He continued his glare at me but still didn't speak.

"Killing Captain Ekaterina Norikova and sticking her behind the wheel of that yacht was a nice touch, Colonel. I'll admit it got my heart rate up for a minute. You wanted me to believe she was Anastasia Burinkova, and it would've worked except for one small detail. Well, actually one huge detail. I know exactly where Anya is."

"*Fignya!*"

I moved my face closer to his. "No, it's not bullshit, and you know it. Now, here's what's going to happen. You're going to call off your goons, and I'm going to live a long, happy life. In return, I'm going to give you Anya on a silver platter."

"You cannot negotiate with something you do not have," he growled.

"I'm not negotiating, Colonel. I'm telling you what's going to happen. In fact, I just thought of something extra to make my life insurance policy a little stronger. Excuse me for just a second."

I sat back on my heels, never taking my eyes off Sokolov, and pressed the speed dial button on my phone for Pierre. "We're going to need an exfil off the beach in front of Sokolov's dacha in seven minutes." I ended the call. "I've decided I'm taking your lovely bride with me when I leave in"—I glanced at my watch—"seven minutes."

Tatiana burst into horrified gasps, and I stuck a needle in her thigh, quieting her cries and leaving her a helpless, unconscious mass on the floor beside her broken and bloody husband.

I shoved the muzzle of my gun into Sokolov's mouth, and he gagged on the blood and steel. "Call off your goons, and you get Anya, and maybe you'll get Tatiana back alive. If anyone so much as points a finger in my direction, I'll find you again, just like I did tonight, and I'll gut you like pig. If I see anybody sneeze in my direction, your wife gets a bullet to the brain, and her daddy's fortune will never make it into your Swiss bank account. Oh, and even though Tatiana knows all about your mistress, she doesn't know about your bastard child with her. I think it might break her heart to learn you gave your girlfriend a baby when you wouldn't do the same for your wife. Yeah, Colonel, that's right. I know all your dirty little secrets."

I made a show of glancing across Sokolov's shoulder at my partner. "Did I leave anything out?"

Hunter shook his head. "Nope, I think you covered everything. Time to hit the road."

I whispered, "Good night, Colonel," and nodded to my partner.

Hunter sent the butt of his pistol crashing into Sokolov's temple, and I shoved my two remaining syringes into the colonel's thighs. With Tatiana Sokolov's limp body slung across my shoulder, I headed for the stairs.

The bow of Pierre's boat hit the sand as if we'd practiced the timing for weeks. We stepped aboard, and the engines revved, carrying us into the waiting darkness of the Mediterranean Sea.

Chapter 20
North to Alaska

"What am I going to do with a Russian colonel's wife?" demanded Pierre.

"You're the best babysitter I know," I said. "Surely you can come up with something for a few days."

"No," he protested. "I will imprison a Russian spy for you, but not the wife of an SVR colonel. You do not have enough helicopters to bribe me."

"You're right," I admitted. "Let's drop her off on Îles d'Hyères. Do you have any smelling salts on board?"

Pierre nodded his approval of the plan. "That is a marvelous idea, and no, I have nothing like that on board."

"What are you thinking?" asked Hunter.

"I want to plant a seed and see if it sprouts," I said.

"I'm going to need you to *sprechen sie* English I can understand."

"I need Tatiana to be awake but still a little groggy when we drop her off."

Hunter looked at his watch. "She's been out for almost thirty minutes. That's how long that stuff lasts, right, Pierre?"

The Frenchman looked down at the hundred-pound Russian. "It last for one half hour for you, but for her is much longer."

"How much farther to the port?" I asked

"Ten minutes at this speed, but I can go faster," said Pierre.

"No, definitely not faster. In fact, let's slow down, and give me something I can use as a blindfold."

Hunter tore a piece of cloth from a towel and tossed it toward me. I managed to get the towel tied across Tatiana's eyes, and step one of the plan to plant my seed was done. I propped the woman against the gunwale and unscrewed the cup from the top of Pierre's coffee thermos. Holding the small, plastic cup overboard, I allowed it to fill with cold sea water, then I slowly poured it across Tatiana's neck and shoulders. Slowly, her breathing changed as consciousness returned. Her hands were still bound behind her, and the blindfold was securely in place.

As we motored slowly toward the port, Tatiana Sokolova shivered in the cool night air.

I tugged Hunter toward the woman and whispered, "Play along."

I began planting. "So, as long as we can keep them from finding out about Sochi, we should be able to pull it off."

My partner grinned, suddenly understanding the game. "Yeah, I think it'll be fine. There are enough sailboats in Sochi to blend in long enough to make it work."

A few seconds later, I lifted a cell phone to my ear. "Hang on a second. I have to call Sergei."

The phone was dead, but that didn't matter. The monologue wasn't for anyone named Sergei. It was an act intended entirely for Tatiana. It was time to plant a little seed in her loyal head and let it find its way to Colonel Sokolov's ear.

In my best Russian, I spoke into the worthless phone. "That's right. We'll be in Sochi no later than May fifteenth."

As we approached the darkened port, I cut the flex-cuffs from our prisoner's wrists but left the blindfold in place a few minutes longer. Pierre let the gunwale brush alongside the dock, and I pulled the blindfold from Tatiana's face just before I shoved her toward the dock. She stumbled and collapsed on the wooden dock, blinking and still trembling in fear.

The seed had been planted. I just hoped it was in fertile soil.

We flew out of Marseille on the Canadian passports and landed in Cairo, where Skipper had arranged a hop to Morocco aboard a Doctors Without Borders cargo plane. Two days later, we were back at Bonaventure Plantation telling our teammates how boring the South of France had been.

"You really busted a vodka bottle across his teeth?" Clark asked, unable to hold back his laughter. "That's priceless."

Maebelle came through the kitchen door with a tray of shot glasses and a bottle of Ketel One vodka. "It's Dutch, and not Russian, but it'll have to do."

She passed out the shot glasses, and I held mine in the air. "Here's to success in phase one, and to Hunter for sending our favorite Russian colonel to the dentist with a mouthful of broken teeth."

"Cheers!" came the unanimous return from the team.

"Okay, guys. I know we want to celebrate, but we'll have to cut it short for now. We've got to keep the ball rolling and try to find Anya. Skipper, how's the ice situation in the Bering Sea?"

"Thank God for global warming," she said. "The Bering Sea is once again completely liquid, and I just happened to find a deal on a pair of bus tickets to the Aleutian Islands for you and Hunter."

"Bus tickets?" Hunter and I groaned in unison.

"Yeah, boys. You can't go everywhere in first class. You've got to learn how the other half lives from time to time."

"I'm not riding a bus to Alaska," I said. "I'd rather ride Pecan, the horse that hates me."

Skipper couldn't contain her laughter. "I think you'll ride this bus. It's an Airbus out of Jacksonville tomorrow morning."

Hunter picked up the vodka bottle and shook it at Skipper. "I've got a history with these things, so don't make me give a repeat performance."

"You know better, big boy."

He gently returned the bottle to the table. "Okay, maybe you're right, but I do have a history."

She made a pistol with her finger and thumb and pointed it toward Hunter. "Yes, you do, but if you want to have a future, you'll think twice before waving a bottle at me."

We briefed the plan for Alaska, the Aleutians, and Siberia with Skipper and Clark while Maebelle cooked dinner.

"We know she's in town—or at least she was seven months ago. We just don't know where," Skipper said.

Hunter scratched at his chin. "If Anya is what you say she is, I don't think we'll have any trouble finding a thirty-year-old beauty queen in a Siberian fishing village. She's gonna stick out like a sore thumb."

"I don't think we should expect her to look like I remember her. She's been living off the grid in one of the most remote places on Earth and trying to hide from the Kremlin. I'd say there's a pretty good chance she's changed her appearance significantly."

Skipper nodded. "I'd say you're right, Chase, but the only way to know is to find her, and that's up to you guys. Let's move on to the infiltration plan."

Hunter and I leaned in as Skipper turned her monitor toward us and pointed at the screen. "This is Adak, Alaska. It's the last U.S. outpost before even the sea lions start speaking Russian. That's where you'll meet your contact, a CIA agent on the station under the guise of being a climate researcher...whatever that is. He'll have your kits and a seaplane for you. I wanted you to take the Caravan, but it would take a week to fly that thing all the way up there."

Hunter and I made mental notes and listened as Skipper continued.

"I've been monitoring the satellite imagery, and there's no signs of life at the old seaplane training base, so I think that's your way in. Low and slow from the northeast as quietly as possible."

I stared at the imagery as she flipped through the scenes. "That place looks like a mess, but I agree, no signs of intelligent life."

Hunter laughed. "What kind of intelligent life would live in Eastern Siberia?"

"Good point," I said.

Hunter clicked his tongue against his teeth. "Okay, so let's say we get in without being seen, shot down, or drowned, and let's say we find this Anya chick. How do we get her out, even if she agrees to come?"

Skipper pulled an envelope from her desk drawer and tossed it toward me. "She's got a passport that says her name is Ana Fulton. Or at least she did when you turned her loose last year. And, even if she doesn't, here's another. Just get her back to Adak, and our friendly neighborhood climatologist will get the three of you on a plane to Cyprus. From there, you'll fly to Sevastopol on visas I'll have waiting for you in Cyprus."

Hunter held up his hand. "Whoa. This is a lot of moving parts. And isn't Sevastopol in Russia?"

"The moving parts are my specialty, so don't worry about those. As far as Sevastopol belonging to Russia, it depends on who you ask. Ukraine thinks Crimea belongs to them, but the Kremlin has a different opinion. It doesn't really matter. The only reason you're going there is to get on the boat."

"What boat?" I asked.

"The boat to Sochi where you'll meet Dominic with the dunker. This is where the moving parts get a little close together."

She paused to bring up another screen. "We're working on the details, but it looks like your seed germinated and took root. Sokolov has added a Sochi trip to his agenda. He'll feel safer in Russia than in France, so if all the other moving parts fall into place, Anya will be able to get a face-to-face with the good colonel and cut a deal of her own. That's when the real fun begins."

"Why does everyone keep calling it fun?" I said. "Hunter and I go chasing Russians all over the world, with bullets flying in every direction, and everyone back here calls it fun. To quote Inigo Montoya, I don't think that word means what you think it means."

A soft knock sounded at the door to Skipper's room, and Singer poked his head inside. "Sorry to interrupt, but when you guys finish up, I need to talk to Chase for a few minutes."

"Sure," I said. "We'll be done in a few minutes. Is everything all right?"

"That's what I want to know," said the singing sniper as he closed the door.

"That was weird," Skipper muttered.

"Snipers are weird people," Hunter returned. "Especially that one."

"Okay, then, so it's off to Alaska tomorrow morning, right?"

"You got it," Skipper said, "but I think it'd be a good idea to spend some quality time with your wife tonight. She's still a lit-tle...okay, a lot uneasy about you seeing Anya again."

"Thanks, Skipper. I'll do that. Do you have any questions, Hunter?"

He shook his head. "No, it's all as clear as mud. What could possibly go wrong? Atlanta, Alaska, sneak into Siberia, kidnap a blacklisted SVR red sparrow, jet off to Cyprus, then some place Russia's been fighting over for two hundred years, and finally to Sochi to sink a boat with our kidnapped, blacklisted spy with no exfiltration plan at all. Sounds perfect."

"Exactly," Skipper and I said in stereo.

Hunter shook his head. "I like this group more every day. I think I've finally found a home."

Before my foot hit the floor at the bottom of the stairs, Singer took my arm. "Let's go for a walk."

"Okay, but I need to spend some time with Penny," I said.

"It won't take long. We just need to talk about a few things."

We walked out the front door of the plantation house, a door I rarely used, and took a seat on the steps leading down to the pecan tree-lined drive.

"What's up, Singer? Is something bothering you?"

"No, everything's fine with me. It's you I'm worried about. You're carrying a big burden on your shoulders by looking out for all of us, trying to work out this thing with the Russians trying to kill you, and keeping your young wife happy through it all."

I started to speak, but he held up a finger. "Just listen for a minute. I know how you were raised until your parents were killed…"

I felt a lump form in my throat, but I kept listening.

"I know your folks were believers and good Christian people. They found a way to keep their faith in the middle of hell, and that's a struggle. Believe me, I know. I live it every day. It's my job to send bullets downrange to human lives. No matter how black their hearts are, those are still humans I'm putting down, and I fight the battle every day to square my faith with my missions. Sometimes that ain't easy. I know you've got a lot of doubts and questions dancing around in that head of yours, and that's normal. You and me live in a world most people never see. Most people never have to pull a trigger and take another man's life, but we do, Chase, and that weighs heavy on those of us who believe. And you're one of us."

He patted my chest with the palm of his hand, the same hand he'd used to pull countless triggers and stop countless beating hearts in pursuit of what he believed was right.

"Chase, I know in your heart you believe you'll see your momma and daddy and little sister again, and I believe it, too. Keep the faith, even if it's only the size of a grain of mustard seed. Keep it, and let it bring you home. I told you before that you belong to the angels, and it's true. Your soul does belong to them, but your body belongs to this Earth and to your wife. The angels and the Earth don't always have the same agenda, but when you have to look at yourself in the mirror and meet yourself eye to eye, it's up to you to see the difference and pick the right side."

He took his hand from my chest and looked into my soul. "Don't ever think you're alone, because you ain't. Just because you've never seen those angels doesn't mean they're not picking you up when you fall. And just because Penny doesn't have wings growing out of her back doesn't mean she's not one of 'em."

He patted me on the back and stood. "Now, let's go get some supper before we hurt Maebelle's feelings."

I put my arm around his shoulder. "Thanks, Singer. You're a good man."

He smiled. "I may not always have the answers, but I'll always listen, Chase."

* * *

Dinner was another feast beyond compare. The team had grown to love Maebelle as much as they loved her food—especially Charlie, the black lab. The two of them were practically inseparable.

"I'm sure you've made something incredible for dessert, Maebelle, but if you'll excuse Penny and me, we're going to turn in for the night. We've not seen much of each other lately, and I'd like to change that."

Penny smiled and took my hand. We spent the remainder of the evening talking about everything except work. We laughed, we sang, we made love, and most importantly, we enjoyed being alone together, if only for a few hours.

"I love you, Chase, and more than that, I respect you for who you are and what you believe. I'm proud to be your wife, and I'll be right here when you come home from wherever life takes you. All I ask is that you take me with you in your heart and come home when it's over. Just come home to me, Chase."

We fell asleep in each other's arms and let the world and everything in it disappear.

Instead of the smell of Penny's coffee and bacon waking me the next morning, I slipped from our bed and delivered breakfast to her for a change.

"It's not as good as Maebelle's, but it's the thought that counts, right?"

"Oh, you didn't have to do this. I was going to make breakfast for you, but thank you."

We ate in silence, listening to the birds singing and the fish jumping outside the boat in the North River.

Finally, she looked up, a tiny smile on her beautiful face. "Thank you for last night...and this morning."

"I promise you a million more nights like that and mornings like this."

"No, I don't want more mornings like this one. I have to tell you goodbye and watch you fly away this morning. I want a million mornings when you don't have to leave."

I moved our trays from the bed and kissed her gently, taking her in my arms for another moment before I had to wade into Hell.

Chapter 21
Nothing to It

Adak, Alaska, feels like the edge of the Earth. It's twelve hundred miles from Anchorage and nine hundred miles from Ust-Kamchatsk and Anya. Skipper had called it the last American outpost in the Aleutians, but she wasn't exactly correct.

Hunter and I were greeted by Bob, the climatologist in Adak. He said he'd been there almost two years and had learned absolutely nothing about the weather, except that it was cold. The one thing Bob did know, however, was the Russians. Although he vehemently denied being an employee of the agency, Bob told us everything we could want to know about Ust-Kamchatsk. He outfitted us with every piece of gear we could need, including a turbocharged Cessna 206 Stationair on amphib floats.

Bob stared off into the western sky. "I've not been fully read-in on your mission, but I'm envious, whatever it is. You'll like the folks in Ust-Kamchatsk. Their lives are simple and far removed from the politics of the rest of the world. If this woman you're looking for is there, Yuri will know how to find her."

"Who's Yuri?" I asked.

Bob looked down at his boots as if he were trying to decide how much to tell us. "Yuri is an interesting man. When you meet him, he'll be a bartender in the only hotel in town. Go to the hotel. Don't try to hide or blend in. You can't do either one in a place like Ust-Kam. Yuri was a card-carrying communist until…." He paused, staring back at the sky. "Until he wasn't. Now he's a bartender—among other things. Go see him, and tell him the weatherman says '*privet.*' He'll help you find this Anya character."

Bob spat between his boots and ground the spittle into the ground. "What is this Anya woman to you? There's always more to every Siberian story, but there's something behind your eyes when you talk about her. What is it? Did she try to kill you or something?"

I mimicked his spitting and grinding. "Or something."

He shrugged off my nonanswer and then gave us the best news we'd had so far. "They'll top you off at Casco Cove."

I looked at Hunter, and he returned my stare. "What's Casco Cove?"

Bob closed one eye and stared us down. "You mean your analyst didn't brief you on Casco Cove?"

"Nope."

He let out a huff as if he knew an inside joke he wasn't willing to tell. "It's the Coast Guard station on Attu, a mountain sticking out of the ocean about four hundred and twenty miles west of here as the crow flies, but I recommend keeping as much dry ground under you as possible. Sticking to the island chain will only add about thirty miles to your trip. And trust me, it's worth it. You don't want to go down in water that cold. You won't last long, even in a survival suit."

"I didn't know we had a Coast Guard station that far out there."

"Not many people do," Bob said, "and even fewer people care. I think there's about twenty Coasties on the island. It's a pretty good runway, and the gas is clean. Don't drink their coffee, though. I don't know what they put in it, but it'd knock the rust off a Buick."

"All right, then. Casco Cove it is for gas and coffee."

"When you take off out of Attu, the only chunk of dry ground between there and Ust-Kam is an island called Komandorskiye Ostrova."

"Commander Island?" I said.

Bob nodded slowly. "Two American spies—one of whom speaks, or at least understands Russian—sneaking into Siberia, looking for one particular Russian woman." He inspected his well-chewed fingernails. "Are you sure you don't need a hand? I've been stuck out here on this rock for a long time without anything to do."

"We're not spies," Hunter and I said as if we'd been practicing for years.

"Yeah, me too," Bob mumbled. "If you change your mind, you know where to find me. Keys are in the plane, and she's full of gas. There's a LORAN station on Attu. You can't miss it."

I stuck out my hand. "Thanks, Bob. We'll be back in a few days if everything goes well. If not, well, you know."

He ignored my offered hand. "Yeah, I know."

The Stationair wasn't your run-of-the-mill seaplane. She was overpowered, overequipped, and exactly what I wanted if I couldn't have my Caravan. We landed at the Coast Guard station and rolled to a stop outside the operations building. A pair of coverall-clad Coasties strolled out, obviously surprised to see us.

I shut down the engine and popped open the door. "The weatherman from Adak said you guys have the best coffee and the cheapest gas within a thousand miles."

The younger of two men elbowed his partner, and they both relaxed. "Welcome to Casco Cove. We heard we might be getting some visitors, but none of us believed it."

Hunter and I climbed down from the plane. "Well, you can believe it now. I'm Chase, and this is Hunter."

"I'm Petty Officer Third Class Jason Mills, and this is Petty Officer Second Class Mike Thompson. What brings you guys way out here?"

"Whale watching," Hunter said. "We're tracking a pod of humpbacks for *National Geographic*. Wildlife photographers is what we are."

Both Coasties shrugged. "Whatever you say. We'll tie your plane down and top you off. You two wildlife photographers can go on inside. We'll find you some grub and a bunk for the night."

We climbed the six steps from the parking apron to the sidewalk.

"Wildlife photographers? Really?" I said.

"Hey, it's what came to mind in the moment. Don't crush my dreams of working for *Nat Geo.*"

"If you get us busted, I'll crush more than your dreams."

He laughed. "Are you serious? Getting busted by some Coasties is what you're worried about? We're about to sneak into Russia to meet up with a bartender named Yuri on the advice of a spook-turned-weatherman, and you're worried about what a couple of Coast Guard petty officers think we are?"

"You've got a way of putting things in perspective, Hunter. I kinda like having you around."

"I kinda like being around."

Bob was right. The coffee tasted like melted shoes, but the food was good. When we left the next morning, the two petty officers wished us well.

"Stop by and see us on your way back out," one said. "Maybe you can show us some of those pictures of the whales you're tracking."

Hunter pointed toward the pair. "We might just do that, but don't hold your breath."

We blasted off into the bluest sky I'd ever seen. The snow-covered peaks of Attu were unimaginably beautiful.

"I wish Penny could see that," I said, pointing toward the highest peaks.

Hunter pushed my hand out of the air. "Maybe you can bring her on your next whale-watching expedition."

"Hey, the whales are your fantasy, not mine."

He rolled his eyes. "I fantasize about a lot of things, but whales aren't one of them. Let me fly for a while. You don't get to have all the fun."

I laughed. "Sure. You have the controls."

"I have the controls."

The Bering Sea was dead calm without a breath of wind disturbing its surface. From my seat, it was easy to pretend the whole world was covered with blue water. And from our position so close to the North Pole, every direction seemed like south. The advanced avionics of the Stationair made navigation far easier than it would have been with a compass. Hunter was a good pilot and preferred hand-flying instead of letting the autopilot do the work. He was proving to be an asset, and I was looking forward to seeing him on the ground in Siberia.

"There they are," he said. "The Commander Islands at ten o'clock and maybe seventy or eighty miles."

The visibility was limited only by the curvature of the Earth. The islands peeked out of the sea like toys in a bathtub, and we turned north to avoid overflying the first Russian territory I'd seen since breaking Anya out of the Black Dolphin Prison.

I double-checked the transponder to make sure it was off. "Make sure you keep us low enough to avoid radar on that island. They do have an airport over there, so I'm pretty sure they've got a radar antenna. We don't need a pair of MiGs coming to say hello."

Hunter pulled the power and let the Stationair settle toward the sea. Radar antennas are line-of-sight tools. If we couldn't see the antenna, it couldn't see us. Forty-five minutes later, no MiG fighters had come out to play, so I believed we'd made it across—or beneath—our first hurdle.

I pulled out the aerial photos Skipper printed for us and studied the terrain northeast of Ust-Kam.

"Let the autopilot do the flying for a few minutes, and take a look at this picture. We're planning for the lake just northeast of the town. The abandoned seaplane base is on the northwest shoreline. Do you see it?"

Hunter took the picture from my hand and studied it. "Yeah, I see it."

With the tip of my pen, I touched the mountains east of the town. "I think we can use that mountain for cover until the last minute, and then chop the power and glide into the lake. I think that's our best chance of not being seen. What do you think?"

He squinted at me over his sunglasses. "My opinion hasn't changed since the last forty-seven times we looked at these pictures. I agree. Now let's make it happen."

"I have the controls," I said, disengaging the autopilot.

"You have the controls."

"Okay, there's our friendly mountain. It's showtime."

He grabbed a pair of binoculars from beneath his seat and scanned the terrain in front of us. "It doesn't look like there's been a living soul out there in a thousand years."

"How about behind us?" I asked. "Can you see Commander Islands?"

He spun in his seat and pressed the binoculars to his eyes. "Nope. Go ahead and start up. I'll tell you when I can see it."

I added enough power to make the Stationair climb at three hundred feet per minute. At thirty-one hundred feet, Hunter said, "Level off here. The island is just coming into sight."

Using the curvature of the Earth to hide from the radar antenna on Komandorskiye Ostrova, and the mountain to shield us from prying eyes in Ust-Kamchatsk, I continued northwest until the battered, rusted roofs of the old seaplane base came into sight.

"There it is," I said.

Hunter scanned the area with the binoculars. "Not a breath of wind. It's going to be a glassy water landing."

Water without ripples looks like a mirror from above, making it all but impossible to judge our height above the surface on final approach. We'd been taught to set up the airplane in the landing attitude and slowly hold it off the water with power until the floats kissed the surface, then to add power as the water tried to drag the floats to a stop. The problem with that method was it was noisy, especially with a monstrous, turbocharged engine spinning a three-blade prop. Arriving unheard wasn't a possibil-

ity. I just hoped the weatherman's predictions about the tempera-
ment of the townspeople was on the money. If not, we would
find ourselves in a gunfight before the prop stopped spinning.

I set up for a five-mile straight-in approach, shoved the propeller control full forward, and closed the throttle. The airplane
followed my commands to the letter and settled toward the lake
as if she wanted to be on the water.

I was silently praying for some wind—any wind—from any
direction. The glassy water was the worst possible condition for
what I was about to attempt. I had less than three dozen water
landings under my belt and zero on the Stationair. I expected it
to behave like my Caravan when the floats met the surface, but I
had no way to know for sure.

"I should've done a couple of water landings back at the Coast
Guard station."

Hunter peeled the binoculars from his face. "What?"

"I didn't mean to say that out loud, but I should've done some
water landings with this thing before we came blasting in here
like a freight train."

He rubbed his hands on his pant legs. "It's a little late for that
now."

"I just hope those angels Singer talks about are watching
over us."

"If anybody's watching, I hope it's them and not the Russians."

We crossed the shoreline, still gliding toward the lake a mile
ahead, and I started through the final landing checklist.

Fuel selector on both tanks.

Gear up. Water rudders up.

Flaps set.

Prop set.

Seatbelts secure.

Speed: seventy-five knots.

Hunter began calling altitudes. "Fifty...forty...thirty...
twenty..."

I eased the nose up a few degrees. The shoreline and dilapidated buildings of the base were coming at us faster than I liked, and the need to look out my door at the water beneath was almost more than I could resist.

"Watch your speed!" Hunter bellowed.

I shot my eyes to the airspeed indicator and saw us inching dangerously close to stall speed. If I stalled the airplane this close to the water, we may never survive the crash. I lowered the nose to regain some speed without adding power.

Hunter dug his fingertips into his thighs. "We're running out of water."

The enormous buildings filled the windscreen. I could add power and maybe climb out over the buildings, or I could lower the nose another few degrees and let the floats hit the water and ride it out. But I had to make a decision.

The angels made it for me. The left float kissed the surface, followed less than a second later by the right, and my hand flew to the throttle, but Hunter caught my wrist the instant before I advanced the throttle. With no power, the water grabbed the floats and snatched us from the sky, turning our seventy knots of forward speed into zero in less than five seconds. Our bodies lunged forward against our harnesses, and the big floatplane settled into the water with the idling engine still propelling us forward fast enough to wrap a wing around anything we hit. I shoved the water rudder control down, giving me at least some degree of steering, and then shut the engine down. Before the prop stopped turning, Hunter was out the door and standing on the float, waiting for us to collide with something.

I pressed the left rudder pedal to its stop, and the big plane settled alongside what was left of a floating dock. Relieved and finally able to breathe again, I stepped from the cockpit and onto the float. We tugged the plane into an overhanging shed in four or five feet of water.

After tying the plane securely to a pair of bollards, Hunter grabbed my shirt. "I may not have a license, but I'm doing the landings from now on. You almost killed us."

I shoved Hunter backward and ran toward the nose of the airplane in near panic.

He staggered two and a half strides and stared at me in disbelief. "What's wrong?"

"It has to be here," I insisted.

"What has to be there?"

I frantically ran my hands across the smooth surface of the cowling. "The damage from the crash. It has to be here, otherwise, that was a perfectly good landing."

Hunter let me know I was number one. At least I think that's what that finger meant.

Chapter 22
Closing Time

We snagged the gear we thought we'd need from the plane, crammed some food down our throats, and set out for the three-mile hike into Ust-Kamchatsk.

"Do you think anybody saw us?" I asked.

"If they did, they would've thought we died in the crash. You better hope nobody saw that train wreck, or you'll never live it down when we get into town."

"Thanks for the support."

"Oh, I'm supportive. I support the idea of never trying that again."

"I agree. Let's find Yuri. If he's really the local bartender, I'm sure he can make you feel better."

We walked for almost an hour before the buildings of Ust-Kam came into sight.

Hunter was the first to speak. "Whew, that's a rough-looking place."

"This is a rough part of the world," I said.

A little girl of perhaps five was the first Russian we encountered on the northern reaches of the village. She was wearing boots that were clearly made for someone with feet twice the size of hers. Her blonde hair was pulled back and braided into two neat ponytails, and she wore a long-sleeved dress that may not have been washed lately...or ever.

I smiled at the girl. "*Privet. Ty simpatichnaya. Mne nravitsya tvoye plat'ye.*"

She blushed, covered her face with her tiny hands, and squeaked, "*Spasibo.*"

Hunter said, "I see I need to learn to *sprechen sie* Russian if I'm going to keep hanging out with you."

"I told her she was pretty and that I liked her dress, and she said thanks."

"Hmm, that could come in handy," Hunter said. "You'll have to teach me that much Russian, at least." He poked his chin out as if thinking about what I'd said. "You're pretty, and I like your dress. Tie simpatico emmy TV plate. Is that it?"

"You nailed it, partner. You're a natural, and you'll be fluent before we leave this town."

"Yep, that's me. A regular prodigy."

I drew a candy bar from my pack, knelt in front of the little girl, and opened the wrapper. "What's your name?" I asked as I offered her a piece of the candy.

She stared at the chocolate but didn't reach for it, so I tossed it into my mouth. "Mmm."

She giggled and extended her hand. "*Zhelaniye.*"

I broke off another piece and placed it on her outstretched palm. She slowly moved the candy to her lips and bit off a tiny corner. The girl's eyes lit up, and she grinned as if it was her first taste of American chocolate. I suspected it was her first taste of anything American and I was the first *Amerikanskiy* she'd ever met.

Her bright blue eyes stared at the remainder of the candy bar in my hand. I folded the paper wrapper back around the chocolate and handed it to her.

She whispered, "*Spasibo.*"

"You're welcome," I answered in Russian. "Do you know a man named Yuri?"

She tucked the candy into her dress pocket and nodded.

"Can you tell me where he is?"

She continued bobbing her head up and down, but this time, she reached for my hand and wrapped her fingers around my thumb. "I will take you to him."

A pair of Americans showing up in a Siberian fishing village and holding hands with a five-year-old girl wasn't the first impression I wanted to give the good people of Ust-Kam.

I pulled my hand away. "No, you should stay here, but you can tell me where he is."

She shrugged her little shoulders as if to say, "Okay, whatever you say," and then aimed her finger toward the southwest. "*Siniy otel'.*"

"The blue hotel?"

"*Da.*"

"*Spasibo,*" Hunter said.

I looked up at him in surprise.

"Hey, what can I say? I'm a prodigy."

We left the little girl licking chocolate from her fingers and smiling as if she'd never been happier.

Hunter said, "What do you think her mother's gonna say when she finds a Hershey's bar in her daughter's pocket?"

"She'll probably think American spies crashed a seaplane on the lake and bribed her daughter with chocolate for local information."

"Yep, I'd say that's about right."

Ten minutes later, after passing a dozen people on the street—some who ignored us and others who couldn't keep their eyes off of us—we found the only big blue building in town.

I unshouldered my pack. "This has to be the place."

The muddy streets and weathered buildings made the village look like a cross between a town in an old Western movie and something out of *Mad Max*.

As if we were old regulars, we scraped the mud from our boots before pushing through the door. The lobby was poorly lit and not exactly up to health department code, but it wasn't too bad. The clerk, a man of perhaps thirty with rotten teeth and greasy hair, stood behind the counter staring at us.

"We're looking for Yuri," I said in my friendliest Russian.

The clerk lit a hand-rolled cigarette and motioned to doors to the left of the lobby.

"*Spasibo.*" Hunter punched my arm. "I'm getting good at this Russian stuff already."

"Yes, you are, but I recommend not branching out too much. Just stick with *spasibo*. It's hard to go wrong with thank you."

We pushed through the doors and into a cantina where everyone in the room, except us two, was smoking something. Most had cigarettes, but the bartender—a big, burly man with four or five days of growth on his head and face as if his only grooming product was a worn-out razor—held a long, dark cigar between his teeth, an inch-long ash dangling from the tip.

The only other exits were a small door to the left of the bar and two tall windows spaced irregularly on the front wall. Bowls of borscht rested on most of the occupied tables with half-empty glasses and bottles. Most of the occupants of the room ignored us, but a few cast curious glances our way. The bartender, far more than curious, glared through us as if we'd just walked in to drag him to the gallows. Never taking his eyes off us, he wiped a filthy towel across the bar, pretending to clean.

Unsure what was about to unfold, we walked to the bar and set our packs on the floor beside a pair of stools.

Hunter broke the ice. "Mind if we sit down, Yuri?"

To the man's credit, he didn't flinch. Instead, he motioned to the barstools, and in Russian-accented English, said, "Let me guess. For you, martinis, shaken not stirred."

I tried not to smile. "Is it that obvious?"

"Look around. If you are not fisherman or fur trapper, you do not belong in Ust-Kamchatsk. You two are definitely not trappers, but maybe on fishing trip, no?"

Hunter pushed the dirty towel from in front of him. "You can hold the martinis, but I'll take a Miller Lite if you've got it."

For the first time, the bartender smiled, showing at least two missing teeth and a broken one. "Yeah, sure. Can I get you Big Mac while I am at it?"

"I'm Chase. He's Hunter. A mutual friend of ours from Adak, calls himself the weatherman, said to tell you *privet.*"

He eyeballed Hunter and me several times. "Is that so? The weatherman, you say?"

"*Da,*" I said.

In throaty Russian, the man said, "If you know this man, the weatherman, you saw him spit on ground behind himself when he walks, no?"

I could feel Hunter on the verge of spitting out the only Russian word he knew, or perhaps trying to tell the man he liked his dress and that he looked pretty, so I stepped in to prevent an international incident in a rathole bar on the far side of the world.

In what I believed was perfect Russian, I said, "No, the weatherman always spits between his boots and grinds it into the dirt with the toe of his right foot."

If we were Freemasons, we'd have been exchanging the secret handshake and passing codes, but in the world of espionage, the rituals are a bit less formal.

Spitting between your own feet is unique enough, so Yuri poured two glasses half full of what I assumed was vodka. "Would you like also cigar?"

"*Spasibo,*" Hunter barked.

Yuri almost laughed.

The cigars he produced weren't run-of-the-mill scraps wrapped in flammable leather; they were Cubans. Excellent Cubans.

I toasted the tip and savored the first draw. "We're a long way from Havana, Yuri. How'd you come up with cigars this good all the way out here on the edge of godforsaken nowhere?"

The man stared at me through the smoke. "My friend, since nineteen fifty-nine, Havana has been closer to Russia than Miami."

"Touché."

I was right. It was vodka in our glasses, but it wasn't as good as the cigars. Or perhaps my palate isn't refined enough—or Russian enough—to know good vodka when I taste it.

When we'd taken our seats at Yuri's bar, Hunter turned his stool just enough to keep one eye on the front door. Sitting with one's back to the door is an unforgivable—and sometimes deadly—sin for spies, gunfighters, and gamblers. In the past week of our lives, we'd checked at least two of those boxes, and I had a feeling we'd cover the third in the next few days.

Believing we'd moved past the butt-sniffing so common in the intelligence world, I held up my glass, swirling the clear liquor inside. "So, how does a former KGB officer end up pouring second-rate liquor in a bar at the end of the world?"

He pulled the cigar from his mouth and cradled it between the index and middle finger of his left hand that reached for my glass. I offered no resistance as he pulled the glass from my grasp with his cigar hand and swallowed the remaining vodka. Then he leaned down and reached beneath the bar with his right hand while never taking his eyes from mine.

From the corner of my eye, I watched my partner slide his hand beneath his coat, reaching for his pistol. I appreciated the gesture, but if Yuri pulled a gun from beneath the bar, there wasn't enough firepower in the state of Georgia to get us out of that bar alive. We were strangers in a strange land and neck-deep in somebody else's muddy pond.

To my relief and great delight, when Yuri returned to his full height, he was holding an unopened bottle of Jack Daniel's Single Barrel. He removed the cork and tossed it across his shoulder and into a plastic bucket overflowing with cigarette wrappers and empty bottles. "Maybe you like better, no?"

Hunter emptied his glass of the remaining vodka and slid it toward Yuri. "The Ruskies are 'bout to see Brown Liquor Stone up in here."

I'd heard a story or two about the antics of Stone W. Hunter on spirits aged in oak. I was more than certain Siberia wasn't ready for Brown Liquor Stone, but after nearly killing Hunter in my first Stationair water landing, I figured he deserved a little single-barrel Tennessee sipping whiskey.

Yuri filled my glass and then Hunter's. "You asked me question about KGB. I do not know what this is, but I know American CIA. Is same, yes?"

I shrugged. "I wouldn't know. I've never been part of either one."

Yuri held up the ornate Jack Daniel's bottle. "Then we are same. *Zdorov'ya!*"

Hunter and I touched our glasses to his bottle, and I echoed the Russian "To your health," while Hunter declared, "*Spasibo!*"

Although I should've expected it, I didn't realize we'd broken out the ruler to measure our manhood. I enjoyed a mouthful of the near-perfect whiskey, but Hunter and Yuri locked eyes and continued swallowing Jasper—Jack, to his friends—Newton Daniel's finest.

I was intrigued by their contest, and the Yankee Doodle Dandy in me wanted to put my money on Hunter, but I would've lost. Yuri drained the bottle and then smashed it into a thousand pieces on the bar before Hunter managed to find the bottom of his glass.

Yuri wiped his mouth with his forearm. "Ha! I like your friend. His name is Hunter, yes?"

"Yeah, Hunter," I said.

"Then he is the *okhotnik*! Tell him. Make him understand."

My partner patted my arm and wiped his mouth. "Yeah, yeah. I got it. *Okhotnik*. That's me."

Yuri roared in laughter as if he'd been saving up for years. "We are three men, far from home, and drinking whiskey from America. Now we are comrades, yes?"

"Comrades! And I'm *okhotnik*!" Hunter coughed as a tear left his eye.

I checked over my shoulder and leaned into the bar. "Say, Yuri, is there some place we can have a little chat? We'd like to ask you about a friend of ours we think might be here in town."

"Do not be fool," he said. "Is much too early for talking. For now, we drink. I pour good vodka now for comrades."

He reached into his pocket for a ring of keys, one of which opened a cabinet behind the bar. From the cabinet, he produced a bottle with no label and a black cork shoved in the top. The bottle was slightly more than half full. He motioned toward my glass with the top of his bottle. "Drink. Drink. So I can pour for you vodka."

I held up my hand. "No, thanks, Yuri. I'd rather just sip my whiskey."

The inner edges of his eyebrows came together, forming a v that didn't stand for vodka.

My partner slid his empty glass toward him, and Yuri raked the glass from the bar, ignoring the sound and the mess the breaking glass made when it hit the floor. "Is okay. I pour clean glasses for new friends."

He pulled out two double shot glasses and slammed them on the bar, then topped them off with the vodka from the locker.

Hunter reached for his glass, but I slid my hand over the top of it. "How about this, Yuri? You drink it first, and then we will."

"No, no. Do not be fool. Drink, drink. Is much too good for me."

I locked eyes with him, my eyebrows arching toward each other. "No, really, I insist. You first."

Clearly at an impasse, I picked up the glass and held it out toward him.

Never taking his eyes from mine, he lifted the glass from my hand and carefully poured the contents back into the bottle before doing the same with Hunter's. After locking the bottle back inside the cabinet, he pounded his flattened palms on the bar as if he were playing patty-cake with a giant. "*Bar zakryt! Ubiraysya, Ubiraysya!*"

Apparently, when Yuri says get out, it's time to get out, but Hunter and I didn't budge.

Chapter 23

Say Ahh

"Okay, you are not fool, and maybe you are spy. Maybe not. What do you want?"

"No, Yuri, we are not fools, although *okhotnik* here may be a little drunk. I'm looking for a beautiful Russian woman."

"All Russian women are beautiful, and all American men are looking for one. You are no different," he huffed.

I didn't smile, and he got the message. "No, Yuri, I'm very different. I have a feeling you know the woman I'm talking about."

I reached across the bar and pulled his credit card machine from beside the cashbox, holding it in front of his face. "The woman I'm talking about made a four-hundred-thousand-ruble transaction on this machine last fall."

Yuri's Adam's apple rose and fell as he studied my face. In a movement so quick his hands turned to pale blurs, he grabbed the back of my neck and palmed my chin, pulling me from my seat and forcing my abdomen against the bar, making it impossible to draw my pistol. Hunter's drinking competition had dulled his reflexes. His reaction was a little slow, but by the time I realized my predicament, he had the muzzle of his pistol pressed to Yuri's temple.

"Take your hands off of him right now," Hunter growled, "or die where you stand."

Yuri didn't release his grasp. "Go ahead and shoot me. You will be dead before I stop bleeding, and you will never find girl."

"Let him go, or I'm willing to take that chance, you bastard."

"Show me tongue, American."

I pulled against his vice-like grip and muttered, "What?"

"Let me see tongue."

Hunter said, "You've got one second to turn him loose, or I'm going to show you what the inside of your skull looks like."

"Wait, Hunter," I managed to grunt as I stuck out my tongue, exposing the scar Anya left with the razor-sharp blade of her favorite knife."

The Russian released his grip on my head, and I placed my hand on top of Hunter's pistol, lowering it to the bar.

My partner sat spellbound, mesmerized by what he'd witnessed. "What the hell was that about?"

"It was about making sure I'm the guy Anya told Yuri would be coming."

"And clearly you are," Yuri said. "Come with me."

Hunter, in his partially inebriated state, looked more confused than ever. "Is this normal for you?"

I had to chuckle. "Yeah, pretty much. Were you really going to shoot Yuri?"

"I don't know. I was torn between stopping him from snapping your neck and my crazy need to see what was going to happen next. But, yeah, I would've messed him up."

I put my hand on his shoulder as he tucked his pistol away. "Thanks, but next time, don't hesitate. Pull the trigger."

"Whatever you say, boss."

We followed Yuri through the small door beside the bar and through a dimly lit hallway that seemed to grow smaller the farther we walked. Yuri pulled his keyring from his pocket again. He removed a padlock from a steel hasp mounted high on a wooden door that could've been the hatch of a pirate ship two hundred years ago. He motioned through the door with his chin. "Go inside."

I leaned around the door into a room only slightly brighter than the hallway. "Yeah, I'll pass. I'm not a fan of waiting in a room with only one door and no windows."

Yuri shrugged. "Suit yourself, but it would be shame to not find her after you come this far."

He made a good point, but he'd already tried to poison us once, and even though I'd shown him the scar, I was a long way from trusting him.

"I'll tell you how this is going to work. We'll wait in your bar where there are plenty of exits, and you're going to tell her we're here. You're right, we've come a long way, but she's been expecting us for a long time. We'll let her make the decision, but I'm not going through that dead-end trapdoor."

Yuri looked back down the long hallway toward the bar. "Is not good idea, but is your life, not mine. I will tell her."

From our darkened position, I could barely see down the corridor leading into Yuri's bar. I planned to use that to my full advantage. I motioned for Hunter to lead the way, and I followed closely behind.

When we were far enough away from the big Russian, I whispered, "Sidestep the door and hold."

His barely perceptible nod made me glad he was on my team. When we reached the end of the hallway, Hunter made a show of opening the door, silhouetting himself in the light and then slamming the door hard enough to ensure Yuri heard the noise. What the Russian didn't see—we hoped—was my partner and me sidestepping into the shadows of the hallway and pressing our bodies against the wall. We could clearly see his outline, but we were in almost pure darkness.

I bent down and untied my boots, silently slipping them from my feet as Hunter did the same. When Yuri's shadow disappeared to the left, we drew our pistols and crept the length of the hallway with our footfalls, leaving no sound of movement. I quick-peeked around the corner and gave Hunter the hand signal for stairs. He ducked and rounded the corner like a cat. I trained my pistol over his left shoulder as we took each tread of the staircase with our feet pressed solidly against the walls, leaving no room for the old wooden stairs to betray us with an echoing creak.

At the top landing, we watched Yuri knock twice on the first door on the right and then insert his key into the knob. "Anastasia, the man you have been waiting for is downstairs, but his partner is not the man you described. His name is not Clark. It is Hunter. Also, they insist on waiting in the bar. It is closed and locked. No one else is in there."

I couldn't hear her response, but he said, "*Da,*" and pulled the door closed as he backed into the hallway.

Hunter slipped a syringe of Pierre's sleeping meds from his pocket, and we waited for Yuri to round the corner onto the stairs. The instant his chin turned the corner, I exploded upward, throwing the best uppercut I could produce and landing it perfectly beneath his jawbone. I was afraid he might not go down, but as big as he was, he was no Apollo Creed. The man's knees turned to pudding, and he collapsed like a felled oak. I caught his bulk before he landed and began tumbling down the stairs. Hunter drove the needle home in his neck, and I laid him on his left side on the landing.

We moved in silent strides toward the apartment door, and I encased the doorknob in my left hand, expecting it to turn easily. Instead, it was like trying to turn an anvil. Hunter saw my white knuckles and sent a thundering right-heel kick just below the frozen knob. The door exploded inward, and we charged the opening, Hunter low with his pistol drawn, and me high with a thousand drums pounding inside my head.

Would Anya be standing inside the door with a throwing knife leaving each hand as soon as I made entry? Would the whole room be a trap? I had a thousand other fears swarming in my mind, but I had to focus on the task and deal with what lay behind door number one.

As Hunter landed on one knee in front of me, I looked into the smoky blue-gray eyes I never believed I'd see again. Anastasia

Robertovna Burinkova stood six feet inside the doorway with her hands folded angelically. She was just as beautiful, and perhaps more terrifying than I remembered, and in a moment, my mouth went dry and the heart in my chest pounded as if I'd just come face-to-face with the only force on Earth I feared.

"Have you brought to me my death, Chasechka? Why else would you come?"

Her English was that of a woman who'd not spoken the language in nearly a year.

I willed my words to come. "Perhaps, but not now, and not by my hand."

"Put away guns, close door, and come inside."

I tapped Hunter's shoulder, and he lowered his pistol but didn't holster it. Mine, on the other hand, found its way back into the soft leather that was its home.

Some power *that* woman held over me forbade me from turning my back to her, if only for the instant it would take to close the door. I'll never know why I couldn't turn. Perhaps I believed she would turn to smoke and drift into nothing if I took my eyes from her. Perhaps I feared her knife would land at the base of my skull if I gave her the target. Perhaps every truth I knew was but a fragile ornament in her folded hands, and if I turned away, my reality, my world, would fall from her hands and disintegrate into countless shards of madness, chaos, and irrevocable ruin. She once held that power in her hands, her eyes, and her body, but that was when I was a man of innocence and naïve faith, driven by lust and an ancient yearning for the forbidden, the dangerous, the unpossessable.

She stood as motionless as a statue, her eyes calling until at last she smiled and tilted her head, just as she'd been taught— just as she knew almost no man could resist. I was no longer the man she'd seduced, the man who'd willingly laid his heart at her feet. That man perished; he died a thousand deaths reliving the reality of how close he'd come to ultimate ruin in her hands, in her mind, and in her bed. The sinew of scars resists the blade like innocent flesh cannot. I had earned my sinew, my scars, my armor. I'd proven in the arena where no mercy exists that I was more than I'd been, that I could strike and be stricken without retreating and without hesitation. Everything I had been in the shell Anya had known as a target, a mission, was no more, and I turned, unafraid, unfettered, and slowly pressed the door of the apartment back into its jamb and twisted the lock.

"We will have tea," she said, "and you will tell me what I am to do."

Chapter 24
Zhena

Hunter couldn't take his eyes off Anya as he and I sat at the small wooden table in the cramped kitchen of her apartment. "She's going to kill us both and feed us to that bartender sleeping in the stairwell, isn't she?"

"Maybe," I admitted, "but she does make good tea."

"If she doesn't poison it."

"I will not poison you, Mr. Hunter. I kill with only knives and my hands. Tea is safe for you."

I couldn't suppress the smile. "Oh, yeah. I forgot to tell you she has superhuman hearing, too."

The teakettle whistled on the two-eye gas stove, and Anya lifted it by its battered wooden handle. Three mismatched mugs rested on the table beside a wooden box.

She motioned toward the box with the spout of the kettle. "Choose."

After lifting the lid, I thumbed through two dozen individually wrapped teabags, each labeled in Cyrillic. I selected three identical packages and dropped one into each mug. Anya poured the steaming water into the mugs, leaving an inch at the top of each.

"For you, Chasechka, is honey." She slid to me an oddly shaped glass jar with foil wrapped loosely around the top and a wooden spoon handle protruding. I remembered seeing her lick honey from the tips of her fingers aboard my boat, and I tried to imagine the ruin my life would be if Clark hadn't pulled me from the pit into which I'd fallen.

"For me also honey. You will do, yes?"

I spooned the golden syrup from the jar into her mug, then mine, and motioned toward Hunter's cup.

He waved his hand over the mug. "No, none for me."

Anya placed the kettle back on the stove and returned with only one spoon. I took it from her hand and then stirred her tea before doing the same to mine. Although he knew very little of our history, Hunter was right to be afraid of her. Underestimating that woman could be the deadliest mistake of anyone's life.

She pulled a three-legged stool to the table between Hunter and me and reached for his cup. "*Okhotnik* is *hunter* in Russian. Do you know this?"

I couldn't tell if the look on his face was one of fascination, fear, or lust, but any combination would've been appropriate. Instead of speaking, he only nodded.

"*A ty govorish' po Russki?*"

Somewhere between a Jack Daniel's buzz and fear for his soul, Hunter said, "*Spasibo*," and laughter exploded from the table.

Anya reached for Hunter's mug, her eyes pinned to his. She lifted the mug, took a sip of his tea, and placed it back in front of him. She licked her lips, savoring the unsweetened tea. "See? Is not poison, *okhotnik*, and is okay you do not speak Russian. I will speak only English, but if I do not know word"—she put her hand on top of mine—"Chase will teach me."

I slid my hand from beneath hers and lifted my mug to my lips. The feel of the earthy hot tea and sweetness of the honey warmed my mouth and made me think of Penny. Perhaps it wasn't the tea. Perhaps it was the fact that I could look at one of the most beautiful women and confidently pull my hand away from hers, knowing the life I was building with Penny Fulton outweighed anything that could've ever been with Anya Burinkova.

"I made a deal with Nicholai Sokolov."

Anya bit at her bottom lip, stared into her cup, and slowly raised it to her mouth. She let the tea warm her tongue before allowing it to slide down her throat. "Which one?"

I shot a look at Hunter before asking, "What?"

Anya pushed her mug away, and for the first time, turned to face me. "I know two men of this name, Nicholai Sokolov. Both are dangerous men. You have made deal with which one?"

"Colonel Sokolov."

Anya swallowed hard. "Is better with that one. Other one is man like Dmitri Barkov. Rich, and uh...*besposhchadnyy.*"

"Ruthless," I said to Hunter.

I could see the imagination playing behind his eyes. If a man could be more ruthless than the one we'd cornered in France, he wasn't a man we wanted to lock horns with.

"What is deal you made with Colonel Sokolov?"

I stalled, using a sip of tea. "I, well, *we* killed several of his guards in France and kidnapped his wife."

The corners of Anya's lips curled into a vindictive smile. "You and *okhotnik*? Why did you do this?"

"That's a long story," I said, "but suffice it to say, Sokolov has put a price on my head, and there are plenty of his people who want to make a name for themselves by killing the American."

She folded her hands together and leaned slightly toward me. "How much is price? I could kill you and collect money."

That made the corners of my mouth want to curl upward, but I didn't want her knowing she was playing directly into my hand. "They killed your sister."

"No," she said, shaking her head.

"Yes, Anya, they killed her. I saw her body aboard a yacht they tried to use to kill me."

"No, Chasechka, you do not understand. They did not kill her. She killed herself when she allowed you to bring her to Black Dolphin. It was death sentence for her. She knew this. I cannot mourn her. I do not know her, but I understand why Colonel Sokolov will do this."

"Tell me."

"You say you find body of Ekaterina Norikova on boat. That means Colonel Sokolov wanted your body to be found near hers so the Americans would believe it was me. This is what you believe also, yes?"

"It's a good theory," I admitted, "but I'm not sure that's exactly what he had in mind. The more I think about it, the more I believe it wasn't really an attempt on my life. I believe it was an attempt to make me *believe* it was an attempt on my life, and you were the perpetrator."

Anya's English was good, but the look on her face made me restate my theory in Russian.

She considered my idea. "Is good result for him if you die or do not die. If die, he gets what he wants, and if you do not die and think it was me, you lead him to me, and he can kill me."

Hunter let out a low whistle. "This is getting deep."

"This did not happen in America, no?"

"No, we were in Honeymoon Harbour in The Bahamas."

She pressed her lips tightly together. "Who?"

"My wife, Penny, and me."

"*Zhena?*"

"Yes, my wife. Her name is Penny."

She stared into the grain of the wooden table and traced the lines with the tip of her finger. Her reaction wasn't what I'd expected. I thought she would ignore the news, pretending I hadn't said a word, but my declaration clearly had an effect on her I couldn't have predicted. It was easy for me to believe there wasn't a real woman beneath Anya's arresting exterior. After what I'd been through with her, I'd learned through pain that she could be robotically cold. But I also believed that the news I was married and had taken my wife to the same anchorage Anya had claimed to be the perfect honeymoon spot affected the woman inside the shell of an assassin.

Anya shot her eyes to mine. "Did you bring him here? Is that deal you have made with him?"

"No, Anya, I didn't bring him here, but I did tell him I'd deliver you to him."

"Why would you do this?"

Her dramatic change of subjects didn't surprise me at all. "I did it to buy myself some time."

"Time to spend with wife, Penny?"

Her return to the previous subject, however, did surprise me.

"No, Anya. I needed time to find you. You left quite a breadcrumb for me to find, by the way."

"What is breadcrumb?" She seemed genuinely confused.

"The four-hundred-thousand-ruble transaction in the credit card machine downstairs coded 'Katerina's Heart.' *That's* the breadcrumb."

She allowed herself to look at me. "I hope you are very happy with Penny, your wife. I am sorry I could not—"

To my surprise, Hunter spoke up. "Uh, guys. I'm sorry to break up whatever this is, but your friend, Yuri, is going to come bursting through that door any minute, and he'll probably be ready to kill me and Chase. It might be nice if you called him off before one of us has to shoot him."

Anya shot a glance toward the door. "What did you do to him?"

Hunter pointed toward me. "Chase knocked him out with a bad-ass uppercut. You would've been proud. Then I hit him with some French sleeping meds, and we left him on the stairs."

Anya's eyes widened. "You hit Yuri in face?"

I held up my right hand, showing off my battered knuckles.

She let out a girlish chuckle—something I'd never heard her do.

"You are much better fighter now, or Yuri is very drunk."

Hunter said, "Oh, he's drunk all right. He had half a bottle of—"

I interrupted. "Yeah, let's just say I'm not the same guy you knew, and we'll leave it at that."

She reached for my fist with both hands and touched her lips to the bloody knuckles.

I pulled my hand from hers. "We can't do that, Anya."

She nodded slowly. "*Da*, I know. But inside heart I have dream you come back. That was reason for breadcrumb."

"I'm sorry, Anya. After everything…"

Hunter's prediction suddenly became reality, and the big Russian barreled through the door. He had a shotgun tucked tightly against his hip as he thundered toward the kitchen.

Anya leapt to her feet. "*Stoy, Yuri! Stoy!* They are my friends!"

"*Tvoi druz'ya umrut.*"

Even Hunter knew that meant Yuri was going to kill us.

He and I drew our pistols simultaneously, but Anya's speed left everyone in the room in awe.

She stopped the big Russian with the tip of her knife pressed against his left cheekbone and a piece of broken glass from the honey jar barely breaking the skin over his jugular. "I said they are my friends, Yuri."

The beast of a man slowly backed away from the deadliest woman I knew, never taking his eyes off me as he slipped into the hallway.

"I am sorry about that. He is angry man sometimes when he is embarrassed. He will have drink and forget everything. Now tell me why you are here."

I turned on the faucet and dampened a towel that was hanging from a hook. Cleaning the spilled honey from the table was more work than I anticipated.

"Thank you, Chase. I will clean later. For now, tell me truth. Why are you here?"

I rinsed my hands and returned the sticky towel to the hook. "I'm here to give you a chance to come in out of the cold and give me a shot at staying alive."

"I am listening. What is plan you have? You have always plan."

I lifted a knife from the countertop and held it toward the most dangerous woman I knew. "This one is simple. I want you to kill me right in front of Colonel Sokolov."

Chapter 25
The Serpent Behind

"We now should have vodka," Anya said, pulling open a cabinet door.

"I thought you didn't like vodka. You told me you were a terrible Russian because you hate the cold, vodka, and caviar."

"That is why I am better spy than you. I remember everything perfectly, and you remember only some things and sometimes not perfectly. I told you, I do not drink vodka. I detest cold, and I cannot eat caviar. Is terrible. I drink tea. Vodka makes my mind soft. I eat chocolate because it tastes better than fish egg. I rather chase you through Caribbean than build *snegovik* in Mother Russia."

I replayed the moment in my mind's eye, and every detail was as clear as if it were playing on a movie screen.

"You also believed I didn't know that *snegovik* is a snowman."

She unscrewed the cap from a bottle and tossed it at me. "No, Chasechka. I let you believe this, but is not true. You are terrible spy just like I am terrible Russian."

I rolled my eyes. "The difference is, I'm not a spy. But you are Russian."

She poured three small glasses. "I am not Russian so much anymore. I am, I think word is *outcast*."

Anya handed a glass to me and then Hunter. He sniffed the clear spirit and drank a third of it immediately.

"Now you trust me to not poison you?"

"Yeah, after nearly cutting Yuri's goozle out, I figure you're all right."

She turned to me. "Goozle?"

"He means you were going to gut him like pig," I explained.

We drank, and I laid out my plan. "We have a boat that will be in Sochi soon. It's an exact replica of *Aegis*, with two significant differences. First, the interior is completely unfinished, and second, it's designed to sink itself on command. Hunter and I planted the seed in Lady Sokolova's head that we'd be in Sochi, relying on her to pass the word to her husband."

Anya held up a finger. "But you said you kidnapped Colonel Sokolov's wife."

"Yeah, we did, but only for an hour. We dumped her on an island just south of the colonel's dacha on the French Riviera. I'm sure she was safely back in her bed two hours later."

"Is strange kidnapping," Anya said.

I shrugged. "Well, you said I was a terrible spy."

"Okay, so you have sinking boat in Sochi. What else is plan?"

"Anya, your English has gotten terrible. What's happened to you?"

"My English is better than your Russian. It is just sleepy from not using. Is nice again to use English."

If she weren't a murderous, devious, Russian spy, Anya Burinkova would be on the cover of every fashion magazine in the world with men falling at her feet like flies. It was difficult not to be distracted by her looks and practiced, feigned charm.

"So, the plan isn't quite as simple as sticking me on the boat and sending me to the bottom of the Black Sea. Sokolov believes I'm going to deliver you to him on a silver platter, and in return, he thinks I trust him to let me live. I have trust issues with Russians these days."

There it was—that dead, cold stare only Russian women have perfected.

"Anyway, what I want you to do is contact Sokolov. Tell him you'll kill me if he allows you to return to work for the Kremlin. He'll take the deal because it'll give him everything he wants. I'll be dead. He'll have double-crossed me and pulled a fast one on the Americans, and you get to come in from the cold and stop living on the edge of nowhere. The only thing the Kremlin would like more than having you and me dead is having me dead and you back inside Red Square. They've invested a lot of time and money in you, and if there's one thing I know about Russians, they are not wasteful. Oh, there's one more thing I know about Russians. They hate admitting when they're wrong."

Anya stared through my chest as if she could see into my soul. The three of us sat in silence for an interminable amount of time as she thought.

"You are correct. We are not wasteful, and we are never wrong. I do not like your plan, but plan will almost work."

"What do you mean, it'll almost work?"

"Is not important for you. Is good plan, and I will do it for you, Chasechka. When?"

I stared through my empty vodka glass and then through the tiny kitchen window at the darkening northern sky. "I've had too much vodka to fly...."

"Fly?" Anya asked. "You have airplane here in Ust-Kamchatsk?"

"Yes, we have a floatplane at the abandoned seaplane base three miles north of town."

She wrinkled her forehead. "This floatplane will fly all the way to Sochi?"

"Well, I suppose it could with a couple of fuel stops and permission to fly an American-registered airplane in Russian airspace. But we'll be flying the other direction...at least initially."

"There is nothing other way from Ust-Kamchatsk except sea."

"That's not exactly true," I said. "There's a nice little string of islands stretching from here all the way to Alaska, and a couple of those islands have some particularly friendly natives who can't wait to help us out."

Anya's eyes became the eyes of a child. "You are taking me to Alaska?"

"Yes, we'll fly to Adak in our floatplane and then take a bigger plane to Anchorage before we head for the Mediterranean. But we can't do any of that tonight with this much alcohol in my body and the long Siberian night less than an hour away. We'll leave before the sun comes up and hike back out to the lake."

Anya shook her head. "No, we do not hike. I have car you give to me in Sol-Iletsk."

"You still have that piece of crap?"

She smiled. "Yes, I still have everything you give to me."

I wondered how literal her statement was, but I didn't pursue it. "What do you think the chances are Yuri will rent us a room for the night and not kill us in our sleep?"

Anya snapped. "No, no Yuri. Is too many things for in his head."

Hunter closed one eye and stared at Anya with the other. "What the hell does that mean, too many things for in his head? Say that in Russian to Chase-Catch-A-Catch, or whatever you call him, and let him explain it to me."

It made a lot more sense in Russian. I said, "Yuri can't be trusted with information this important."

Hunter smacked his forehead. "Why couldn't she just say that?"

I lowered my chin, scowling at my partner. "You expect me to explain communication problems between you and a Russian woman? Really?"

He held up both hands. "Hey, I'm the pretty one. You're supposed to be the smart one."

Anya huffed. "Now I am pretty one *and* smart one."

Hunter raised his eyebrows. "She's got a point."

"Yeah, well, that may be true, but what we don't have is a place to sleep tonight."

"You will sleep here," Anya said. "I have only one bed, but couch makes bed, and I have many blanket."

I turned to Hunter, but his blank expression gave me no direction as I considered her offer.

"Maybe your Penny will not like you sleeping with me, no?"

"No," I said, "I'm sure she wouldn't approve of me sleeping with you, but I don't think she'd be upset about me sleeping on your couch. That's not what I'm worried about."

Anya smiled. "I promise I will not kill you in sleep if you promise same."

Hunter let out a nervous sigh. "That's good enough for me. How about you, Chase?"

"If she were going to kill us," I said, "we'd already be dead."

"Is true. You have given many opportunities. I do not want you dead. I like you, *okhotnik*, and Chase has new wife who needs him. I have to ask question. Is okay, yes?"

"Of course," I said. "What is it?"

"I try not to make you sad, but why is Hunter with you and not Clark?"

"Clark was injured in a bad accident on the Khyber Pass. He broke his back."

"He is alive or no?"

"Yes, he's alive, but it'll be a long time before he can work again. Hunter is my partner now."

"I would be sad if he is dead, but I am also sad he is hurt. And is Hunter surname or Christian name or not name?"

I could see it in his eyes, Hunter considering the necessity of revealing personal information.

"*Da,*" he said.

Well done, Hunter. Yes *and* thank you *can get you a long way in any language.*

"Yes, I like you very much, *okhotnik.*"

Anya insisted on feeding us, so we ate black bread and borscht topped with sour cream and dill. It was hearty, but not exactly what we'd be having back at Bonaventure Plantation with Maebelle in the kitchen.

"Your Penny cooks for you, yes?"

I couldn't decide if it was idle conversation or an attempt at competition. I'd never known Anya to speak without a reason, so I was leaning toward it being a comparison.

"Yes, Penny is a wonderful cook," I said, trying to stop the game of twenty questions before it got started.

"Is good for you. Wife should cook for husband. I do not have husband, but I would cook for him if he follow breadcrumb and come for me."

In what I assumed was Hunter's twisted attempt at having fun at my expense, he said, "I'm sure you'd make a terrific wife, Anya. This soup is fantastic."

My size thirteen boot landed against his shin hard enough to get my point across.

"She makes for you lemonade and stew of fish and potatoes?"

Changing tactics, I opted to let her have the small victory. "No, Anya. You're the only woman who's ever made that for me."

With one sharp nod punctuating her superiority, she said, "Yes, I am better spy *and* wife."

Part of me wanted it to simply end, but I couldn't let it go. "You were never my wife, Anya."

Without a word, she stood and paced from the kitchen.

Hunter leaned in. "What's happening, Chase? I'm not sure I like whatever this little pissing match is supposed to be."

I grabbed his bread and shoved it into his bowl. "You're the one poking the Russian bear. Give me a break."

He shoved the bread into his mouth and mumbled, "I made for you stew of fish, Chasey-Catch-A-Catch."

For a moment, I considered putting a bullet through my own partner's knee. Stone Hunter was doing a fine job of filling Clark's role of torturing me at every opportunity.

Anya returned, and beside my bowl she laid a Florida driver's license and American passport, both in the name of Ana R. Fulton.

"I am only Russian girl in Siberia with Florida driving license and surname Fulton. Same as Penny, yes?"

I gave Hunter one more shin kick for good measure, then wiped my mouth. "I think I'm ready for bed."

Anya looked at me with that utterly irresistible smile she'd no doubt perfected at State School 4, where she learned exactly how to find any man's kryptonite and turn him into putty in her hands. It had once worked on me. I didn't know if she was trying to seduce me or if the behavior had become so deeply ingrained in her personality that it was impossible to do otherwise. Either way, I wouldn't be sleeping—or doing anything else—in Anya Burinkova's bed, regardless of the last name on her passport and driver's license.

* * *

Hunter pulled a blanket tightly beneath his chin. "Let me make something perfectly clear to you, Chasey-Chiquita. You'll be keeping your hands—and everything else—to yourself tonight, no matter who or what you dream about. Otherwise, I'll give you a scar that'll make you forget all about that little scratch she left on your tongue."

"What? You don't want to snuggle?" I said, feigning disappointment.

"Go to sleep, lover boy. You've got a lot of flying to do tomorrow."

I laughed. "I thought you said you weren't going to let me fly anymore after that landing this morning."

"No, that's not what I said. I said I'll be doing the landings from now on. You can still do the flying, but I'd like to live to tell my grandkids about this grand adventure you're dragging me on."

"Good night, Hunter."

"Oh, and another thing," he said. "You'll be keeping your big butt right here in this bed all night. There'll be no creeping down the hall to check on your kryptonite. If you live through what I'd do to you, I promise you'll never survive the wrath of Penny, the *real* Mrs. Fulton."

I rolled over and pulled the blanket into place. "Not even tempted a little bit."

"Yeah, right," he scoffed. "The way she smiles at you, there's not a man alive who wouldn't be tempted. So, don't lie to me."

Barely above a whisper, I said, "Her smile doesn't frighten me. It's the serpent behind that smile that sends waves of terror down my spine."

Chapter 26
Shotgun

I lay in the silent darkness, haunted by the terrifying thought that our airplane may not be where we left it. If someone discovered our magic carpet and wanted it for himself, getting out of Siberia, especially with Anya along for the ride, was going to be more challenging than anything I'd ever attempted. Merciful sleep finally came just before sunrise, as exhaustion conquered irrational fear.

"Hey, Superman, wake up. It's time to rock 'n roll."

I blinked and almost begged for just five more minutes, but it was too late. Hunter was up, and when Hunter is up, everyone is up.

"Why'd you call me Superman?"

"Because you survived the night without getting melted down by your kryptonite. I'm starting to believe there's hope for you yet."

"Yeah, okay, I'm coming, but I could really use another hour."

"It's too late for that. Besides, your ex-wife made coffee and something I can't identify in a bowl."

I threw the blanket at him. "She's not my ex-wife."

"Yeah, well, she's your ex-something. What is that thing she keeps calling you? Chase-Chickity-Chonga or whatever?"

"I can't catch a break, can I? It's a Russian thing they do with names. Instead of calling someone *darling* or *sweetheart*, they add *echka* to the end of their first name. I don't understand it, either, but it's what they do."

He shook his head. "Well, it may be what they do, but if Penny ever hears that Russian call you that lovey-dovey little name, she'll chickity chop the chit out of her."

"You're a funny dude, Hunter, but never the twain shall meet."

He pointed his finger at my nose. "You better hope they don't."

Anya's apartment had a bathtub the size of a cereal box and no shower, so I washed my face in the sink and brushed my teeth with my finger.

I heard Anya explaining breakfast to Hunter.

"Is kasha. Like for you, I think oatmeal."

He sniffed at the contents of the bowl. "Okay, if you say so, but do you have any more honey after turning the jar into a potential murder weapon?"

She giggled, removed another jar of honey from the cupboard, and turned to greet me. "*Dobroye utro*, Chasechka. You are ready for kasha, yes?"

"Absolutely," I said. "After finger-brushing my teeth, nothing's better than a big steaming bowl of kasha."

"It's like oatmeal, but Russian," Hunter said as he dipped honey from the jar.

"You're becoming quite the wealth of Eastern European knowledge there, partner. You'll be moving to Moscow before you know it."

He took his first bite and pointed his spoon at me. "You never know. If the women in Moscow look like Anyachka, you may be right."

She shook her head. "No, *okhotnik*, Anyachka is not same. I will teach you later."

He shrugged, offered a "*Spasibo*," and dug back into his porridge.

Anya turned back to me with a look of puzzlement. "You made teeth clean with finger?"

"Yes. I seem to have forgotten my toothbrush."

Mischief replaced puzzlement on her face. "Man should be like brush for teeth."

"What?" I asked, thoroughly confused by her bizarre statement.

"Yes, man should be like brush for teeth. Is for only one woman. If for more than one woman, he is brush for toilet."

Hunter pointed his spoon again. "Now there's some wisdom, Chasey-Choo-Choo. You should remember that one."

"Eat your kasha, and stay out of this."

Obviously amused with herself, Anya giggled and handed me a bowl of kasha. "*Spasibo*, you little Russian toothbrush philosopher."

Hunter helped Anya clean the few dishes we'd used for breakfast, and ten minutes later, we were in her LuAZ-969, an odd-looking, Russian all-wheel-drive truck I'd left with her after breaking her out of the Black Dolphin Prison. Although ugly, it was a vehicle more than capable of handling the rugged Siberian terrain and carrying practically anything that would fit inside its canvas-covered cargo compartment.

Fortunately, my fears of someone stealing our airplane were unfounded. The plane was right where we'd left her, and as I discovered during my thorough preflight inspection, completely unmolested. We untied and pushed the plane from the shed. Hunter stood on the remains of a dilapidated dock, holding the wing strut while I climbed aboard and started the engine. Seaplanes don't have brakes, so once the engine is running, the plane starts moving. Hunter hopped aboard the starboard float and discovered Anya occupying the front seat, relegating him to passenger status in the back.

He donned his headset and pulled the mic to his lips. "I think you got my chair, lady."

Anya looked over her shoulder. "I called *drobovik*, but maybe you did not hear."

He sighed. "Well, I guess I just learned the Russian word for *shotgun*."

Unlike the conditions during our arrival, there was a breeze from the northeast, so I pointed the prop into the wind and added full power. As the northeastern shoreline grew ever closer, we continued picking up speed until the water gave up its grasp of our floats and our boat became a flying machine.

I continued climbing to the northeast with the mountain off our right side. With the autopilot managing our climb, I programmed the Casco Cove Coast Guard Station into the GPS and ignored the magenta line pointing directly to the airport.

Anya noticed my deviation from the course. "Why are you not following line?"

I pointed toward the east, where the islands would soon be visible on the horizon. "I can't exactly fly across the Komandorskiye Ostrova in an American airplane."

She reached beneath her seat, pulled the handle, and slid her seat forward toward the panel. After readjusting her seatbelt, she tuned a new frequency into the communication radio and pulled the mic to her lips.

Three radio transmissions later, we were cleared directly across Russia's easternmost airport, with Anya's perfect Russian voice doing all the talking.

"Is nice to have friends sometimes, no?"

I motioned to the yoke. "It sure is. You have the controls."

She held the yoke with one hand and flew the Stationair straight down the magenta line.

"Clark was right," I said. "You can fly."

"Yes, but I could not tell you before."

"How about helicopters? Can you fly one of those, too?" I asked.

She offered a wry smile. "I think you know truth about that."

"So that *was* you in the pool in Virginia."

Her smile broadened. "So that *was* you in plane in sky and you who killed Colonel Tornovich, no?"

I removed my sunglasses from the case and slipped them on. "I have no idea what you're talking about."

Putting the Commander Islands astern, I reclaimed the controls then descended low enough so the Russian radar couldn't watch us cross the International Date Line into American airspace. We landed to the north at the Coast Guard station as we'd done on our westbound leg.

I shut down near the fuel pumps. "Anya, it might be best if you stay in the airplane while we fuel up. You might be hard to explain. These guys think we're wildlife photographers for *Nat Geo*."

She stuck out her bottom lip. "But you know how much I love man in uniform. I will not speak. Only stretch legs, okay?"

Making Anya Burinkova do something she didn't want to do was like negotiating with a king cobra. You may play your flute and believe she's dancing for you, but she'll strike whenever she wants, and there's nothing you or your flute can do about it.

It was no surprise the Coasties ignored Hunter and me. Anya had a way of garnering attention from young men, especially if those men hadn't seen a woman in months.

Adak looked as it had the day we met the weatherman. He was happy to get his airplane back in one piece, and he was, of course, intrigued with our passenger.

"Be careful, boys. I've been in this business a long time, and I know a honey trap when I see one. That girl has honey oozing from every pore."

"You've got a good eye," I said. "I got my foot stuck in that trap a few years ago, so I know exactly what she is."

He looked me up and down. "Yeah, I bet it wasn't your foot she trapped, boy. Was it worth the ride?"

"No, sir. It never is."

He patted me on the back and laughed. "You may be wise beyond your years, son. You keep your...foot out of traps like that, and you may end up living long enough to tell your grandbabies about your wild adventures."

"Thanks for the plane. I can pay you now, or you can send me a bill."

He laughed from his heels up. "A bill? Now that's a good one. You don't owe me anything for using that plane. I don't even know who owns it. I just figured you'd have it back before anybody knew it was gone."

I stuck out my hand. "Nonetheless, we appreciate it, and we'll be glad to return the favor someday. Oh, I almost forgot. Your friend, Yuri, said *potseluy yego v zadnitsu.*"

The weatherman slapped his leg. "Yes, I'm sure he did. Good luck to you boys. And remember, both of you stay out of that honey trap."

Now that I was back on American soil, it was time to make my first call home for the operation.

"Chase! Are you okay? Where are you? Is Hunter okay?"

Penny's excitement never failed to make me smile. I doubted she really wanted me to answer all those questions in precisely that order, so instead, I said, "I love you."

That was good enough. The anxiety in her voice softened. "I love you, too. I've been so worried."

"There's no need to worry. We're fine. We're back in Adak and should be in Anchorage in a few hours. Skipper arranged a spot for us on a King Air."

"Did you find…her?"

"We did, and she's agreed to do what we need."

Penny huffed. "Oh, I'm sure she did. I'm sure she'd agree to anything for you…"

I let her carry on for several minutes, knowing better than to interrupt her.

When she finished her tirade, I said, "She's got a whole new group of admirers at the Coast Guard station, so she has no interest in me."

"Yeah, she better not."

"Hunter is a good chaperone, so you have nothing to worry about. Is Skipper around? I need to talk with her, too."

"She's here, but I want to talk to you again before you hang up, okay?"

"Anything you want, Penny."

Skipper came on the line. "It's about time. Is everything okay?"

"Yes, we're fine. The op is going as planned. We have Anya, and we're back on Adak. If your King Air shows up, we'll be in Anchorage in time for dinner."

"Good. Did you have any trouble in Siberia?"

I glanced at Anya and took a deep breath. "Surprisingly, no. There were no bullets and no dead bodies this time."

"Well, that's better than I expected. The King Air should be there any minute. The dunker is in the Black Sea, but Dominic says it was damaged on the crossing. I'll have more details later, but other than that, everything is going as planned. Penny and I brought *Aegis* back home, and you're going to love the new sails. They're awesome."

I secretly hoped Skipper never outgrew that girlish excitement for everything around her, but sooner or later, life's cruel reality would diminish one of the most beautiful things about the woman I'd always see as my little sister.

"I can't wait to try them out. I'll call you from Anchorage, and you can fill me in on the agenda from there."

"Oh, I almost forgot the most important part. You're gonna love this. Your new friend from the Pentagon called and offered a little help in Sochi. I'll tell you all about it when you call back."

"What friend?" I asked.

"Duh, Chase. The chief of naval operations. Who else? To be so smart, you sure are dumb sometimes."

"I get that a lot," I said. "If there's nothing else, put Penny back on."

"Okay, here she is."

"Hey, I know you're busy and all, but I just want to hear your voice again and tell you I love you. Did I hear Skipper say you were calling back today?"

"I love you, too, Penny. And yes, I'll call from Anchorage later this evening. We have to nail down the itinerary for the other side of Russia. How's Clark and the guys?"

"Everybody's doing fine. Maebelle won't let Clark overdo it, so that's good. But there is one thing, and I know I shouldn't be telling you bad news while you're on a mission, but the Judge isn't doing well. He got sick while he was in Atlanta, and he's in the hospital."

"Is he going to be okay? What's wrong?"

I could almost hear her deciding how much to tell me. "They don't really know. Try not to think about that. Just get this thing done and come home, okay?"

"Okay, baby. We'll talk tonight."

Skipper was right. The King Air landed and taxied up to the terminal only minutes after I'd pocketed my phone. After refueling, the pilot motioned for us to come aboard, and we followed his direction.

The flight from Adak to Anchorage is just under 1200 miles, close to the maximum range for the King Air, but we made it in four hours. Hunter and Anya slept most of the way, but my mind was consumed with thoughts of the Judge and what assistance the CNO could be offering. As with most of life's mysteries, only time would tell.

With a little help from Skipper and someone she referred to as a "friend" at Immigration and Customs Enforcement, Anya's —Ana's—passport was stamped, and for the first time in years, or perhaps for the first time ever, she was legally inside the United States.

Anya was a study in contrasts: terrifyingly deadly yet breathtakingly beautiful, and devoted to her craft yet childlike in her curiosity about America. She sat for several long moments, staring with admiration at the purple ink as it dried on her passport. I wanted to know what was happening inside her head—what she was dreaming, planning, scheming.

Something in my gut kept warning me that she was going to run. With a perfectly legitimate passport and two million dollars in a Cayman bank, she could spend the rest of her life doing anything and everything she wanted in the U.S. without enduring another Siberian winter over Yuri's bar.

Trusting Anya was something I would never again do. Even if she proved herself worthy of my trust in a thousand operations, I would always expect her loyalties to be lying elsewhere and her brilliant mind to be planning her next coup. If she ran, my operation was doomed. Everything about the mission relied on her involvement. She was the hinge pin. Without her, I'd spend the rest of my life, though short it may be, running from Sokolov's hit men.

I couldn't trust her, but I hoped she'd be true to her word long enough to convince the Russian colonel my bones were rotting in the frigid depths seven thousand feet beneath the surface of the Black Sea.

Chapter 27
Prettier

If she hadn't been one of the best young operational analysts on the planet, Skipper could've made a comfortable living as a travel agent. Five minutes after our King Air landed at Anchorage International, we were airborne in a Sikorsky S-76 helicopter and climbing eastward.

In the previous decade, I'd spent a lot of time not knowing what was happening around me, but thankfully those moments were growing rarer. I wasn't entirely sure where we were headed, but I knew Skipper had arranged the perfect accommodations.

My faith in my analyst was once again rewarded. We landed at the Girdwood Airport and were carried in style to the Alyeska Resort forty miles east of Anchorage. Although very few things were impossible for Anya, running from Alyeska would be far from easy. The resort was tucked away on a postcard-perfect setting at the foot of a glacier overlooking a beautifully pristine mountain lake. Finding a corner of the world more beautiful than the Caribbean wasn't easy, but Alyeska came close.

"What does word *Alyeska* mean?"

I slipped a nice tip into the bellman's palm. He pocketed the cash and looked at me with expectation pouring from his eyes.

"Is there something else?" I asked.

"I was waiting to answer your wife's question, if you want."

I stared at him, bewildered. "What question?"

He motioned toward Anya. "Mrs. Fulton asked about the origin of *Alyeska*."

"Oh, no. She's not my wife. We're just traveling together."

The man blushed. "Oh, I'm sorry, sir. I didn't mean to—"

Anya placed her hand on the young man's forearm. "Is okay. I am ex-wife."

His expression turned from blushing to voyeuristic intrigue, so I intervened before the situation grew more uncomfortable.

"You were saying? About what *Alyeska* means. For *Ms.* Fulton."

"Oh, yes, *Alyeska* is an archaic spelling of the Aleut word *Alaska*, meaning mainland, great country, or great land."

"See, that wasn't so hard, now was it?" I patted the young man on the shoulder, encouraging him to turn for the door of the suite.

The accommodations were magnificent. If I didn't harbor the world's deepest hatred of cold weather, I could see myself spending some quality time at Alyeska.

After I surveyed the suite, noting every possible exit, I threw a pillow at Anya. "Ex-wife? What was that all about? I should kill you in your sleep."

"I am not so easy to kill. Not even when I am sleeping."

"I'll give you that one. You do have a way of coming back from the dead."

She reached across her shoulder, fingering the place where the scar of the 9mm entry wound above her shoulder blade would always be. "I was almost dead, but you saved my life, and again you saved me from death in prison. I think you do not want me to die, so you will not kill me in sleep or any other time."

"Yeah, well, I think we'll be even if you come through on this operation and convince Sokolov I'm dead."

"He will watch you die with own eyes, so he will tell only lie to himself, and I will not have to. And then I will be returned to Moscow for rare second chance in SVR."

I tried to detect anything in her tone, body language, or facial expression that would lead me to believe she was planning a run for the hills, but everything about her said she was in for the long haul. No one is more perfectly deceptive than a Russian red sparrow, but I believed she was telling the truth.

* * *

"How's your new home away from home?" came Skipper's infectious tone through the speaker of my phone.

"It's perfect. How did you find this place?"

I could almost see her pretending to brush the dust from her shoulders with a swiping hand. "It's what I do."

"Yes, it is, and I appreciate it. So, let's hear about this damage the dunker sustained on the Atlantic crossing."

"I just got off the phone with Dominic. They left the mast up for the crossing aboard the cargo ship, and it took a lightning strike. It fried some of the circuitry, but Tommy is working it out."

"Ooh, I don't like the sound of that. How long does Tommy think it'll take to make the repairs?"

"I know. I don't like it, either," she said, "but it's not like it could've been prevented. If we had taken the mast down, we would have to wait for a crane to put it back up, so we'd have the delay either way. Who could've known they'd take a lightning strike?"

I sighed. "I'm sure you're right, but sitting on Anya for three days in Alaska isn't exactly what I had on the agenda."

"You could come home," she said.

I gave her idea a moment's consideration. "I don't know if that's a very good idea, but you and Penny could come here."

Skipper sucked air through her teeth. "Ooh, catfight. Penny and Anya on the same continent is scary enough, but in the same hotel? That's a recipe for fireworks."

"Okay, we'll revisit the idea after we finish the briefing. Tell me about the CNO's offer to help in the Black Sea."

"Oh, you're going to love this, Chase. We've got a pair of nuclear subs conducting ops in the Mediterranean. That means instead of a surface support vessel—which was our original plan—we can pluck you off the dunker with a sub, air-lock you aboard, and exfil silently back to the Med."

"That news is good enough to offset the lightning strike, but how did you pull that rabbit out of your hat?"

"I didn't," she said. "The rabbit hopped into my lap. Imagine my surprise when I got a call from Admiral Galloway offering up the use of one of his subs."

"They're going to want something in return, but it's too good to pass up. It's the perfect exfil plan."

I could hear her tapping furiously on her keyboard.

"Okay, so the weather window is great. The water's gonna be cold, but if everything goes right with the sub, you won't be in the water long enough to kill you."

"That's encouraging."

"Hey, I got you a swanky resort in the Alaskan interior and a nuclear submarine. Now you want me to warm up the Black Sea. Even I can't pull that one off."

I laughed. "But if anyone could, it would be you, Skipper. Is there anything else?"

"Thanks for the vote of confidence, but I know my limits… what few there are. I think that covers everything for now. I'll keep you posted on the repairs to the dunker. I know I should've talked with you about it first, but I gave Admiral Galloway a hard yes on the sub. I hope that's okay."

"Yes, that perfect. You made the right call. Let me talk to Penny."

Penny came on in her usual mood. "Hey, Chase. Are you settled in at the resort? Skipper showed me the pictures, and it looks amazing."

"Hey, sweetheart. Yes, it's very nice. As always, Skipper hit a home run, but it looks like we'll be camped out for a few days waiting for Tommy to get the dunker back up and running. I was thinking maybe you'd like to come up and see the place."

Her cheerful tone suddenly turned uncertain. "Uh, and *she's* there, right?"

"Yes," I said. "Anya's here."

She took a long breath. "Not that I care if I make her uncomfortable, but I don't want to do anything to put the operation at risk."

I had no illusions of Penny and Anya ever being best friends, but I hadn't considered the potential for a confrontation to screw up the op. My gears started turning and cranked out a solution. "I want you to come up and bring Skipper. If it looks like there's any chance of endangering the mission, we'll get you out of here."

"Okay," she answered quickly. "We'll be on the next flight, but promise me you'll tell me immediately if you think it's going south."

"I will, Penny, but promise me you're not going to try to kill her."

"You know me better than that. Class, not trash, right? I will admit I'm curious to see what she looks like. Is she prettier than me?"

"Nobody's prettier than you, Penny. Nobody."

"You're sweet, but you're a liar, Chase Fulton. I'll see you tomorrow."

Throughout my conversation, Hunter had been shifting his gaze between me in the bedroom and Anya in the kitchen. He was good at a lot of things, but hiding how he felt about anything wasn't one of his strengths.

"That's a hell of a plan you've hatched there, cowboy. Throwing a honey badger and a queen cobra in a pit together. What could possibly go wrong?"

I feigned pulling my pistol on him. "There's no such thing as a queen cobra."

He motioned toward the kitchen with his chin. "Are you sure about that, Pistol Pete?"

I pulled a barstool away from the island separating the kitchen from the living room. "Anya, we need to talk."

She formed a bipod with her elbows and rested her chin on top of her folded hands. "Is time for me to call Colonel Sokolov, no?"

"Yes, we have to make that call, but there's something else."

"You are afraid, Chasechka. I see it in eyes."

"No, it's not fear. It's concern."

"No, is fear."

I rubbed my palms across the quartz countertop, forming wax on, wax off motions until she trapped my hands beneath hers. "Tell me what is it."

"Penny and Skipper are coming here tomorrow."

She giggled—something I'd seen her do only a handful of times. "Wife and ex-wife in same house. Is like situation-comedy television show in America, no?"

"I don't see the potential for much comedy, but I agree, it's a great premise for a show. Are you going to behave?"

She didn't move her hands from mine. "Chasechka, I am happy for you to be content. You can never believe me, I know this, but love is not for me what you think. For me—for most Russians in service to country—first love is for Russia. Is inside our mind from birth, and is always inside us. Is for you, patriotism, I think, but for Russians, much bigger."

"What are you talking about?"

She pulled her hands from mine and looked toward the ceiling, perhaps for inspiration. "Is not easy for me to say in English."

I sat back in my barstool. "Okay, then. My Russian is good enough to keep up, so let's hear it."

Her confidence in her native tongue was evident. "When I came to you, it was for an assignment, and I believed in the validity of that assignment. I had been trained to do a job, and I was very good, but I did not think I would come to care about you. I had spent my whole life training to do exactly what Colonel Tornovich sent me to do to you, but I was never taught how to not fall in love with a man who was so kind to me as you were."

I held up my hand. "Don't. It doesn't do any good for you to lie to me anymore. Those days are long behind us. You're not going to get inside my head again, so telling me you fell in love with me is a waste of your time and mine."

Still in Russian, she said, "No, Chase. Listen to me. I did not choose to fall in love with you, and maybe what I felt wasn't really love. I do not know, but I feel for you things I did not know I could feel, and it was not a decision for me. What I am trying to tell you is that I know you are happy, and you have a very good life with Penny. I will not damage that life for you. I am now nervous to see her, but I want to know the woman who can make you happy. Is she prettier than me?"

I slapped the countertop. "That's exactly what she asked me about you."

She pinned her eyes to mine. "Is she?"

I didn't blink. "Not only is she prettier, she's never lied to me."

Chapter 28
The Second Knife

Twenty-four hours later, Skipper was first through the door, but only by a few inches. Penny was hot on her heels.

She was quick to throw her arms around me, but her distraction was more than obvious. "Where is she?"

"She's outside, on the deck overlooking the lake," I said, catching her hands in mine. "Listen to me. I know there's a whirlwind of emotion going on in that head of yours, but Anya is going to be quiet and cold. That's how she is. Don't take that as something negative directed at you."

Penny squeezed my hands. "Class, not trash, Chase. I'm not going to make a scene, but I have to see her. I have to know if she's as threatening as her half sister."

"Except for the scar, they're practically identical," I said. "Come on, let's get this over. Hunter can't wait for the fireworks."

"I'm sorry to disappoint Hunter, but there won't be any fireworks from me," she said.

I led her toward the deck, my heart bucking inside my chest, but when we reached the door, the scene unfolding outside stopped us in our tracks.

"You are wife, Penny?"

Skipper took a step forward and crossed her arms. "Uh, no, I'm not. I'm Elizabeth, the analyst, code name Skipper. And you're Anya Burinkova."

Anya stood. "Yes, I am, and I know who you are, but I thought maybe you were also wife. I am sorry for what happened on Island Cumberland. I could not let that man, Michael Anderson, kill you, but I should not have left you tied up."

Skipper, immediately disarmed, leaned against the rail. "I held you in my lap on the way to the hospital in Miami after you were shot. I held pressure on your wound, but...."

"Thank you for that, Elizabeth...or Skipper. You saved my life."

"No, you saved mine. Those men would've killed me and Chase in that house. If you hadn't come in when you did, we never would've made it out."

Anya licked her lips. "Was long time ago, and cannot be changed. I am happy you are alive."

"I'm glad you're alive, too, but only because you're essential for this mission."

"Yes, I will do for Chase, and now also for you."

Penny led me through the door and onto the deck.

Anya stood, folded her hands, and faced Penny. "You are wife, and I am..."

My heart stopped. If Anya said the word *ex-wife*, Penny would throw her into the lake.

"...Anastasia Burinkova."

The two women stood, each silently appraising the other until Penny glanced at Skipper and then me. "Could we have a drink and a few minutes alone?"

I would've preferred Penny throwing Anya into the lake. The idea of those two women having a drink alone terrified me.

Skipper stepped toward Anya and reached for her. "Don't resist. I just need to know if you've got a gun."

Anya looked down at Skipper's hands. "I do not have gun, but I have knife. Is here." She pointed toward her back pocket and raised her hands.

My analyst and little sister pulled the knife from the deadly former Russian spy and tucked it into her pocket.

Hunter delivered a pair of wineglasses as Skipper and I left the two women alone on the deck. I imagined how many ways Anya could use the stem of a wineglass as a weapon. If she could turn a broken honey jar into a blade, the wineglass offered limitless possibilities. Hunter set the glasses on the table between the two deck chairs and made a show of dropping the napkins. He quickly recovered them, placed them on the table beside the glasses, and wordlessly pulled the door closed behind him.

Still uncertain if my heart would ever beat again, I glared through the heavy glass of the window onto the deck. The thought of Anya saying or doing something to hurt the woman I loved chilled me to my core.

"I'd give a million bucks to be a fly on the wall out there."

Hunter spun on his heel, then stared onto the deck. "A million bucks, huh? Okay, I'll take it." He tossed something small and round from his palm into the air toward me. I snatched it from its flight and immediately thanked Singer's angels for my new partner.

The earpiece slid into my ear as if it had been custom made just for me. In fact, it had been. The transmitter attached to the underside of the table on the deck—thanks to Hunter "dropping the napkins"—was the next best thing to being a fly on the wall.

I listened as the two women tentatively started circling. "Thank you for what you're doing for Chase."

"I have no choice. He saved my life. I must do for him same."

"He's the most important person in the world to me, Anya. I know how he remembers you, and he probably always will, but I need you to know and understand that the life he has with me is good, and I love him with no conditions."

Anya lifted her glass to her lips and set the drink back on the table with a thud in my earpiece. "He is brave and kind man who is also noble. He is good man for any woman, but for you is best man. I see in his eyes when he speaks of you. You are his person, and he needs you."

Penny stared at her. "I don't know what I expected you to be, but this isn't it. I wanted to hate you, and I was nervous to finally see you in person."

Anya smiled. "I was also nervous and afraid. I care for Chase because he was kind to me, but I did terrible thing to him. It was right thing for my country, but terrible for him. I am sorry for that, and I am now happy for him to find his person and to know you are good person who will never hurt him."

It was Penny's turn to have a drink, but I was smart enough to snatch my earpiece before she put her drink back on the table.

"I need you to tell me the truth when I ask you this next question, okay?"

"I will tell truth," Anya said. "I promise."

"Will they kill you?"

Anya stared across the lake, then slowly nodded. "Probably they will, but is okay."

"Why?"

"Is what happens in Russia. I am *izgnannik*. Is word meaning, uh…not in good feeling with Kremlin."

"Outcast."

"Yes, I am outcast. If they let me live, I will be clerk or maid in service, but never again trusted SVR officer."

"That's not what I mean," Penny said. "I wasn't asking why they would kill you. I was asking why you're doing this for Chase."

"He did for me same in Sol-Iletsk. I would die in that prison if he did not come to free me. Now he will die at hands of SVR if I do not do this for him. Is what is right."

Penny gazed out over the lake. "I wish it could be different."

"Do not wish for things that cannot be."

Neither woman said a word for several minutes, then Anya suddenly let out a schoolgirl giggle. "Does he drink always from same cup?"

Penny smiled curiously. "He does."

"I left for him note inside cup on first *Aegis* boat. Drink from different cup. Always same is pattern, and pattern is dangerous."

Penny chuckled. "He's a little stubborn, but I love him."

To my surprise, Anya lifted her glass and tilted it toward my wife.

Penny followed suit and touched the rim of her glass to Anya's. "Here is to a man who is stubborn but easy to love."

Penny said, "*Zdorov'ya!*"

Anya's face lit up. "Do you speak Russian?"

Penny emptied her wineglass into her mouth, swallowing in animated satisfaction, then grinned. "Nope, but you're going to teach me. And hey, I'm sorry about the knife thing with Skipper. She's a little protective of Chase and me."

Anya reached for her shoe then handed an identical second knife to Penny. "Is okay. Tell her you took this one from me in fight."

It may have been the sight of the second knife or the reality of the moment, but something brought Penny back to serious business. "I know you could kill me whenever you want, but don't play with Chase. He's my husband, and I will fight for him."

Anya's eyes narrowed. "I cannot make him happy how you do. I would not do that to him and to you. I will keep him alive on Black Sea, I promise to you this. But I will not do more than this."

Hunter, Skipper, and I watched the two women stand from their seats and head for the door. I snatched the earpiece and tossed it to my partner. When they came into the room, we stood, anticipation in our eyes.

Penny glared at Skipper, then pulled the knife from behind her back and threw it onto the floor, sticking the point in the hardwood planking. "You missed one."

Skipper flushed pale and stared at the knife in horror. "Penny, I'm...."

Penny let out a muffled giggle. "I'm just kidding, but you did miss one."

The sound of a second knife sticking into the floor only inches from the first shocked everyone in the room except Anya. "You missed actually two, but is still okay."

I pulled the knives from the floor and made a show of depositing them onto the highest shelf in the kitchen. "I think we've all had enough excitement for one afternoon. Let's have dinner and get some rest. We've got a couple of days before we have to be on the other side of the world, and I thought maybe we could climb the glacier tomorrow."

My suggestion was well received, but things never seem to work out the way I plan. The Seven Glaciers Restaurant at the Alyeska Resort wasn't prepared for two American covert operatives, a Russian spy, an operational analyst, and Penny.

As we walked from the tram—our chariot from the hotel to the mountaintop restaurant—Anya took Hunter's arm. "I will be for tonight your date."

Skipper wriggled her way between the two, hipping Anya to the side and lacing her arm through Hunter's. "Uh, I don't think so. You can be the fifth wheel."

Undeterred, Anya took Hunter's unclaimed arm. "You can be envy of every man in restaurant."

Penny peered at Anya. "Well, not the envy of *every* man, but maybe every man other than Chase."

Dinner wasn't exactly a reunion of old friends, but it wasn't unpleasant. The food was unforgettable, and the conversation, although uneasy at times, grew less strained as the corks left the wine bottles.

A two-hour dinner gave way to sunset in the northernmost latitudes of the United States at 10:15 p.m., followed by my first sighting of the aurora borealis. It turned out I wasn't alone.

"Oh, my God, Chase! Look at that." Penny stood in wide-eyed wonder as the northern lights danced their haunting green hues across the polar sky.

Hunter seemed entranced, and even Skipper was left in stunned silence.

"When I was child, I saw first time in city of Salekhard, and I cried in fear. There, the lights are called *Nger Harp*, which means *light of dead* in English." Anya had everyone's attention. "Is too far from winter. Is only green now, but in long dark winter, is beautiful, like spirits playing together in sky."

The northern lights weren't visible from the resort back at the base of the mountain, but I'd never forget that night at the top of the glacier.

For the sake of his sanity, I hoped Hunter went to bed alone. He didn't need his for-tonight date crawling around inside his head for the rest of his life, and with her, it's likely his life would be far shorter than otherwise.

Penny laid her head on my shoulder and played with my hair. "Thank you for inviting me to come up here."

I kissed her forehead. "If I'm not getting shot at, I always want you to be wherever I am."

She kissed my cheek and sighed.

"What is it? I know this is a lot for you to deal with, meeting Anya and all, but what's going on in that head of yours?"

She traced her finger down my chest and then rolled over onto her back. "Isn't there some other way, Chase?"

"Some other way to do what?"

She pulled at a curl of hair dangling across her shoulder. "Can't you think of some way to not give her back to the Russians?"

"What are you talking about?"

She rolled over, propping herself up on my chest. "I'm talking about Anya. Chase, they're going to kill her, and she's willing to let them. Isn't there something you can do?"

Chapter 29

Our Ex-Wife

The sun was up before anyone in the suite. At those extreme latitudes, days and nights don't have the same meaning as in the Lower Forty-eight.

I ordered breakfast from room service and asked the concierge if there was a guide who could take us for a glacier hike.

"Of course, sir. I'll arrange it all for you."

Six hours later, we were eating sandwiches on a mountain of ice high above the resort.

"How old do you think this glacier is?" our guide asked.

Skipper was the only one brave enough to answer. "Like a hundred million years old or something, right? They're left over from the ice age."

"That's what most people believe," said the guide, "and you're sort of right, but not really. Think of a glacier like a river—the Nile, for example. Is the river the gap in the Earth where the water flows, or is it the water itself?"

Hunter jumped in. "A river is water. The gap in the Earth is the riverbed."

The guide snapped his fingers. "Bingo. You're exactly right, and a glacier is the same thing. It may take a drop of water a few months to flow the length of the Nile and empty into the sea. The same is true of glaciers in a phenomenon known as *glacial flow*. The ice is formed by the enormous volume of snow as it builds up and crushes itself into ice. The southernmost extent of the glacier melts and falls into the sea, just like the drop of water in the Nile, and it's replaced by more ice upstream. This process of ice forming at the northern extreme of a glacier, and eventually thawing at the southern extreme, takes about a hundred years in Alaska, so believe it or not, most Alaskan glaciers are about a hundred years old."

After our picnic, we were plucked off the glacier by another Sikorsky S-76 and delivered safe and sound to the resort, where it was time for pre-dinner showers and cocktails. By some twist of timing, I found myself alone at the kitchen counter with Anya.

"Is this for you how every day you live?"

I poured a pair of cocktails. "What do you mean?"

"Is eating food in restaurant and climbing on glacier what you do every day?"

"Well, it's not a glacier every day, but when I'm not working, I try to enjoy every minute of my life. In my opinion, experiences like climbing a glacier for a picnic lunch at the top is a pretty good way to spend a day."

"It is all so strange to me, how you live life. And is for Penny same?"

I laughed. "Is what the same for Penny?"

Anya looked up at me as if I was supposed to know exactly what she was talking about. "Is for her the same? She climbs always these glaciers with you?"

"Yeah, pretty much. If I'm not on a mission, we spend most of our time enjoying everything we can about our life together. This is our first time in Alaska, but I'd say we'll be back. It's beautiful here."

She stared out the window as she stirred her drink with her fingertip. "She is very fortunate woman. This is not how most people have for life, no?"

"No, I guess not. We're still young, and we have the financial means to do pretty much whatever we want, but you don't have to be wealthy to enjoy life. Sometimes the simplest things are the best."

She let her hand land on my arm. "Like watching sun go away over ocean with you on first *Aegis* boat, no?"

I pulled my arm away. "Yeah, like that."

She flinched. "I am sorry, Chase. I didn't mean to—"

"It's okay, Anya. I know."

We touched glasses and drank in silence, listening to the showers running in the rest of the house.

"She wants me to find another way," I said, staring into my drink.

"What are you saying, Chasechka?"

"Penny. She wants me to find a way to pull this off without you going back to Russia when it's over. She's afraid they'll kill you."

Disbelief filled her eyes. "Why would she want this for me?"

"Because she's a good person, Anya. She's never going to invite you to the spa for a girls' day out, but she doesn't want you to die."

"But I told her is no good to want something that cannot be, and I must go back to Moscow. Maybe they will let me be clerk. Is better than living in Siberia."

I took another drink. "Do you really think that's what's going to happen, Anya, or are they going to put a bullet in your head at the first opportunity?"

She pushed her glass in tiny circles on the countertop. "Do you believe glacier is only one hundred years old?"

I put my finger under her chin and made her look at me. "If there is another way, will you take it?"

She pulled away. "I will do what is necessary for you to be alive, Chasechka."

"I know, Anya, but if I could come up with a way to keep myself alive and you out of Moscow, would you do it?"

"Where would I go?" she asked in a child's voice. "I do not want to go back to Siberia. Is muddy in summer and ice in winter."

"I don't know yet, but I have an idea I'm working on. I just need to know you'll take it if I can make it happen."

"If this will mean I can live life to eat in restaurant and climb glacier every day, I will take it."

"Okay, good. Now, we've got to get you on the phone with Colonel Sokolov, and here's what I want you to tell him."

I laid out my plan for her, and she agreed. Skipper established an untraceable connection to Sokolov's cell phone, and Anya went to work.

"Colonel, is Anastasia Burinkova, and I have a gift for you."

The conversation continued in rapid-fire Russian. I pieced together most of it, but hearing only one side of a conversation between a former Russian assassin and the current commander of Directorate KR left a few gaps my language skills couldn't fill.

When the conversation was over, she handed the receiver back to Skipper, who quickly cut the connection.

Anya started talking. "He told me you are working for him to deliver me to SVR. He says you are errand boy for him now."

"I'm no one's errand boy," I demanded.

"Do not get upset. Colonel Sokolov is man of arrogance and believes he is to maybe one day be president. I say to him I will kill you if I can come in from cold to again be SVR officer, and he agreed at once."

Penny had been quietly listening to the exchange, but suddenly lost the ability to hold her tongue. "He's lying. You know he's going to kill you. Chase, you know it, too."

"Yes, Penny, you are correct," Anya said. "Was test from me. If I say to him I want to come back to be clerk or work in kitchen, he maybe say yes and let me live, but I say to him I want to be SVR officer again. He cannot let me be officer again, but he say yes, regardless of truth. Is clear he will kill me."

Penny grabbed my shoulders. "Chase, you have to do something."

I turned to Skipper. "Walk with me."

My analyst and I walked in lockstep through the front door of the resort and down to the small lake. A pair of bald eagles soared across the water, wingtip to wingtip, and one plucked a fish from barely beneath the surface. With the fish firmly clasped in the smaller bird's talons, they climbed away from the lake until they reached a nest I hadn't noticed.

"They must be feeding their chicks," Skipper said, mesmerized by the sight. "This place is amazing."

"Yes, it is. We'll definitely be coming back."

"Not without me."

"So, listen. Penny's right. We can't let Anya go back to Russia when this is over, but there's only one way I know of to pull this off. I need to talk to General Beaufour."

Skipper raised her eyebrows. "You want me to call the director of Central Intelligence? Chase, I'd have a better shot at getting the Black Sea warmed up for you than getting the DCI on the phone."

I shook my head. "I don't need you to get him on the phone. I have his number. What I need from you is advice."

"Advice? You're asking me for advice?"

"Yes, I am. You're the operational analyst. It's your job to analyze the operation, so here it is."

I laid out my plan, and she never stopped shaking her head. "Are you out of your mind? Do you expect me to believe this is what Penny Fulton, your wife, and my sister-in-law—well, sort of—wants?"

"Yeah, it is. In fact, it was her idea."

"You've clearly flipped. You've come up with some crazy ideas in the past, but this one takes the cake. Call Clark and see what he has to say about it. Meanwhile, I'm going to climb that tree and eat part of that fish with the eagles. That makes a lot more sense than your crazy-ass plan."

She was right about my plan being crazy, but I didn't need Clark's confirmation, so I returned to the room and dialed another number from Skipper's secure line.

"General Beaufour, Chase Fulton here."

"Chase, I'm surprised to hear from you. I recently learned our deal may not be quite as concrete as you led us to believe."

I cleared my throat. "I worked all that out with the president, and he has my full cooperation in almost anything except handing my team off to the next administration."

"Is that so?" the general said.

"It is. In fact, we're working with Admiral Galloway on an operation in the Black Sea as we speak. Are you up to speed on that one?"

"I've not been briefed on the up-to-the-minute, but I have a general knowledge of the operation."

That was agency speak for "I have no idea what you're talking about, but I expect you to fill me in."

"In that case, General, I'd rather have the admiral brief you up. I'm afraid I'd leave out important details, but what I need is to include one foreign national in the exfil plan. Admiral Galloway authorized the op, but I'm sure he did it with the president's approval, so I'll be in touch in twelve hours to confirm we're a go for the extra body in the getaway car."

"Go ahead and give me the highlights, Chase. I'll be better prepared for the conversation with the president that way."

I found bureaucrats to be amusing. "You'll probably want to talk Admiral Galloway instead of going to the president on this one, General. I have to run. I'll be in touch."

I disconnected the line before he could put forth any further argument, but I was intrigued the president and chief of naval operations had kept the director of Central Intelligence out of the loop when it came to an operation off the Russian coast involving a former Russian spy. That was, by definition, the CIA's playground. I needed Washington's support, but I secretly enjoyed stirring the political pot.

It didn't take twelve hours. In fact, it took less than three before a call from the CNO appeared on Skipper's secure line.

I pressed the receiver to my ear.

"Chase, it appears you've invited a few new guests to our party. General Beaufour isn't happy with me since I conveniently forgot to tell him we were fishing in his pond."

"I'm sorry about that, Admiral."

"Don't worry about it. Those West Point grads are easy to get spooled up. It took a glass of good whiskey and two miles of pacing the Oval Office rug, but the president has okayed your op. Make it happen, Chase, but if you start a shooting war over there, General Beaufour's gonna stick you in a uniform and hand you a rifle."

"Thank you, Admiral. Oh, and tell the general I'm a fifty long with a thirty-seven-inch inseam."

"Will do. We'll talk again soon. The president says to keep your head down and your powder dry, son."

"Aye, aye, Admiral."

I spun around in my chair and met Penny's anticipatory stare. "He said yes."

She folded her hands beneath her chin and whispered a prayer.

When I looked around the room, I realized Penny and I were alone. "Where is everybody?"

Penny looked at her watch. "Hunter's learning Russian in the bar with our ex-wife, but I don't know where Skipper went."

"Last time I saw her, she was climbing a tree to eat a fish with a family of bald eagles, and what do you mean, our ex-wife?"

"I saw her passport and driver's license. You may have never had a ceremony, but she's got the credentials."

"That wasn't my idea," I argued. "Dominic did that when we believed she was defecting."

She giggled. "I'm just bustin' your chops, big boy. Don't get all huffy and defensive."

I pulled Penny from her chair. "Go get dressed. It's date night. I'm pretty sure I'll have to go to work tomorrow, so let's take advantage of the one night we have left in Alaska."

The concierge resisted recommending any restaurants other than the Seven Glaciers, but after handing him a hundred-dollar bill, he magically came up with several good choices.

Later that evening, Nicole Bethany "Penny" Thomas Fulton made my last night in Anchorage one I'd not soon forget.

As I lay trying to catch my breath, Penny nestled herself into my arms and whispered, "You're going to be alone with *her* for the next several days. I can't have you getting ideas about trading in your North Texas girl for whatever she is."

Chapter 30
Bond Girl

Just as the weatherman from Adak arranged, Anya, Hunter, and I
landed in Cyprus, met our contact, and claimed our local passports. The flight to Sevastopol was a little less posh than the first-
class ride we had across the Pacific, but thankfully, it was much
shorter at only six hundred fifty miles.

Sevastopol was a city like nothing I'd ever seen. If there's a city
on the globe with more bays, I can't imagine where it would be.
The jagged coastline was peppered with marinas, shipyards,
ports, and waterfront facilities of every description. Mega yachts
rested alongside rusting Soviet-era warships so dilapidated it was
hard to believe they could remain afloat. *Aegis*'s near-twin, the
dunker, was tied up in a marina with five hundred other boats in
the back of Strilets'ka Bay. The place looked like Detroit and
Hong Kong's love child, but nobody spoke anything resembling
English.

Walking down the seemingly endless dock, I could see her
mast rising from the array of boats that weren't designed to sink
on command. From that distance, it was impossible, even for
me, to find an ounce of difference between her and *Aegis*. Every
derelict vessel we passed seemed to have a guy with four teeth
and a cigarette hanging from his mouth, while every yacht had at
least two Eastern European beauties as cute as the former Rus-

sian spy walking between Hunter and me, but in various stages of undress.

Hunter was drooling at a quartet of bikini-clad Ukrainian girls serving drinks aboard a billionaire's three-hundred-foot bath toy. "Does every woman in this part of the world look like you?"

Anya grinned. "Yes, Hunter, we are all beautiful, but not all of them know how to…" She leaned in close and whispered something perfectly filthy into his ear.

Hunter slapped his forehead. "Yep, I'm definitely staying. Never going home. But I'm going to need more language lessons."

"Get on the boat, you horndog. You're worse than Clark."

Dominic and Tommy greeted us from the cockpit.

"You finally made it," Tommy said. "Come aboard! Come aboard!"

"Yeah, we had a little layover in Anchorage while you guys were putting the boat back together. How'd that go?"

Tommy wiped his brow. "Not good. It's a mess, Chase. There's no chance of repairing it without a truckload of parts from home. Everything has to be done manually. I'll teach you, but it increases the difficulty of the operation exponentially. It's going to take one person in each hull and one at the helm to pull it off. Is she…" He paused, apparently unsure how to finish his question, so Anya spoke up.

"She is."

"Okay, well, I guess that settles that," Tommy said. "You must be the notorious Anya."

"I am Anya, yes, but I do not know this word, *notorious*. Perhaps I am not that."

I laughed. "Oh, you're definitely that. I'll explain later."

"Are you guys hungry?" Dominic asked.

"Yeah," Hunter said. "It's been a while since we strapped on the feed bag."

Dominic rolled his eyes. "Okay, I'll get food while Tommy goes over the systems with you."

The shipwright wasted no time, beginning with the EPIRB. "This is the same emergency position indicating radio beacon you had aboard *Aegis* that kept phoning home to Mother Russia. I've kept it semi-jammed for the last few days. Whoever's listening knows we're in the Black Sea, but there's no way to pinpoint our location until I turn it loose."

"That's genius," I said.

"We've got to keep their noses in the air. We can't let them completely lose our scent. They'd get bored, and what fun is that?"

"Okay, so the EPIRB is just a switch flip away from telling the whole story, right?"

"Yep, and here's the switch." Tommy pointed to a panel just inside the door to the main salon. "You'll also notice we did up the salon to look like *Aegis* from the outside. It's a mock-up, but it's still decently comfortable. You will have to live aboard her for a couple of days at least."

"Nice touch," I said. "Now, let's get to the all-important floodgates."

He led us down the portside stairs to the complicated set of valves. "Look at the plastic wire ties sticking off each valve. This one has one, this one has two, and all the way through four. That's the order the valves have to be opened. Any other order, and you'll end up bobbing like a soggy boot near the surface. Got it?"

Hunter and I looked over the valves, counting wire ties as we went. "Yeah, we've got it," I said, "but why not just write the order on a piece of tape or something?"

"Because tape is hard to see in the dark, but that's not the only reason. Before you get this first valve all the way open, your ankles are going to get pretty cold. By the time number two reaches its stops, you'll be knee-deep in the Black Sea. I've learned people tend to get a little nervous when they find themselves going down with the ship, so wire ties are easy. Reading numbers on tape is not."

"Okay, I get it now. So, will we be fully submerged by the time we get number four open?"

"I'm glad you asked." He pointed to a hook on the bulkhead. "Here's your scuba gear. I recommend having it on before you turn the first valve, and have the regulator in your mouth before you turn number four."

Tommy sized up Hunter, Anya, and me. "All three of you do know how to dive, right?"

Hunter and I nodded and turned to Anya.

She glared back at us. "I am Russian James Bond girl. Do not worry about me."

"Okay," Tommy said. "I'll take that as a yes, and we'll move on." He spun, pointing behind him toward the engine compartments. "See this seam? It'll blow apart when the water is about nipple deep." He turned to Anya. "No offense, ma'am."

She rolled her eyes. "I am not only one with nipples on boat."

Tommy rocked his thumb toward her. "I like her."

"Everyone seems to like her these days, Tommy. Even my wife. Let's not get sidetracked."

"Okay, so you've got your gear on and regulator in your mouth before you throw the final valve. Every fiber of your being is going to be screaming at you to get up those stairs where there's free air. Remember, nothing is free. The only thing waiting for you up there is the Russian boat ready to pick *her* up. Your only exit is through that seam when it blows apart. That happens when the top of the mast disappears. I call that periscope depth."

I said, "So, before we bail out, we're supposed to hang out in the hull of a sinking ship until she's eighty feet underwater? Is that what you're saying?"

"That's really up to you. I'll be on a plane back to Miami later tonight, so I won't make those decisions for you. If you decide to swim out the top, please make sure you're deep enough to be un-detectable from the surface. Either way, you'll be a little disori-ented when you get out of the boat. Try to stay neutrally buoyant and not cork to the surface. There's a magnetometer on the console of each set of scuba gear. That'll point you toward the largest metal object in the area. With any luck, it'll be your friends in the submarine."

"Once she's submerged, how fast will she sink?" Hunter asked.

"Once she's fully flooded, she'll head for the bottom a little faster than one foot per second. There'll be some burping as she spits out her last gasps of trapped air at the surface, but after that, she's pretty much a rock. If you're still on board two minutes after she takes her last breath, you've probably taken your last one, too."

He showed us the other set of valves on the starboard side. They were arranged in a mirror image of the portside set.

"Where is my diving equipment?" Anya asked.

Tommy took a long breath. "That's the tricky part. To pull this off, you'll have to be visible on deck when things start coming apart. Your buddies will expect you to be swimming away from the sinking boat while your boyfriend heads for the bottom."

I expected Anya to object to the terms *buddies* and *boyfriend*, but she let it go.

"So, Russian James Bond girl, when the ship heads for Davey Jones's locker, you'll need to get inside the main salon and out of sight before you stick a regulator in your mouth. Your gear is in this bin. You can stow it wherever you want, but make sure it's ready to go before these guys start turning valves."

Anya nodded without a word.

Dominic yelled from the cockpit, "Chow's here!"

We climbed the stairs to find him holding two buckets of KFC chicken.

"Would you look at that?" Hunter said. "The colonel is worldwide. I hope you got mashed potatoes and gravy. That's my favorite."

"Extra crispy in this bucket, and original recipe in this one," Dominic said as he spread out the food on the table.

"This is first time for me," Anya said.

"Your first time in Sevastopol?" Dominic asked.

"No, first time eating KFC. I think I like original best."

We needed a laugh, and we got one.

I ran the mission through my mind a thousand times, imagining everything that could go wrong. "How will we know when the sub's beneath us?"

Dominic licked his fingers. "You won't, but they'll be hovering offshore when you leave Sochi. The sub commander will be floating a satellite buoy and listening for your EPIRB signal, just like the Russians. When he hears it, he'll creep his sub under your hull and shadow you into the depths. I recommend staying afloat until you're at least thirty miles offshore. The bottom's about six thousand feet at that point, and that's plenty deep to keep the Russians from poking around the wreckage once it hits the bottom. The sub will be hovering at one hundred feet with her lights on. You should be able to see it if you get within a couple hundred feet of her. Outside of that range, just follow the magnetometers until you see the lights. You'll enter the airlock just behind the conning tower on the upper surface of the sub. Once you're inside, they'll pump it dry, slowly decompress you, and then open the hatch and invite you inside. The skipper of the boat is Commander Jenkins. And get this. His first name is Noah."

Hunter slapped the table. "Oh, Singer's gonna love this. We're getting saved by Noah's ark. I wish he could be here for this one."

Anya stared blankly at the four Americans who'd apparently spent enough time in Sunday school to know the story of Noah's ark.

"You have no idea what Noah's ark is, do you?" I asked.

"Something American?"

"Actually," I said, "it's not American at all. About five thousand years ago, a very large ship came to rest on a mountain in Turkey, not far from here."

"Maybe you will tell me this story when we get to America, yes?"

"We have a friend who knows all about it. Maybe you should hear it from him. Do you remember the singing sniper from Sol-Iletsk?"

"Of course I do."

"Well, he's a bit of a scholar when it comes to that part of history, and I'm sure he'd love to tell you all about it."

She smiled. "I will look forward to hearing the story."

"Your English is getting better," I said.

"Yes, everything is better with practice. I think maybe soon, my Russian will not be so good."

Chapter 31

Dive...Dive...Dive!

It took just over thirty-six hours to sail the three hundred fifty miles between Sevastopol, Ukraine—or whatever country claimed it that day—and Sochi in the Krasnodar Krai oblast of Russia. The dunker didn't sail identically to *Aegis*, but it was close. Perhaps if Penny had been aboard, she could've coaxed another knot out of the boat.

The closer we got to Sochi, the more time the EPIRB spent broadcasting. We anchored in the Port of Sochi near the Sochi Grand Marina just before sunset. At 3:00 a.m., I flipped the switch on the EPIRB for the final time. It would spend the rest of its life, but hopefully not ours, telling the Russians exactly where we were.

We kept Hunter hidden inside the boat, never letting him see the light of day. For the ruse to work, we couldn't risk having anyone spot him. With the exception of half a dozen Americans, the whole world needed to believe Anya and I were on the boat alone.

Just before sunup, Anya placed the call we'd been waiting to make for over two months. "Comrade Colonel Sokolov, we will sail from Sochi on morning wind to Samsun, Turkey, where the American is to meet CIA officers. Boat will only make ten knots. I will be in command of boat at noon when the American will sleep. One hour later, I will administer drugs and blow up boat. You will have men there to rescue me, yes?"

I understood every word of her end of the Russian conversation and could read the comrade colonel's responses from the looks on her face.

She drove her fist into the table. "He is fool, and he thinks I am fool. He will not send men to rescue me, but he will send them to watch us die."

"Yes, Anya. They've turned against you, but that happened when they sent you to the Black Dolphin Prison. The good news is, it will all be over soon."

"It will never be over, Chasechka. It will always be true in my mind, and I can never forget. All of my life, from age of five or maybe four, I was trained to serve the Rodina. It is at center of me, and now I am nothing."

I'd never seen Anya like that. It left me on the verge of lowering my guard and offering her my sympathy, but the damage she tried to do not only to me, but to my country, kept me from surrendering.

"We've all made decisions that resulted in less-than-ideal consequences, but in a few days, you'll be in America with two million bucks in the bank. Compared to most of the people on the planet, Anya, your life isn't looking all that bad."

She reached for my hand, but I pulled away. "Chasechka, imagine if American director of Central Intelligence was following boat to watch you die."

* * *

The wind blew from the northwest at twelve knots when we motored from the Port of Sochi and unfurled our sails. The dunker made eight knots on the morning breeze, and I prayed there was an American nuclear submarine lurking about. Unless he was directly beneath the boat so the depth-sounder could reflect from the hull, I'd never know if he was there.

Anya's words rang in my ears as I watched the city of Sochi disappear behind us. That would probably be the last time she would ever see the country of her birth, the country she served and loved, the country that turned her into something no one should ever have to become. I tried to imagine how it would feel sailing away from Saint Augustine or Saint Marys, knowing I'd never see American again.

"I'm sorry, Anya."

"For what are you sorry?"

"I'm sorry I've been less than kind to you, and I'm sorry you have to watch your home disappear forever. It's not fair, and no one should ever have to endure that."

"Is for me what life is, Chasechka. I made the choice to turn against my country for a short while, and that choice will make for me the rest of my life."

"No, Anya, that's not true. Your country turned you into an assassin and forced you to use your body and mind to do things no one should ever be asked to do. You didn't deserve that. They forced that upon you. You made a decision to grasp a moment of freedom, something you'd never known, and you shouldn't have to suffer for that. I'm going to get you back to America, and I will make sure you have a home where you can do whatever you want. After that, the decisions are all yours."

"I can have cat?"

"What?"

"In America, I can have baby cat for pet, yes?"

The absurdity and simplicity of what freedom meant to someone who'd never experienced it astonished me, and I laughed. "Yes, Anya, you can have a thousand baby cats if you want. They're called kittens."

"They are *kotenok* in Russian, but that does not matter now."

Just as Sochi disappeared over the northern horizon, in our wake I watched a sea serpent rise from the depths, its head a bulbous, black eye protruding a few feet above the surface. I stared at the unearthly figure, believing it must be an optical illusion, until it became a bright white flashing light: Short-short-long-short-short-short-short-long. Short-short-long-short-short-short-short-long.

That's Morse code for USA!

I forced my finger toward the periscope of the submarine that would be our home for the next several days. "Anya, look!"

She gasped. "Is submarine, yes?"

"It sure is," I said through a huge red, white, and blue grin.

Although hers wasn't star-spangled, yet, she grinned in excitement and leapt toward me with outstretched arms. I caught her and hugged the woman I once believed I loved.

When I opened my eyes, the periscope was gone with no evidence of ever having been there. The confidence of knowing she was just feet away changed my outlook on everything about the coming afternoon.

As the morning wore on, the wind increased, and so did our speed. There was no chance we'd outrun the nuclear sub beneath us, but something about the dread of running for deep water with the intention of scuttling our ship felt accelerated.

The radar suffered its demise during the lightning strike, so I had no way to know if there was a Russian boat, or any boat, following us. I scanned the horizon every ten minutes with the best binoculars money could buy and finally caught a reflection dead astern. I marked its position on the stern rail and checked again every three minutes. The reflection became a speck, and then an outline, and finally, the steel hull of a Russian warship. They'd bought a ticket and came to watch the show.

When the sun reached its zenith, noon had been called, and Anya took her seat at the helm for the noon to four watch—the final watch to ever be manned aboard the dunker.

At three minutes past noon, I saw the sun over the Black Sea for the last time and closed the doors to the main salon behind me. Hunter was asleep in the portside hull.

"Wake up, lazybones. It's almost showtime."

He yawned and raised his watch to his face. "Oh, I guess it is. How's your girl?"

"She's not my girl," I said, "and from the looks of things back in Anchorage, she's got her eye on you."

"Oh, no, she's not my type. I prefer women who've not been trained to kill Americans."

"Well, there is that."

We crammed a couple of MREs down our throats and finished off our supply of bottled water. We'd need the calories to keep our bodies as warm as possible in the frigid water we were on the verge of experiencing, and staying hydrated had been beaten into both of us in every tactical training class we'd ever attended.

"Oh, I almost forgot to tell you. The sub came up to wink at us. She stuck her periscope in our wake about two hundred feet astern and flashed USA."

Hunter flashed a thumbs-up. "It's good to know we've got a ride out of here."

"Yeah, it is, and there's a Russian warship astern as well. I suspect our old friend, Colonel Sokolov, may be aboard to watch the show."

"We're sure gonna give him one, aren't we?"

I glanced at my watch and called, "T-minus ten minutes. Let's gear up."

Hunter headed for the starboard hull, and I slid down the stairs in front of the portside valves. I had just over 3,000 pounds of air in my tank, Hunter had 3,100, and Anya's console read 3,250. It just seemed right that she'd have more air than we did. I knew Hunter was practically a dolphin, and I was as comfortable underwater as on the surface, so we'd be fine no matter what happened in the murky depths. But I didn't know how Anya would react when the world around her turned black, cold, and wet.

At precisely one o'clock, Anya came through the main salon door, closing it behind her. She checked her gear tucked behind the door, then leaned into Hunter's side of the boat. He flashed the okay signal, and she nodded.

Seconds later, she was standing in front of me, looking up at me the way she had more times than I could remember. "Thank you, Chasechka. It doesn't matter what happens now except you and Hunter are safe. You cannot believe me, and I know this, but this does not make it lie. I love you, Chasechka. I will see you on submarine."

"Don't miss the boat, Anya. They won't wait for you if you're not at the airlock. Tell me you're comfortable in the scuba gear."

She placed her hand on my chest. "Do not worry. I will find submarine. I am very good diver. I have to hear story of ark of Noah."

She stood on her toes and kissed my cheek. "Is drug I told Colonel Sokolov I would give to you." Anya smiled and disappeared up the stairs.

Two minutes later, I heard the flash grenade explode on the bow, followed by the modified smoke grenade designed to initially release a slow plume of white smoke and then grow in intensity until submerged.

"Dive! Dive! Dive!" I yelled, and opened valve number one.

Just as Tommy had predicted, the water was almost instantly rising above my ankles.

"Number two!"

I had to believe Hunter was opening his valves in conjunction with me. When the second valve was fully open, the water covered my thighs.

"Three!" I yelled as I leaned back to try seeing my partner across the salon. I couldn't see him, but the surface of the water in my hull was level, so that left no question that he was flooding his side in sync with mine. The third valve put the water nipple deep on me, so Hunter was up to his chin.

I yelled, "Four!" the second before sticking the regulator in my mouth. My heart pounded, and I double-checked my pressure gauge: 3,000 pounds of air.

The water was cold and dark and tumultuous. As the final trapped air escaped the hulls, gasping and gurgling as it went, the boat creaked and moaned its death throes. There was no way to know if Anya had made it inside the main salon and donned her gear. I could swim up the stairs and feel for her, but it didn't matter if she was there. My fate lay in my ability to wait for the hull to open up and let me out, and then to find the submarine.

I closed my eyes and sent up a silent prayer asking the God who hears the prayers of an assassin to put Anya and Hunter on that submarine, no matter what it cost.

As if He'd heard my prayer and sent a mighty clap of thunder as an answer, the watery world around me exploded, and the bulkhead I'd been resting against vanished in the chaos. Then, just as suddenly and violently as it began, silence filled the space around me, and I was alone, cold, and blind. It took a minute, or perhaps an eternity to gather my wits and reach for my console. The dim light of the gauges was blurred and distant. I cracked the seal at the top of my mask, allowing a rush of water in, clearing the fog inside my mask. A glance upward and a single exhalation through my nose sent the water cascading from my mask, bringing the world in front of me into focus. There was little to see other than my console telling me I was at ninety-two feet beneath the surface with two thousand pounds of air left. The magnetometer pointed straight ahead, and I descended to one hundred feet and started finning for the sub.

I spent more time looking around and behind me than at where the sub should've been. I had to know Hunter and Anya were somewhere close and swimming for our only chance of freedom and survival. I activated the strobe chemlight I'd forgotten was attached to my shoulder, and the soft green light made me feel as though I were swimming in the northern lights…in Anya's lights of the dead.

Fifteen hundred pounds of air. Magnetometer still pointing straight ahead. Depth, one hundred five feet. No green glow behind me.

Twelve hundred pounds of air and a misty white light loomed ahead like the single headlight of a car in the snow. It grew ever brighter with each fin kick, but there was still no soft green glow of a chemlight from Hunter or Anya.

The black behemoth of an American nuclear submarine appeared out of the mist, and I slid my hand across its smooth surface as I finned for the conning tower and the airlock that was my doorway to warmth, safety, and home.

As I swam across the upper surface of the sub, I caught a faint green light, and I commanded my legs to kick with every ounce of strength inside of me. The green light grew brighter and finally outlined the form of my partner, the combat controller and warrior. Hunter was alive and had found the sub before I had. I should've expected no less.

He reached for my hand and drew me toward him as if our team had won the Super Bowl. When he let go of me, I raised both hands, palms up, and looked around, asking if he knew where Anya was. His only reply was a mirror image of my questioning motion.

Eight hundred pounds of air. Depth, ninety feet.

I kicked away from the sub and swam back the direction I believed I had come, hoping, praying to see Anya's faint green light dancing in the black, bottomless void. She wasn't there. Nothing was. Only emptiness and death for anything that breathed air.

Something strong grabbed my ankle and yanked me backward with a violence I couldn't have expected. I turned to see Hunter reaching for my tank valve. He gave another mighty jerk, forcing me back toward the sub and shaking his head. He shoved me toward the airlock and slammed his finger into his pressure gauge.

Five hundred pounds of air. Our time was up, and the airlock was our only option. Just the two of us, Hunter and me.

We swam inside, and he pushed the hatch closed and spun the wheel, sealing the hatch. The water around us began flowing out of the chamber, leaving our heads above the frigid water.

"I'm sorry, Chase. She didn't make it. I never saw her again after she checked on me in the hull before we sank. I'm sorry."

I pounded my fist against the steel bulkhead of the airlock until an echoing voice came over a speaker. "Gentlemen, how much air do you have left?"

I looked around for the disembodied voice and watched Hunter grab his console. "Eight fifty."

I focused on my gauges and yelled, "Four seventy-five."

The voice returned. "Stick your regs back in your mouths, boys. There's a *Rusalochka* banging on the hatch, and I intend to let her in."

Water poured again into the airlock chamber, and I stuck the regulator back into my mouth, breathing as slowly as possible. Four hundred seventy-five pounds of air at one hundred feet was barely enough to give the chamber time to flood and drain again. In four minutes, I would be breathing aluminum dust from inside my tank.

The instant the water level reached our eyes, I lunged for the wheel. It felt like it took a thousand turns to open the hatch, but the instant it opened a foot, Anya squeezed her thin body inside. Hunter had the hatch closed and sealed only seconds later. Anya threw her arms around us, pulling us tightly against her. We squeezed back, and I felt the diaphragm in my regulator snap closed. I was out of air.

As calmly as I could manage, I reached for Anya's alternate air source and stuck it in my mouth. The new regulator delivered half of one breath and froze. Anya's eyes widened, and I turned to Hunter. He took a full breath and pulled the regulator from his mouth, shoving it toward Anya. She opened her mouth, accepting his reg, and took a full breath. She instantly pulled the regulator from her mouth and placed it at my lips. I met Hunter's gaze as he stuck his alternate in his mouth. I took a breath and passed it back to Anya. We continued buddy breathing until the airlock had evacuated the water below our chins.

Hunter spit out his regulator. "Puff, puff, pass, baby! And what the hell is a *Rusalochka*?"

"*Rusalochka* is Russian mermaid." Anya swayed side to side, emulating the mythical seductress. "But now I am American mermaid."

About the Author

Cap Daniels

Cap Daniels is a former sailing charter captain, scuba and sailing instructor, pilot, Air Force combat veteran, and civil servant of the U.S. Department of Defense. Raised far from the ocean in rural East Tennessee, his early infatuation with salt water was sparked by the fascinating, and sometimes true, sea stories told by his father, a retired Navy Chief Petty Officer. Those stories of adventure on the high seas sent Cap in search of adventure of his own, which eventually landed him on Florida's Gulf Coast where he spends as much time as possible on, in, and under the waters of the Emerald Coast.

With a headful of larger-than-life characters and their thrilling exploits, Cap pours his love of adventure and passion for the ocean onto the pages of The Chase Fulton Novels series.

Visit www.CapDaniels.com to join the mailing list to receive newsletter and release updates.

Connect with Cap Daniels

Facebook: www.Facebook.com/WriterCapDaniels
Instagram: https://www.instagram.com/authorcapdaniels/
BookBub: https://www.bookbub.com/profile/cap-daniels

Made in the USA
Columbia, SC
19 February 2020